"Give me one good reason why I shouldn't have you court-martialed.

"I'm waiting," Admiral Janeway said.

Kirk decided to rely on a tried-and-true technique: He answered the question he felt she *should* have asked him.

"I think I've done a good job of fulfilling my obligations to you."

"Captain," Janeway said, more than a hint of annoyance in her tone, "I came all this way because you *haven't* fulfilled your obligations."

She leaned forward, punctuating her words by tapping her finger against the galley table. "I gave you this ship so you could be the eyes and ears of Starfleet where and when we can't send an identifiable ship of our own."

"You gave me this ship so I could investigate Spock's disappearance."

Janeway would not be deflected. "Captain Kirk . . . Ambassador Spock is dead."

OTHER BOOKS BY WILLIAM SHATNER

with Judith & Garfield Reeves-Stevens

Star Trek: Totality
Captain's Peril
Captain's Blood

Star Trek: The Mirror Universe Saga
Spectre
Dark Victory
Preserver

Star Trek: Odyssey
The Ashes of Eden
The Return
Avenger

with Chris Kreski
Get a Life!

with Chip Walter
Star Trek: I'm Working on That

STAR TREK®
CAPTAIN'S GLORY

WILLIAM SHATNER

WITH JUDITH & GARFIELD REEVES-STEVENS

Based on *Star Trek*
and *Star Trek: The Next Generation*®
created by Gene Roddenberry

POCKET BOOKS
New York London Toronto Sydney

Pocket Books
A Division of Simon & Schuster, Inc.
1230 Avenue of the Americas
New York, NY 10020

First Pocket Books paperback edition October 2007

POCKET and colophon are registered trademarks of Simon & Schuster, Inc.

For information about special discounts for bulk purchases, please contact Simon & Schuster Special Sales at 1-800-456-6798 or business@simonandschuster.com.

Cover art by Jerry Vanderstelt

Manufactured in the United States of America

10 9 8 7 6 5 4 3 2 1

ISBN-13: 978-0-7434-5376-9
ISBN-10:   0-7434-5376-X

Elizabeth and I sat down to dinner with our friends
Michael and Jane, and I was reminded how important
my friends and family are to me. Gar and Judy,
Ben and Frally, Leonard and Susie, Scottie and Tracie,
are some of my friends, all of whom are dear to me.
To them, whom I treasure, and the treasure
of my family, I dedicate this book.

ACKNOWLEDGMENTS

Carmen LaVia
Fifi Oscard (in memoriam)
Margaret Clark
But especially Judy & Gar Reeves-Stevens:
the best of the best

... *from land and sea on Earth our home*
to worlds beyond forever roam;
O hear our plea from reaches far
For those who journey to the stars.

— THE NAVY HYMN
M. BRACK, 2154

CAPTAIN'S GLORY

Prologue
Hailing Frequencies

Sometimes it was Harry Mudd, and sometimes it was Kodos. But this time, when the turbolift doors parted, it was the Gorn who charged him.

Kirk stumbled backward as ivory claws slashed the air.

He lost his footing, fell to the deck in the corridor of his ship, scrabbling back to avoid the inevitable.

The Gorn advanced, one heavy, deliberate step after another. Its obsidian blade flashed with each strobe of the red-alert warning lights, gleamed with the deep, rich color of blood.

"I weary of the chase."

Each word was guttural, hissed.

"Wait for me . . . I shall be merciful and ssswift."

Kirk froze, no longer able to move, even to save himself. The Gorn towered over him, arm raised for the killing stroke, its muscles bunched beneath its scales. Its breath

1

enveloped him with the stench of rotting meat, of death, defeat.

But defeat was nothing Kirk could accept, and in his primal rejection of death, he regained control of his body, kicked at the creature's knees.

Startled by its prey's defiance, the Gorn twisted to the side.

Kirk seized his chance. Leapt to his feet. Ran from the turbolift.

"We destroyed intrudersss, as I will destroy you!"

But the Gorn's vicious threat was drowned out by the blare of alarms.

Kirk staggered as the Enterprise shuddered beneath his feet.

Even with no communication with his chief engineer, Kirk knew Scotty was pushing the ship's engines past their limits. He could feel their vibrations as they strained to break free of the planet's crushing gravity.

At the same time, Kirk heard the rising howl of wind that told him his ship was entering the atmosphere—a trajectory she'd never survive. Not at this speed without shields to protect her.

"Captain Kirk to the bridge."

Uhura was calling him, but he had no way of replying. There were no com stations on any of the bulkheads, only phaser and disruptor scorches from the battle with the Klingon boarding party.

Kirk ran down the corridor until he reached another turbolift.

Instinctively, he braced himself as its doors slipped open.

The car was empty.

He rushed inside, twisted the activator.

2

"Bridge." The word was little more than a gasp.

"Captain Kirk!"

Uhura's voice was more insistent. But Kirk still couldn't answer her. The com station in the turbolift car had been shattered by a sword blade.

The decks pulsed by. The car slowed.

Kirk had just an instant to realize that he couldn't have reached the bridge so quickly when the doors parted and the Gorn lunged in, a tidal wave of green.

"Earthling captain!"

Kirk ducked and the deadly blade carved empty air as he rammed his shoulder into the Gorn's chest, trying to force the creature out of the lift. But the doors had already shut. The car began to move again.

Kirk was trapped, nowhere to run.

He blocked the Gorn's downward stab. He punched the creature's muzzle. The car rocked as the Enterprise was buffeted by thickening atmosphere.

"To the bridge!" Uhura's voice cried out over the ship's speakers.

The next slash of the blade caught Kirk across his chest, slicing his shirt, drawing blood.

The Gorn growled in triumph, struck again.

Kirk moved by training, by instinct, deflected the Gorn's follow-through by grabbing its massive green hand, forcing the blade back and up and into the creature's thick neck.

The Gorn's shriek was deafening in the cramped car. Gouts of purple blood sprayed from the gaping wound as the creature threw itself from wall to wall.

The heat of the dying beast burned into Kirk as the Gorn fell against him, crushing him against unyielding doors.

3

Kirk struggled to free himself even as the creature's life ended. The Gorn slid to the floor of the turbolift car. Its huge body shivered once in death, then stilled.

The car slowed.

Kirk looked down at his chest, his shirt smeared with Gorn blood mingled with his own.

The slashing wound was deep. But there was no time to get to McCoy in sickbay. Not with the Enterprise *so close to destruction.*

So close to death.

The car doors opened.

Kirk ran from the turbolift, onto his bridge.

He called for Uhura.

No answer.

Instead, at her station, he saw a white object with pentagonal sides, small enough to fit in his hand.

Instinctively he knew the object was Uhura. She had been reduced to her basic chemical components.

Kirk couldn't remember why it was important that he had that information. He just knew it was.

His gaze shifted to the main viewscreen, where hellish flames leapt among the stars at warp.

The Enterprise *was flying through the galactic barrier. In the very same moment, she screamed through the atmosphere of an unknown planet . . . at the same time that her engines tore themselves apart while her crew was reduced to—*

"It's a dream!" Kirk shouted his realization, held out his fists in protest. "It's the dream."

But this time, unlike all the other times, whether it was Harry Mudd or Kodos who pursued him, the knowledge that he was dreaming was not enough to let him wake.

This time, he still fought to keep his balance on the shifting deck.

Kirk stumbled to his chair, clung to it, staring at the flames on the viewscreen.

"Spock! Analysis!"

Spock turned from his science station, his familiar face ice blue in the glow from his holographic viewer.

"Do I have your attention?" Spock calmly inquired.

"Yes—tell me what we're facing." Kirk took a step toward Spock.

But as fast as Kirk could advance, Spock shrank back, receding from him as the bridge itself began dissolving into a cloud of dark sand.

Kirk felt as if he himself were shrinking, his whole existence swirling down some unseen vortex, into the compression of an all-devouring black hole.

"We're life, Jim," Spock called from the distance. "But not as they know it."

Kirk reached out to his friend, wanting, needing, to understand.

"Spock, explain . . ."

But Spock's only answer was a far-off echo: "Do I have your attention . . ."

The instant the black spiral claimed him, Kirk, at last, awoke on his new ship, the *Belle Rêve*.

He sat up on the side of his bunk in his narrow cabin—the finest on the ship despite its size.

The sweat was cold on his forehead.

His heartbeat thundered in his ears.

The dream had changed. Not just the Gorn . . . Spock.

And that changed what Starfleet and Admiral Kathryn Janeway had steadfastly refused to believe for more than a year.

Somewhere, Kirk knew beyond doubt, Spock was still alive.

Spock had called out to him.

"We're life, Jim. But not as they know it."

Spock had Kirk's attention.

1

The citizens of Alpha Centauri B II, who had not thought of themselves as "colonists" for generations, were unprepared for the violence of the first attack. Nor had anyone anticipated the target of that violence.

Only the grove of fig trees planted by the great man himself more than two centuries earlier survived. The rest of the Cochrane Institute lay in ruins.

But the day that ended with the gathering storm of war had begun as any other on a world complacent and too used to peace.

It was late winter in the Northern Hemisphere of New Montana; the stars Centauri A and Centauri B rose together in the dawn. Only during summer is sunlight present for a full twenty-six hours each day. That's the season when the orbit of Centauri B's second planet places it between the two larger stars of the ternary Alpha Centauri system.

On the island continent of Atlantis, the early morning then was crisp, the forests of Earth maple and birch bare of leaves, their empty branches little more than quick dark brush strokes against the pure blue canvas of a sky that had not been "alien" to humans for centuries.

Outside the main urban centers of the east coast, smoke trailed from the chimneys of housing clusters. The crackle and scent of burning wood added the sensory texture missing from the island's efficient geothermal power plants that provided energy to its scattered communities. It was only at the Cochrane Institute that planet-based antimatter generators were used, a requirement of its cutting-edge work in warp propulsion.

More than thirty major buildings formed the main campus, their dusky red forms sweeping up a gentle rise of green foothills. The structures that commanded the hilltops looked out to Lily's Ocean to the east and the rugged Rockier Mountains to the west. As the first human to journey to Centauri B II, Zefram Cochrane had thoroughly enjoyed exercising his right to name both the planet and its major geological features.

One of the uppermost buildings was a Starfleet installation. The research performed there was restricted, ensuring that Starfleet's capabilities would always remain significantly more advanced than those of civilian ships, privateers, and any potential "peer competitors"—Starfleet's current bland term for the restive Klingon Empire.

Officially known as Facility 18, the building was older than the others, constructed almost ninety standard years earlier. Its historic façade of intricately sculpted, red Centauran sandstone was set off by bold horizontal timbers of the pale, native Lincoln trees praised—and named—by Cochrane for producing logs of exceptional uniformity.

Facility 18's stark and sleek interior, however, revealed signs of regular rebuilding and upgrading. The most recent changes dated from the frantic months toward the end of the Dominion War, eight years earlier. Though the realization was never discussed in public, the leadership of Starfleet was uncomfortably aware that the war's heavy price for survival had also spurred one of the most productive periods of scientific advancement Starfleet had experienced for generations.

On this date, Middleday, Twelfthmonth 27 on New Montana, Stardate 58552.2 for the Federation at large, Facility 18 was preparing to run a static test on a prototype warp core. Little different in principle from those in service on most Starfleet vessels, the experimental device was notable for its size—almost one-third smaller than the standard design for its payload capacity. The anticipation was that, within a decade at the present rate of development, Starfleet would be able to test runabout-size vessels capable of warp-nine velocities. In terms of travel time, the galaxy grew smaller every day.

The prototype warp core was scheduled to come online at 0800 hours. For this test, it would produce a warp bubble approximately four meters in diameter with a field strength of no more than five millicochranes. These specifics were important: A warp field that weak would not be able to pop out of the planet's relativistic frame. Even more significant, the core would remain motionless as researchers measured the field's shape and stability, and the efficiency of the miniaturized synthetic-dilithium matrix—one of the keys to the warp core's smaller size.

If the test were successful, space trials would follow, with the prototype warp core installed on a test sled.

But the test was not successful, and Starfleet's Advanced Warp Development Group paid the price of that failure.

Commander Tresk Drumain was a third-generation Starfleet engineer, and the lead investigator on the current prototype tests. He had arrived at Facility 18 at noon the day before, and had worked through the night to prepare the prototype core for the static test.

As the time for the initialization approached, Drumain needed no coffee or other stimulant to stay awake. He was thirty-four standard years old, and the excitement and the challenge of the moment were more than enough to keep him alert. Even making commander by age thirty-two hadn't been as thrilling as this test promised to be.

Drumain felt confident in his team's preparations. The prototype core was already locked down in the center of the main test chamber—an immense, reinforced, triduranium-sheathed room more than one hundred meters on a side. Even if a miscalculation or a power surge resulted in the core jumping to warp, the chamber was aligned so that the planet's own rotation would cause the core to slam into a vast reservoir containing four hundred thousand liters of water. That reservoir was built into the grassy hillside to the east of Facility 18. Because the core's power supply remained outside the warp field, the field would collapse instantly, allowing for no more than a few hundred meters of travel.

There was no need for concern.

At 0750, in the dimly lit control room overlooking the test chamber, Drumain took his chair at the main monitoring console. As scheduled, the triduranium blast shield slid silently over the large observation window. Now the test core was visible only on the rows of console monitors displaying visual sensor readings from inside the chamber.

Three hours earlier, the atmosphere had been pumped out of the test chamber, leaving the core in a vacuum that was almost the equal of interstellar space. The visual images from inside the chamber were sharp and clear.

At 0755, Drumain glanced again at the message padd propped on the console so all could see. It held the good luck wishes of Commander Geordi La Forge. The man was a legend in Starfleet, and Drumain and his crew had been surprised and encouraged to realize that one of Starfleet's greatest engineering geniuses was paying personal attention to what they were attempting here. La Forge had asked to be informed about the test results as quickly as possible, and Drumain looked forward to making that call sometime before lunch.

At 0759, Drumain polled his team—a group of more than fifty Starfleet and institute personnel. Their responses were instant and reassuring. All systems on the test core were checked and ready. All sensors were operational. The antimatter generator was online and producing the required level of power.

Drumain tugged down on his Starfleet jacket as the final few seconds of the countdown proceeded.

Timecode: zero.

Everything occurred exactly as planned.

For eighteen seconds.

That was when a warning alert flashed on Drumain's board. A minor power surge.

It wasn't large enough for the computer safety subroutines to automatically shut down the test, but the warning prompted Drumain to keep his hand over the large red "kill" switch.

His eyes jumped back and forth between the display showing the power graph and the display showing the test core, but except for the soft blue glow of the Cerenkov emitters running along its side, the core was unchanged from its initial condition.

Around him, Drumain could hear his team's quick whispered conversations as they tried to isolate the reason for the surge.

Mirrin O'Hara was the first to see and report the residue.

At once, Drumain called for the visual sensors to enlarge the view of the core.

What he saw onscreen was puzzling. A dark shadow was forming around the core's casing, growing as randomly as fingers of frost spidering over a window in winter.

Drumain enlarged the sensor image even more.

At closer resolution, the residue resembled grains of black sand. But now Drumain could see that it was accreting into cubes, the largest no more than a decimeter or so across, the others in a range of smaller sizes, some little more than specks.

O'Hara readily identified the chemical composition of the residue: mostly carbon, with traces of simpler elements, down to and including hydrogen.

The warp-field strength began to change.

Drumain immediately checked the vacuum readings in the chamber—it was still holding. He frowned. The residue wasn't particulate matter condensing out of the air. There *was* no air.

The only explanation was that it was being *created* by the warp field.

And that was impossible.

The impossible, however, continued until 0802, when the warp field flared.

That finally triggered the automatic cutoffs, and then—for no reason that Drumain could establish—all the chamber's sensors went offline.

He polled his team again. No one had any explanation for what they had seen or what their sensors had measured.

Drumain needed more information. He ordered the chamber repressurized, then motioned to O'Hara to come with him. They took the stairs down to the main entry doors. Because internal sensors remained inoperative, Drumain was careful to use his tricorder to scan the room behind the doors, verifying that the chamber had full atmosphere and no radiation. O'Hara confirmed his findings.

The doors slid apart, and Drumain felt a rush of chilled air as the slight overpressure in the revealed chamber equalized. At once, he smelled something electric, burnt, the odor unnerving to an engineer.

All the chamber lights were out.

Before he could even request it, O'Hara opened a critical-equipment locker beside the doors and retrieved two palmlights. With their twin beams of light sweeping over the distant test core, Drumain took the first steps into the chamber as O'Hara followed close behind. Their footsteps echoed in the metal-clad chamber.

As they drew nearer and their palmlights revealed more details, Drumain saw that the cylindrical core, nine meters long and two meters in cross section, hadn't shifted from its test bed. But the test bed itself was barely visible. It thrust upward as if trying to escape the mound of dark cubes piled around it like drifting sand poised to engulf a pyramid on Mars.

Black residue clung to the sides of the core like frozen streams of water.

Drumain gestured to O'Hara to circle round the core to the left. He took the right.

Other than the residue, neither of their tricorders detected anything beyond the ordinary.

But tricorders had their limitations.

Drumain reached the front of the core, and nearly dropped the device.

A Starfleet admiral was standing there, waiting.

Before he could even begin to ask her how she could possibly have survived the vacuum *and* the energy fluctuations of the warp field, the admiral smiled at him.

"Hello, Tresk," she said.

It wasn't the tone an admiral used to address a subordinate officer—it was the greeting of an intimate friend. And now that Drumain could see her more clearly in the beam from his palmlight, she seemed far too young to have attained her rank.

"Admiral . . . did you just beam in?"

The admiral's warm smile expanded, and Drumain had a sudden realization that explained the familiarity of her voice—Eleanor Stein.

Twelve years ago, in their last year at the Academy, he had lost his heart to her. But she, like him, had valued a Starfleet career more than passion, and after graduation they had taken separate paths. Drumain still dreamed of her, and had always wondered if she dreamed of him.

"I do," the admiral said, answering his unspoken question.

A wave of gooseflesh swept up Drumain's spine to prickle the close-cropped hair at the back of his neck and scalp. The admiral took a step forward. With that one movement, she no longer *resembled* his long-lost love, she *became* her, just as she had been twelve years ago, her admiral's uniform now a cadet's jumpsuit.

Drumain blinked, incredulous. "Eleanor . . . ?"

"Commander . . . who're you talking to?" O'Hara came around the front of the core, then stopped dead in surprise. She shone her palmlight into the cadet's eyes. "Where'd you come from?"

"Mirrin," the cadet said as she turned away from Drumain to O'Hara.

Drumain blinked again, puzzled, but relieved. The light had played tricks on him. In profile, the admiral looked nothing at all like his memory of Eleanor. Even her jumpsuit looked like a civilian outfit.

"Mom . . . ?"

Drumain recognized a familiar shock in O'Hara's voice. As if relays closed in his brain, triggering his own internal safety overrides, he switched from engineer to Starfleet officer.

He and O'Hara faced a human where no human could reasonably be—a human disturbingly like a lover he'd never forgotten, yet also like his teammate's mother.

There could be only one explanation, one thing to do.

Drumain's finger trembled as he tapped his combadge. He hoped there was still time, but feared there was not. "Drumain to Security. Intruder alert. Test Chamber One."

The intruder turned, and with that motion her features blurred, then focused. She was Eleanor again.

"Oh, Tresk, that wasn't necessary. There's nothing to fear now. . . ."

"O'Hara," Drumain said urgently, "get out of here. Run."

Without taking her eyes off Drumain, the cadet held out her hand to O'Hara—

—*and that hand stretched through the air like smoke.*

Drumain's breath left him as the dark strand writhed toward O'Hara.

O'Hara's palmlight and tricorder dropped, clanging on the triduranium tiles, as she clawed at the black substance that swept over her face.

Drumain found his voice. "Let her go!"

The cadet shook her head. "I know she wants this. So do you."

Drumain heard rustling. He looked down in horror. There, in the slash of light sent by O'Hara's palmlight across the chamber floor, undulating shadows of black residue flowed from the test core to his boots.

Drumain tried to step back, but he felt resistance. He twisted around.

The black cubes were stacking up behind him, already as high as his knees.

He began to fall, but the cadet was suddenly before him, both arms wrapped around him, just as Eleanor had held him on their last night together.

"Accept. . . ." she said.

Drumain's pulse fluttered with fear as he stared past his captor to a small mound of utter blackness that was rapidly dissolving into wisps of smoke.

It was all that was left of O'Hara.

"Embrace. . . ."

Drumain looked into eyes that held all the love he had forgotten, the desire he had tried to banish from his life.

". . . No . . ." he whispered, even as he felt his own body absorbing, dissolving . . .

"Be loved. . . ." Soft lips sought his, and Drumain felt his mouth open wide as black tendrils streamed down to fill his throat and seal his lungs. His vision dimmed, then died as a once-beloved face exploded into dark particles and engulfed him.

At 0808, a Starfleet security team watched helpless in amazement as a slowly moving, cresting wave of black sand began rising in the test chamber. As Tresk Drumain joined Mirrin O'Hara in the Peace of the Totality.

At 0809, the test core exploded.

The surge along the power conduits to the anti-matter generator released magnetic containment.

In the next ten seconds, there were seven more explosions. In less than a minute, all thirty buildings of the institute were in flames.

Two minutes later, eight hundred and fifteen personnel perished.

Over the next three days, three hundred and twenty more succumbed to injuries.

Only the fig trees survived. Planted by the man whose genius had made the United Federation of Planets possible, and now the only living witnesses to the beginning of the Federation's end.

The Totality was finally ready to share its gift with all the species of the galaxy.

And it knew that once that gift was truly understood, it would be accepted without hesitation.

2

In less than an hour, the star would die.

It would take more than five hundred years for the light of its passing to reach Earth, but long before then the star's demise would be analyzed and understood by the astronomers on board the starship now orbiting it.

It had taken less than three months for the *U.S.S. Titan* to reach Salton Cross. And, despite the immensity of space and the multitude of stars, given the unique nature of this one star it was inevitable that the *Titan* would not be alone.

The *Luna*-class starship's classic twin-nacelle silhouette, flattened as if it had been frozen in the moment of its jump to warp speed, was framed both by the immense blue-white star it had come to study and by the gleaming, chrome-finish spikes and vanes of the Araldii ship that had joined it.

The two vessels, their commanders confident in the ability of their ships' engines, were within the destruction zone of the coming supernova. But where there was danger, there was also the opportunity for scientific discovery. That's what their mission was this day.

Neither ship's commander knew of the war that had begun.

As much as Will Riker had enjoyed and treasured his time as first officer of the *Enterprise*, he had no trouble admitting that being captain of the *Titan* was even better.

His command was one of Starfleet's newest class of starships, a return to the ideals of the Federation's past, built for exploration as much as for military missions. Deceptively small, remarkably efficient in design and engineering, it was also home to a unique community of three hundred and fifty of the Federation's best and brightest. Riker took pride in knowing that of the twelve *Luna*-class vessels in service, his ship held the most diverse crew. There were only fifty humans in its company.

That mix of human and aliens of all species—from Ferengi to Syrath, Cardassian to Vulcan, Trill to Pahk-wathanh—filled the *Titan* with a vibrant mood of shared purpose and discovery. There was no greater adventure, no greater calling, than expanding the limits of knowledge, human and otherwise.

For some, Riker knew, the words bordered on cliché, and their grammar was questionable to be sure, but the speech Zefram Cochrane had given centuries ago still served perfectly to define the *Titan*'s mission—the mission for all beings at all times—"to boldly go."

Riker couldn't imagine a better, more fulfilling life. Especially since he shared it with his wife, his *imzadi* for decades, Deanna Troi.

Today, they were starting their workday as they usually did, in Riker's ready room, he with his coffee, she with her tea.

Their topic of conversation, however, was a first for the *Titan*. They were in the midst of planning a formal reception and dinner for the Araldii, the newest species with which the Federation had made first contact.

More to the point, it was the first truly unknown species with which Captain Riker and the *Titan* had made first contact, without any preparation from Starfleet's First Contact Office.

Which is why he and Troi had been joined this morning by Ship Leader Fortral, commander of the Araldii ship the *Titan* had encountered.

"It will be possible to reduce the atmospheric pressure in our reception hall to five hundred torr," Troi said, referring to the notes on her protocol padd. On the *Titan*, Troi served both as ship's counselor *and* diplomatic officer.

There was a brief lag as Fortral listened to the translator device in her headphones. According to the datastreams the ship leader had provided to the *Titan*, Aralda was a large world, twice the size of Earth, yet with gravity only two-thirds Earth normal. Its low density was in part responsible for its equally low-pressure atmosphere. The headphones Fortral wore not only fulfilled the need of providing translation functions, they helped diminish what was, to Araldii, the deafening volume and high pitch of human voices and the background noises of the *Titan*'s environmental systems.

"The low pressure will not cause you discomfort?" Fortral asked in concern. The dark blue, tigerlike stripes that ran horizontally across her pale blue skin glistened as her primary mouth moved. Her secondary mouth, located in what for humans would be the mid-chin region of her face, remained closed, used only for eating and drinking.

Fortral's own voice was a soft, almost impossible-to-hear whisper. Riker's and Troi's universal translators re-created the gentle quality of the ship leader's speech while boosting its volume.

"No," Troi said. "Though it will affect the preparation of some of the foods we plan to serve."

"We appreciate the gesture of goodwill," Fortral said.

"As we appreciate the data you shared with us concerning the supernova," Riker replied with a broad smile.

The *Titan* had arrived at Salton Cross two weeks earlier. The Type O star was eight times larger than Earth's sun and had been catalogued centuries ago. But only in the past two decades had scientists reached the conclusion that the star was about to become a supernova.

Accordingly, the *Titan* had been tasked with ferrying a large contingent of astronomers and astrophysicists to the immediate vicinity of the star in order to observe its death throes.

In retrospect, Riker realized, he should not have been surprised to find an alien vessel already on station, waiting for the end; Araldii astrophysicists were the equal of the Federation's. In fact, they had more detailed acoustic scans of the star's surface than Starfleet's automated probes had captured. Fortunately, the Araldii had been pleased with the historical observations that Riker had been able to share in exchange. The Araldii had not been studying the star for as long as humans had.

One of Fortral's dark blue stripes flickered white for an instant and she held up her three-fingered hand—a human gesture Troi had shown her in the past few weeks—so Fortral could stop humans from talking as an "entangled" message came to her.

The stripes were not a natural part of Fortral's body or coloration, but appeared, instead, to be a type of technology Riker and his science department had never seen. He'd asked his staff to try to determine if the stripes were the result of genetic engineering or nanite implants. They were still working on the matter.

What they were able to tell him was that the stripes functioned as communicators, transponders, tricorders, and even—*Titan*'s chief security officer had informed Riker, though the effect had never been demonstrated—as weapons.

Riker found all this fascinating. The basic tools of modern life aboard a starship could never be taken from the Araldii, because they were already incorporated into their flesh.

"My science leader informs me that the final detonation is approaching," Fortral said.

Reflexively, Riker looked out the ready room's portal. It was dialed down to almost total opacity, but Salton Cross filled more than half the view and the star's blinding light was still hot on his face. The warmth reminded Riker of being on an actual ocean-going vessel, sails snapping, salt spray flying, sun blazing. He knew he would have been an explorer in any age to which he'd been born.

"That's in line with our predictions, as well," Troi confirmed.

Riker blinked as Fortral unnervingly *flowed* from the chair to a standing position. That really was the best term to describe the movement, he decided. His ship's medical scans had indicated that the Araldii did not have a skeletal system, though they did have adaptive muscle bundles that fulfilled the same supportive function. Apparently, however, different postures required different arrangements of muscles. Whenever an Araldon moved from one position to another, it was almost as if air had been let out of her in one place so she could be reinflated in another.

And, Riker reminded himself, the Araldii on their ship *were* all females. Why there were no Araldii males on board was a question that had not yet been solved by either group's translators. It was as if the question made no sense, or had no relevance to Fortral's people.

"I should return, then," Fortral said as her muscle bundles took on her walking configuration. "We will depart ahead of the shock wave as planned."

At a nod from Troi, Riker stood as did she.

The plan that all had agreed to was that the *Titan* would withdraw from the north pole of Salton Cross at just under warp one. Doing so would permit the ship's sensors to record high-resolution, time-expanded data from the star's explosion. Fortral's ship would do the same from the star's south pole.

Riker and Fortral had set a week's time for their next rendezvous. He was looking forward to the exchange of their sensor logs and the celebration of their first contact with a reception. The festivities would necessarily be taking place on the *Titan*. Human visitors to the attenuated atmosphere of the Araldii ship developed the equivalent of mountain sickness within hours.

Riker held out his hands to either side, palms out, as a human might gesture to indicate he carried no weapons; it was the Araldii gesture of greeting and farewell. "Ship Leader Fortral, I wish you a safe journey and look forward to your return."

Fortral returned the gesture to Riker and to Troi as she waited for her translator to finish whispering Riker's words to her. Then she replied, "I wish you the same, and with sincerity, may many males inhabit you."

The Araldii ship leader then distorted her mouth in what some might think was a passable imitation of a human smile. Riker immediately turned to Troi for insight into Fortral's strange statement, but the ship's counselor just shook her head at him. When he turned back to Fortral, all the Araldon's blue stripes were glistening, most of them flickering between dark blue

25

and white. A moment later, she flickered into transparency, caught by her ship's transporter.

" 'May many males *inhabit* you'?" Riker asked.

Troi shrugged. "Whatever it meant, she said it with absolute conviction and well wishes. And I think she was actually trying to smile at you."

"Then I'll feel honored . . . I guess."

The computer display on Riker's desk chimed. *"Bridge to Captain Riker."* It was Riker's first officer, Commander Christine Vale.

"Go ahead."

"Captain, the Araldii ship is withdrawing. Doctor Burke suggests we do the same."

"On my way," Riker answered. He gestured to the door leading to the bridge. "Time to go to work."

Husband and wife, captain and counselor, Riker and Troi stepped onto the bridge of the *Titan*.

Joanna Burke, director of astronomy at the moon's Weiler Observatory, was already waiting, standing by the science station to which she'd been assigned. Her attention was riveted on the main viewscreen, where Salton Cross seemed to pulse as its surface roiled with magnetic eddies large enough to swallow planets.

Commander Vale smoothly stood up from the center chair and moved to the right. "All systems ready for warp-point-nine-five withdrawal, bearing zero zero niner zero."

As Riker sat down in the center chair at the back of the bridge, he thought again that its arrangement was a most comfortable combination of those on the *Enterprise*-D and -E. He spoke to his navigator. "Ensign

Lavena, move us into position above the pole and prepare for warp."

"Aye, sir." Aili Lavena's hydration suit made its characteristic gurgle of slow shifting water as she expertly moved her sheathed hands across her control board. As a marine humanoid at this stage in her life cycle, the Pacifican female was at home only in a fully aquatic environment.

But Lavena's control of the *Titan* was assured and absolute, and in response to her flight commands, Salton Cross appeared to rotate on the viewscreen. The movement stopped only when the *Titan* was eighty million kilometers directly above its north magnetic pole.

"Magnificent," Doctor Burke said. "Neutrino flux peaked one hundred, twelve minutes ago when the star's core collapsed. The shock wave is just about to reach the surface. We can expect the initial blast to begin within five minutes."

"Shields on full," Riker ordered, even though he doubted they'd be required. At a distance of only eighty million kilometers from a supernova, the *Titan*'s shields would likely not protect the ship for more than a minute or two, and he had no desire to stay in place long enough to test the estimate. Riker had learned from his mentor to err on the side of caution wherever possible.

"Shields on full," Commander Tuvok confirmed. As tactical officer, the Vulcan who had served with such distinction on Admiral Janeway's *Voyager* brought a wealth of welcome experience to Riker's crew. He had kept the ship operating smoothly during the first forty-eight hours of the *Titan's* encounter with the Araldii, when the newcomers' intentions had been unknown. Once their peaceful and cooperative nature had been confirmed, both by their willingness to share scientific data and Troi's own empathic sensitivity, Tuvok had concerned himself solely with the safety precautions required for being so close to a star about to explode.

"Neutrino flux has dropped to zero," Burke announced. "This is it."

Riker instinctively wrapped his mind around the relativistic effects he had to account for in the next few minutes. He knew that neutrinos traveled at the speed of light. The fact that the ones produced in the core of Salton Cross were no longer being detected at this distance meant that the fusion reactions at the heart of the star had stopped four minutes and twenty-seven seconds ago. That was the brief time it took neutrinos to travel eighty million kilometers.

The visual image on the viewscreen, however, was constructed by subspace sensor data that propagated at faster-than-light speeds. Most important, that meant he could see the star as it was *now*.

As Riker watched intently, the star—abruptly—began to grow smaller, as if the *Titan* were already warping away.

"There it goes," Burke said with excitement. "The star is collapsing—there's no outward pressure of internal fusion reactions to counteract the inward pull of gravity."

Riker held a hand near his face, as did everyone else on the bridge. Even with visual safeguards in place, the flash of light was going to be strong.

"Criticality in seven . . . six . . . five . . . four . . . three . . ."

Burke's countdown was interrupted.

Two seconds ahead of her best estimate, Salton Cross went supernova.

Over the past few weeks, Riker had come to know Burke well enough to realize that she would be thrilled to have miscalculated and would already be mentally revising her model of the star's interior processes.

The main viewscreen went white.

Thanks to the preparatory sessions Burke's team had conducted for interested *Titan* crew, Riker understood why. Slightly less than four minutes and twenty-seven seconds away, a deadly wave of radiation was streaming toward his ship. It would be followed by a slightly slower though even more destructive wall of ejected solar plasma.

The radiation had the capability to knock out every system on *Titan*, including the shields. And if those failed, every member of the crew would be fatally irradiated within seconds. A few minutes later, when the shock wave hit the ship, the *Titan* would be shattered, likely into its component molecules.

Riker had no intention of waiting for any of that to happen.

"That's it, Aili . . . take us out, warp-factor-point-nine-five."

"Point-nine-five it is, Captain."

Riker leaned back in his chair, smiled at Troi. "Best seats in the house," he said.

In that same instant the main alarm sounded and red lights flashed.

The *Titan* violently pitched forward, then down.

Riker swiftly scanned his bridge. Under present conditions, the strength of that lag in the inertial dampers could mean only one thing: The ship had dropped out of warp as quickly as it had jumped to it.

"Report!" he said, but already his eyes had found the source of the trouble: Every warning light at the engineering station flashed red.

Riker's conn officer fought to keep *Titan*'s dampers and structural-integrity field in alignment.

"Engineering reports warp core offline," Tuvok calmly announced over the alarms.

"Maximum impulse!" Riker ordered. Though they couldn't reach light speed on impulse alone, increasing the distance between the radiation shock wave and the ship would buy his ship a few more seconds. "Bridge to engineering!"

The *Titan*'s chief engineer, Doctor Xin Ra-Havreii, answered at once, his voice uncharacteristically tense. Riker could hear shouted commands and rapid conversations in the background. *"Engineering, Captain."*

"How soon can you bring warp drive back online?" Riker asked, urgent.

"It is *online—the core's building toward a breach! This is a full-scale—"* There was a pause, then Riker heard the Efrosian engineer swear in one of his homeworld's more obscure dialects.

"Stand by, Captain! Initiating emergency core ejection!"

Riker's ship shuddered. All alarms switched off.

"Warp core away," Ra-Havreii said.

A moment later, the ejected core detonated less than a kilometer from the ship.

The too-close explosion drove subspace concussion waves into the *Titan*, overloading its shields and sending a compression pulse through all major circuits.

The lights on the bridge flickered off.

The main viewscreen winked out.

The ship's computer network was down.

Riker was on his feet. Battery-powered emergency lights glowed, but the display screens at all stations flashed with random static.

All hands on the bridge turned to their captain for his orders.

But the *Titan* hung dead in space.

And less than four minutes away, a wall of radiation raced forward at 300,000 kilometers each second to ensure the same fate would soon befall her crew.

3

"Give me one good reason why I shouldn't have you court-martialed," Admiral Janeway said. "In fact, I could use a good reason for not just chucking you out of the airlock right now."

Captain James T. Kirk sat back on his bench in the narrow galley of the *Belle Rêve* and realized he had no answer for the admiral—at least, not one that he'd accept if he were in her position.

He wasn't surprised by Janeway's frustration with him. He knew it had been building for several months, so he couldn't even feign innocence, which was usually one of his better strategies.

He was guilty as charged and that was all there was to it.

A year ago, when he had been on board Captain Riker's *Titan,* Janeway had given him the ship he now commanded. Then, it had been called the *Calypso*, but as the ship's new master he'd changed her name to *Belle Rêve*—Beautiful Dream.

What better name could there be for a ship that sailed among the stars? Except, perhaps, for *Enterprise*.

According to the central registries, the *S.S. Belle Rêve* was a commercial freighter of Rigelian registry. Her main hull was a blunt-nosed cylindrical module about the same size as a single nacelle from an old *Ambassador*-class ship. She had a slightly tapered bulge at the rear of her ventral hull, and two swept-back, outboard warp nacelles. The nacelles were also cylindrical. To Kirk's eye, they gave his ship the look of an antique.

But, more significantly, what the old-fashioned configuration hid was a cleverly engineered distributed-phaser system. Its critical components were spread throughout the ship so that they could be powered up without being detected. Binary quantum torpedoes shared the same characteristic: They didn't go "live" until their warhead components were mated just two seconds before launch. Until that last moment of assembly, even the sensors on Jean-Luc Picard's *Enterprise* would have trouble detecting such uniquely arrayed armaments.

When its *Defiant*-class warp engines were added to the mix, making the small ship vastly overpowered and exceedingly fast, all the ingredients for being one of Starfleet's best Q-ships were in place.

In the vernacular of an earlier time, Kirk's *Belle Rêve* was a spy trawler that sailed where Starfleet chose not to fly its colors.

"I'm waiting," Janeway said.

Kirk decided to rely on a tried-and-true technique: He answered the question he felt she *should* have asked him.

"I think I've done a good job of fulfilling my obligations to you."

Janeway blinked as if she hadn't heard him correctly.

"Captain," she said, more than a hint of irritation in her tone, "I came all this way because you *haven't* fulfilled your obligations."

Kirk spoke lightly, but his words carried serious intent. "Is that what *you* really think? Or is that what Starfleet told you to say?"

Janeway leaned forward, punctuating her words by tapping her finger against the galley table. "I gave you this ship so you could be the eyes and ears of Starfleet where and when we can't send an identifiable ship of our own."

"You gave me this ship so I could investigate Spock's disappearance."

Janeway would not be deflected. "Captain Kirk . . . Ambassador Spock is dead."

Kirk felt his chest tighten, but he restrained any show of frustration. It had been years since he had been subjected to Starfleet's chain of command, even longer since he felt he owed it any particular allegiance.

"We don't know that," he said. The dream was vivid in his memory: *Do I have your attention?*

"I read your report about the events on Remus."

"Then you also know Spock was absorbed by an unknown phenomenon—"

Janeway interrupted to correct him. "Disintegrated."

Kirk continued as if she hadn't spoken. "—and his fate remains undetermined."

Janeway shook her head. "Is that what this has been about?" she asked. "You're not just looking for the people responsible. You really think *he's* still out there?" The admiral's voice held both pity and annoyance. The combination was not lost on Kirk. But he didn't take the bait.

"Of course I do," he said. The dream wasn't evidence he could share with her. But there was other proof. "I saw what Norinda was capable of. The shapeshifting—"

With a wave of her hand, Janeway cut him off again. "I know all this. The changing into clouds of dark smoke, mounds of black sand, cubes of different sizes . . ."

Kirk paused a moment, struggling to keep his vivid recollection of Spock's disappearance, and the revulsion and the fear it came with, from weakening the case he knew he had to make. "Norinda controlled a technology—or natural abilities—beyond our capacity to define them. Spock *might* be dead. But he might just as well have been taken by an alien transporter."

Janeway got up from her bench, then walked to the replicator to study its controls. Kirk understood that the admiral was trying to prevent herself from saying something she might regret. They were both attempting to restrain themselves.

Janeway punched the code for coffee, standard.

"One more time," she said. "You saw him *disintegrated* before your eyes."

Kirk joined her by the replicator, waited until she'd taken her coffee mug. "I've seen Spock 'disintegrated' thousands of times in transporter beams." He punched the controls for a Vulcan espresso—no caffeine.

"Then for all the times you've been 'unavailable' for special duty, why haven't we found you heading back to the Romulan home system?"

Kirk held his coffee cup in a mock toast to Janeway. She merely cupped her own mug for warmth.

"Because," Kirk said, "Norinda failed to provoke a civil war between Romulus and Remus and the *Jolan* Movement fell apart after her disappearance." He took a sip of the hot liquid, detecting as always the loss of authenticity in replication. "As Spock would say, whatever her ultimate goal, logic suggests she's trying to set up a new movement on another world."

Janeway stared at him with something close to suspicion. "At your debriefing, you told the review board exactly what Norinda's ultimate goal was."

"I told the review board what Norinda *said* was her ultimate goal. There's a difference."

"What?" Janeway demanded.

Kirk stayed silent for a moment. He had originally encountered the shapeshifting alien life-form called Norinda in the early months of his first five-year mission as captain of the *Enterprise,* NCC-1701. She had lied to him then, told him a story about having escaped from "the Totality"—an ominous alien force that had somehow conquered the Andromeda Galaxy.

A lifetime later, he had met her again on Remus,

where she claimed to lead a peace movement that had been banished from Romulus. But all the while, it was Norinda and her followers who'd been attempting to start the very civil war that she claimed to oppose.

"She told me she'd make the Romulans and the Remans want peace by exposing them to war," Kirk said. "She said her goal was to leave both planets in ruins, with millions dead, because only then would the survivors realize the value of love."

"But you don't believe that."

Kirk's mind filled with images of all the different forms in which Norinda had appeared to him, remembering how she'd used some kind of subconscious telepathy to assume the appearance of the woman most desired by whomever she happened to speak with.

"She's a monster," Kirk said at last. "The only peace she can bring is that of the grave. She even appeared to my son as his mother."

Kirk had had this discussion a year ago. He had settled it then. He settled it now. "I believe all Norinda wants is destruction. To her, the only world that can be at peace is a world without life."

Janeway hesitated, then seemingly changed the subject of their conversation.

"Have you ever thought that Starfleet's goals and yours might not be that far apart?"

"Admiral, if you're looking for common ground, you're not going to find it. I want to rescue Spock. Starfleet thinks he's dead."

"But it's obvious to me that you're trying to find

Spock by tracking down Norinda. I suggest that's where our goals converge."

Kirk reconsidered what he knew of Janeway. She was shrewd, immensely capable. She had brought her ship and her crew back from the wilds of the Delta Quadrant with honor. Her promotion to the admiralty had been a foregone conclusion. He even found her quite attractive and thought he could find her more so, if she ever decided to stop being an admiral for a day.

But he also knew that she was more solidly connected to Starfleet than he had been or ever would be, now. Like his friend Jean-Luc, Kathryn Janeway could be relied upon to put the needs of Starfleet and the Federation first. Except, of course, in cases of egregious misconduct.

But for Janeway, in those circumstances for which there were no clear-cut divisions between right and wrong, Starfleet would always be right by default, until proven otherwise.

Which means, if Starfleet is searching for Norinda . . . Kirk paused in the midst of that thought.

"I've always suspected there was something you weren't telling me," he said. "The day you offered me this ship, I sensed it. Right now, I'm feeling it even more."

"Now *you've* changed the subject," Janeway said. She gave Kirk a tight smile.

"You've given me seven missions this past year. I took them all."

"You completed four."

"You called off my surveillance mission to the

38

Neutral Zone before I could reach it. The Andorian political prisoner you asked me to 'escort' to Deep Space Nine died en route—complications of torture."

"Suffered at the hands of the Klingons," Janeway said as she carefully placed her untouched coffee on the galley countertop. "Not Starfleet."

"So that only leaves one mission in contention," Kirk said.

"There's no contention. You were ordered to Inver Three. You refused to go. And a Starfleet covert observer team was lost as a result. Which brings us back to your court-martial."

"My *son* is on this ship," Kirk said. "My *friends*, Bones and Scotty. All of us civilians. Inver Three was unsafe. You needed to send in a recovery team. Not a spy ship."

"You *were* the recovery team," Janeway said accusingly. "An extraction team never would have made it through planetary defenses. But the *Belle Rêve* wouldn't have been questioned. Six men and two women would be alive today *except* for your refusal to obey orders."

"If you had asked *me*, I would have gone. But I don't put the innocent in harm's way. And the Starfleet I know wouldn't think of it."

That was when Kirk decided he had had enough of explaining and defending himself—to Janeway, and to Starfleet. He turned his back on such reminders of his old life. He headed for the open door that led to the central corridor, and his new life.

Kirk stepped into the corridor, remembering to duck his head while passing through the small hatch opening; the painful lessons of a year on this cramped vessel had taught him to be more mindful. This main passageway—barely wide enough for two people to stand side by side—was similarly constricted. Anyone taller than two meters had to contend with low-hanging overhead conduits and light fixtures.

Behind him, he heard the clanking of Janeway's boots on the corridor's metal-grid decking.

"Kirk—you can't walk away from this. We had a deal."

Kirk kept moving toward the interdeck ladder. "*My* deal was that I wouldn't place my crew in danger." He couldn't say it more plainly than that. A few quick steps more and he reached the ladder leading up to the bridge. The *Belle Rêve* had a single turbolift, but he preferred to climb whenever he could. The gym on the ship was little more than a treadmill with an erratic gravity adjustment.

"Captain Kirk! Get back here."

Kirk shook his head as he looked up, one hand already on the ladder. "One of us might say something we'll regret."

"Your friends might be civilians, but you're not."

Janeway had reached the ladder. She put her hand over his. "I suspect you refused the mission to Inver Three because you were caught up in following some lead on Manassas."

Kirk steeled himself not to shake off her hand. He had no wish to offend the admiral. But neither would he let her stop him. "This ship is mine to use as I wish between Starfleet missions. You told me that yourself."

"Yes. *Between* missions. But if you refused one because you were on a mission of your own, that is unacceptable."

Kirk felt Janeway's hand give his own a slight push before it dropped away, freeing him.

He took a breath to center himself, was aware of the thrum of the ship's warp generators, idling at standby, ready to burst into superluminal speeds at a single command from their captain. Kirk felt the pent-up energy of those engines move through him. He was unable to distinguish their needs from his own.

He *had* to keep moving.

Like his ship, he had been held in one place too long.

He relinquished his grasp on the ladder and turned to face Janeway. "I've said all I can say. I've filed my report. I've listened to you express Starfleet's interpretation of events. And here we are." Emotion was gone from him, and in that moment of clarity and reflection his thoughts turned once again to Spock. *We're life, Jim. . . .*

"You'll never be able to court-martial me with what you have—even for a Starfleet tribunal, there's too much room for reasonable doubt. So either take my ship from me now, or don't. But let's not waste any more time trying to resolve something that can't be resolved."

"You're willing to give this up?" Janeway said with open disbelief. It was clear to Kirk she meant the *Belle Rêve*.

"I can always get another ship," he said, though he knew he'd be hard-pressed to find one with this vessel's capabilities. "And my friends and my son will come with me. So I really have nothing of value to lose."

Janeway took so long to reply that for a moment it seemed she'd given up. But she'd only changed strategy, and the rules of their engagement.

"What if I told you the Starfleet team on Inver Three *didn't* get killed by rebels?"

Kirk didn't know what point she was trying to make. "Then I'd say you still had a chance to get a recovery team in there to extract them."

"We don't know where they are."

It was a simple statement, but there was something about the way Janeway said it that caught Kirk's attention. He studied her, trying to read her expression. But the admiral had served many years with a Vulcan as well. Her self-control was the equal of his own.

"What I'm about to tell you is classified far above what you're cleared for," Janeway said.

Kirk forced himself to stay silent. If he was about to hear information Janeway thought it was necessary for him to know, how could he *not* be cleared for it? Of all the ills of the past humanity had grown beyond, governmental bureaucracy remained as an echo of the dark ages.

"The entire negotiating team disappeared," Janeway said. "Within days of stopping the civil war on Inver Three, and bringing both sides together, *and* pulling that world back into the Federation."

Kirk was puzzled, and intrigued. Why was Janeway revealing this to him now? Especially since she had spent most of the past hour accusing him of complicity in the team's death.

"A planet's a big place," Kirk said, his tone neutral, all his senses alert to detect whatever else it was that Janeway was hiding from him.

Janeway finally acknowledged their unspoken battle of wills by conceding. She smiled in resignation. "All right. So now, maybe Starfleet will have to court-martial both of us."

Kirk shrugged, waiting, not sure if this was just another ploy on the admiral's part. "You get used to it." He regarded her with curiosity, waiting.

Janeway wasted no more of his time. "Over the past year and a half, one hundred and twenty-eight key Federation personnel have . . . vanished. If we count Ambassador Spock, it's one hundred and twenty-nine."

Irrational hope flared in Kirk. "A pattern?" he asked.

"Circumstantial," Janeway cautioned. "But there is reason to believe that at least some of the disappearances are connected."

Kirk's mind raced as he tried to find something in all he had learned about Spock and Norinda and the *Jolan* Movement of Romulus and Remus. Something that would suggest a link to other events.

He could think of nothing.

"Why did you wait so long to tell me?" Kirk asked. Had he wasted a year looking for Spock without the information he needed?

"We don't know who's responsible," Janeway admitted. "Starfleet Intelligence—"

"Intelligence?" Kirk was surprised to hear that department was involved.

"—is reluctant to declassify their investigations. They're concerned whoever's behind the disappearances might benefit from knowing that . . . we know nothing."

Kirk made himself ask the obvious question. "Has Starfleet Intelligence conducted an investigation into Spock's disappearance?"

Janeway nodded. "As part of their ongoing investigation of the other cases, they have."

"And?" Kirk asked.

Janeway shook her head in exasperation. "I'll say it once more—I think it's time we worked together."

Procedure over the welfare of individuals . . . Kirk felt the familiar heat of anger. *Mindless rules of behavior . . .* "I thought that's what we were doing this past year."

"I don't make policy, Captain. And you do have a reputation for not playing by the rules."

Kirk ignored the provocation to another argument. It *was* time to move on, though it appeared that, contrary to his first thoughts, he'd be moving on with Starfleet after all.

He put both hands on the ladder. "If Starfleet's going to help look for Spock, I want my crew to hear everything. No more secrecy. No more lies." Before Janeway could protest, Kirk started to climb. "I'll see you on the bridge."

By the time he'd reached A Deck, he understood exactly why someone would make one hundred twenty-nine Federation officials disappear over the past year and a half. Even without knowing their identities, Kirk was certain he would find an explanatory pattern in their professions and their areas of expertise—a pattern that would reveal why they were valuable to the Federation.

Which meant that somewhere an enemy was gathering its forces, and the capture of Spock was not just an act of personal revenge; it was the first strike in a war that might already have begun.

4

Riker didn't hesitate. He gave his orders in a steady
stream.

"Send a priority distress call to the Araldii ship.
Scan the radiation burst heading for us—look for any
region where the intensity might be weaker than others. Conn—align us stern first to the direction of the
blast. All personnel are to immediately proceed to the
most forward sections of the main decks."

He tapped his combadge. "Riker to engineering.
When will we have shields?"

*"Working on it, Captain. Two minutes . . . maybe
three . . ."*

"Concentrate on the stern—I want every scrap of
power put into aft shields. Turn off the gravity if you
have to."

Troi was already at the communications station

and had switched over to emergency power. "Captain—the Araldii ship has responded. They're on their way."

More than anything else at this moment, Riker wanted to order his wife to the hangar deck; the *Titan*'s shuttlecraft could travel at warp to reach safety. But with main power offline, there was no time left to manually depressurize the deck to launch the shuttles or the captain's skiff.

Riker drove the wishful thinking and impossible dilemma from his mind. "Troi, ask Ship Leader Fortral if they can use their tractor beam at warp."

Lights flickered on the bridge as main power returned.

Riker tapped his combadge. "Was that you, Doctor Ra-Havreii?"

The chief engineer replied. *"Power's coming back . . . getting ready to divert it all to aft shields . . ."*

Riker became aware of Joanna Burke beside him.

"It won't be enough," the astrophysicist said. "I know the specs of your shields. This close to a supernova . . . they won't be adequate."

Lavena reported from the conn. "Radiation front is three minutes from arrival."

Riker turned to Burke. "You need to get to the mess hall on Deck Seven," he urged her. "That'll put the mass of the ship between you and whatever radiation gets past the shields."

The astrophysicist stood her ground. "If I'm going to die, I'd rather watch the sensors."

"Will, the Araldii ship has arrived," Troi announced.

"Onscreen," Riker said, though he didn't know if those systems had been restored.

But the viewscreen switched on to reveal Ship Leader Fortral, floating among a web of netting on her ship's zero-gravity bridge. Even though Riker had known her for less than two weeks, he could see that she was upset.

"Captain Riker," the Araldon said through the com circuit's translator, "you've experienced a warp-core breach?"

"That's correct, Ship Leader. And there's no time to install our backup."

Fortral's secondary mouth opened for just an instant. It was a disconcerting sight, and Riker felt as if the alien's face had gone out of focus. His eyes struggled to accept the image of two mouths, one over the other.

"I regret we don't have the ability to tow your ship at warp."

"Then tow us at impulse," Riker said. "The farther away we are when the radiation hits, the better the chance our shields will be able to protect us." Riker didn't bother looking at Burke; he knew it was a long shot. Then he thought of another strategy. "Ship Leader Fortral—can *your* shields withstand the radiation at this distance?"

Fortral looked up at something beyond the range of the visual sensor, as if checking a reading. "Barely."

At a nod from her captain, Lavena made her next report. "Radiation front is one minute, ten seconds from arrival."

"I won't ask you to endanger yourselves for us,"

Riker told Fortral truthfully. "But for whatever help you can provide, we will be grateful."

"Understood," the Araldon replied.

The screen went dead.

"They're leaving," Troi said with surprise.

Riker was startled. He had expected some kind of assistance. "Raise them again."

"No response."

The lights on the bridge of the *Titan* dimmed.

"Engineering to bridge. Diverting all power to aft shields."

"Captain, one minute to radiation front," Lavena said. The conn officer's voice, produced by muscle contractions, not airflow, was subdued, uncertain.

Riker leaned forward in his chair. His racing mind considered, discarded, reconsidered all his options, as limited as they were. He ran through everything he knew about supernovas . . . turned sharply in his chair.

"Doctor Burke! If we detonate all our quantum torpedoes just ahead of the radiation front, can we create a pressure bubble? One that might absorb or divert at least some of the energy heading toward us?"

Burke stared back at him, her gaze fixed as if she were attempting to solve all the equations his question required.

"Yes or no, Doctor?"

Burke did not respond at once, still lost in thought.

Riker had no more time to waste. He twisted back to face his tactical officer. "Tuvok . . . fire all quantum torpedoes on my mark, directly astern." He addressed the astronomer, without looking back at her. "Best guess, Doctor—at what distance do they detonate? How much in advance of the radiation front? *Now!*"

Burke's tense voice betrayed that she was flustered, but she knew the stakes. "Detonate as close as you can to the ship." Then she had a question of her own for Riker. "How long for a quantum-torpedo explosion to reach maximum pressure?"

Riker shook his head, frustrated, knowing that Data would have given him the answer at once. He, in contrast, would have to look it up, discuss it with— The answer suddenly came to him. "A tenth of a second!" Whether that was really the figure, remembered from some long-ago lecture, or simply a bad guess, Riker didn't know. But there was no chance to confirm or change it.

"Then set them off two-tenths of a second ahead of the radiation front!"

Riker felt Burke put a hand on his shoulder as if in apology. "It's the best I can do! Sorry!"

"Lavena!" Riker said.

"Twenty-five seconds to arrival."

"Tuvok, can you program the delay?"

"No time, Captain. I will have to do it manually."

"Two-tenths of a second—no more, no less."

"Understood, Captain . . . fifteen seconds . . . fourteen . . ."

Then the whole ship rocked violently, inertial dampers barely keeping up with the change in orientation.

Riker quickly scanned all the displays he could, searching for an explanation for the shock. "Report!"

This time, Burke was first to answer. The astrophysicist was reading from her sensors. "The Araldii ship . . . it exploded . . . directly astern . . ."

"Three seconds," Lavena called out from the conn.

Riker looked over at Troi. From the look on his wife's face, Riker knew she felt as he did, that she longed for one final embrace. But he stayed where he was, as did she. Whatever else they were to each other, first and foremost they were Starfleet officers.

"Two seconds . . ."

Looking straight ahead, Riker stood up, put his hand on his chair arm. Bracing for—

"Firing!"

The capacitor twang of a full spread of quantum torpedoes launching echoed through the bridge. Almost instantly the deck tilted violently as the ship pitched down, and Riker was thrown back, slamming into the step leading down from the engineering station.

The Titan's *shields will be out of alignment! Next time we should . . .*

The utter foolishness of this sudden thought made Riker laugh before he sank into blackness with a different realization filling his mind.

He and his crew and his wife and their ship were finished.

There would be no next time.

5

When Kirk had taken formal command of the *Belle Rêve,* the first thing he had done was reconfigure the bridge. Or, to be accurate, he had had Scotty reconfigure it.

As part of the *Calypso,* the ship's bridge had been a tightly constrained control room, with the captain's office on the aft bulkhead, separated from the crew by a transparent wall. Information flowed in only one direction, from a particular crew station to the captain. Somewhere, sometime, for some other captain, that command structure had been acceptable for the merchant fleet or a private yacht. But Kirk believed in Starfleet's original ideal of sharing critical information among all senior personnel. So now his bridge was almost circular—a drawn-out ellipse, at least—with the captain's chair elevated just back of the center point.

There, Kirk was properly surrounded by duty stations, with all other bridge personnel able to see all displays at all times.

About the only key component left over from the old design was the three-panel main viewscreen. On it now were three different magnifications of Vulcan terrain as the *Belle Rêve* orbited that world. Kirk had come to appreciate having three different sets of critical information available to him, and had asked Scotty to retain that system as it was.

Everything else on the bridge, though, had changed. Most of it had been custom-built by a private shipyard under confidential contract to Starfleet. The result was that all of the ship's brand-new, state-of-the-art, cutting-edge equipment was encased in artistically dented, distressed, and discolored console housings. Kirk smiled, remembering how much Joseph, his child, had been fascinated by that last stage of Scott's installation, when a team of specialists had come aboard with their paints and tools to be sure the *Belle Rêve* looked as old and unthreatening on the inside as she did on the outside.

"I see you've added your own special touches," Janeway said as she stepped from the ladder alcove onto the bridge. She hadn't been aboard the *Belle Rêve* since the refit.

"You signed off on all of them," Kirk reminded her. Somehow, almost everything Janeway said to him felt as if it was the prelude to an argument.

But the admiral didn't seem concerned about the extent of the modifications. Nor did she bring up its cost, which was considerable. Even in an era without money, Starfleet's time and resources were measured and apportioned according to need, and there was never enough of either to accomplish everything required. She was more interested in the duty stations. "You actually have a crew of eight?" That was the number of chairs ringing the new bridge.

"The ship's fully automated for standard operations," Kirk said.

"So there're only the four of you on board right now?"

Kirk nodded. Most of the time, he was happy to take on passengers, especially researchers needing transportation from one system to another for their work. He enjoyed the company of knowledgeable people, especially those in fields he didn't know about or had never even known existed. The more he learned, the more he realized how little he knew, and how much he wanted to know it all. The researchers' presence was also a valuable experience for Joseph, opening the child's eyes to all the possibilities that life held for him.

"Are you going to call them?" Janeway asked.

Kirk complied with her indirect request. Within minutes, ship's engineer Montgomery Scott, ship's physician Leonard McCoy, and Kirk's child, Joseph, were assembled by the tactical console with Janeway and Kirk.

McCoy sat down heavily in the console operator's chair. He claimed his leg implants were troubling him. Though Kirk had never really known a time when McCoy wasn't complaining about something, given that his friend was one hundred and fifty-six years old, Kirk was inclined to believe him.

Kirk was also beginning to suspect that Starfleet Medical researchers were correct when they suggested that something McCoy had experienced during his early service in Starfleet might have had a bearing on his near-record age. In all the worlds of the Federation, there were only ten other humans known to be biologically older. Medical's search for this fact hadn't included Kirk or Scott, since they had arrived in this age through other than natural means.

Personally, Kirk suspected that McCoy's encounter with the teaching device of Sigma Draconis VI could have triggered his longevity. Certainly McCoy had appeared rejuvenated after that event. Though the immediately apparent intellectual aftereffects had rapidly diminished, their final stages had subtly lingered for months afterward. Perhaps his body had been affected as well as his mind.

Scott, in contrast to McCoy, stood by the console, uncharacteristically motionless. More usually, he was to be found immersed in at least twenty tasks at once. Though not a week went by that the veteran engineer didn't talk about finally following through on his plans to retire, there was always something else on the *Belle Rêve* that needed his expertise, another test that he felt he should run.

Privately, Kirk doubted that his old friend would ever retire. For most Starfleet personnel he'd known through the years, retirement was something other people did. Montgomery Scott, he believed, would prove no exception. As long as starships flew, Scotty would be flying with them.

The wild card in Kirk's skeleton crew was his own

flesh and blood, his young son, Joseph. "Wild" because Joseph was also the son of his beloved Teilani, who within her had combined the heritage of humans, Romulans, and Klingons. With an all-too-human father, Joseph truly was more than the sum of his parts.

Further complicating his relationship with his child, Kirk couldn't be sure that Joseph was his *son*. According to McCoy's genetic analysis, it was equally likely that Joseph might be his *daughter*. Joseph's uniquely derived physiology was such that when he matured, his body might develop in either form, or neither. But for now, at a chronological age of almost six and a physiological age almost twice that, Kirk's child was precocious, growing alarmingly fast, and a constant source of amazement to his father.

Joseph was also one of the most striking-looking beings Kirk had ever seen, parental pride notwithstanding.

When Joseph had stepped onto the bridge, even Janeway's first reaction to his appearance was of unconcealed surprise, and Kirk guessed that the admiral had seen almost as many different aliens in her career as he had.

Joseph today was slightly taller than a meter and a half. The details of his musculature, which varied slightly from standard human or Romulan patterns, could not be easily discerned through clothing.

Joseph's face, however, was another matter. The startling red skin of his early years had faded to a more natural—for humans—brown. He remained hairless, though his Klingon head ridges had grown slightly more pronounced, his Romulan ears more pointed, and his Trill-like dappling darker.

But rather than amounting to a hodgepodge mixture of disparate parts that didn't appear to fit together, the overall effect was somehow beautiful and *right*. Kirk often had the impression that the way his child appeared was the way all humanoids were supposed to look. He sometimes wondered if somehow over the aeons, Joseph's pattern had been fractured among many worlds, to create the mutually distinct appearances of different species. Certainly the genetic information McCoy had been given by Beverly Crusher, regarding Doctor Richard Galen's postulated "progenitor" race, bore many resemblances to Joseph's genetic profile.

But Kirk had not encouraged McCoy's efforts to look into that inexplicable connection too closely. Sometimes, he knew, it was best simply to take things at face value. And to himself, if to no one else, he was wise enough to admit that he was concerned about what McCoy might discover. For now, Joseph was simply his mother's and his father's child. Kirk was not in favor of any research or findings that might change that.

Fortunately or unfortunately, other than his compelling appearance, Joseph was no different from any other human child entering his teenage years.

"Hey, Dad" were Joseph's first words of greeting as he arrived on the bridge.

Kirk gave his son a gentle reminder of etiquette. "You remember Admiral Janeway."

Joseph looked at the admiral for a few moments, as

if comparing her image with a vast store of identification pictures in some distant databank, then brightened and held out his long-fingered hand. "Sure. When we went to Remus. Hi, Admiral."

Janeway shook Joseph's hand and, despite years of Starfleet's best instruction in protocol, could only say, "Joseph, you've grown."

"Not surprising, considering he can pack away food like a targ," McCoy said.

Joseph rolled his eyes. "Hey, Uncle Bones, Uncle Scotty."

McCoy patted Joseph on his arm, Scott nodded.

Joseph gave his father a questioning look. "Is this a staff meeting?"

"The admiral has something to tell us about Spock," Kirk said. "I thought we should all hear it." Even absent, Spock remained a part of all their lives. There was an immediate change in the mood of Kirk's friends and child.

"Admiral," Kirk said.

Janeway didn't bother with preambles.

"This is what we know," she said, and the briefing began.

The disappearances had started almost a year ago. If Spock was one of the victims, then it was possible he was the first.

As for the others, one hundred and twenty-eight— or twenty-nine—in all, Starfleet Intelligence had no answers. There was no pattern they could discern that clearly connected all the victims.

Indeed, Intelligence had not become involved in

the investigation until seven months earlier, after at least fifty disappearances had already occurred with nothing to suggest a link between them.

In some instances, a single individual had vanished. An archaeologist on a dig on Bajor. A physician on leave from Starfleet Medical. A computer engineer at the Daystrom Institute who had walked into his office one day, and never left.

Kirk's interest was caught by Janeway's mention of the Bajoran archaeologist. Two years ago, Kirk and Picard had attempted to take a vacation on Bajor and dive among underwater ruins. Several archaeologists had died at that site. At the time, all of their deaths had been accounted for as part of a failed Cardassian plot to obtain a lost "orb," also known by Bajorans as a Tear of the Prophets.

But Janeway added for Kirk's benefit that Starfleet Intelligence had already concluded that the more recent case of the missing archaeologist appeared to be unrelated to his and Picard's Bajor experience.

Kirk noted Janeway's use of the word "appeared," but let her continue.

Starfleet Intelligence had become involved in the scope of the disappearances during their investigation of a disaster at Starbase 499.

On stardate 57503.1, the base had been destroyed. In addition to the entire staff of Starfleet personnel and civilians, the dead included six admirals, four starship captains and their science officers, and three civilians.

In response to his questioning, Janeway confirmed for Kirk that the admirals and captains had been present at the base to attend a classified meeting regarding the disappearance of the *Starship Monitor* almost four years earlier. Kirk knew the *Monitor* and her captain; both had been instrumental in helping him and Picard wipe out the threat of the machine world that had created V'Ger and might also have given rise to the Borg. The details of the *Monitor*'s loss and almost certain destruction were tragic. Her crew and captain were heroes.

At first, Janeway explained, there seemed to be no connection between the subject of that meeting and the disaster that befell the starbase—the inexplicable destruction of its static-warp-field power generator.

The generator failure, however, became the link to a number of other malfunctions—some large, some small—that *did* appear to have a bearing on the other disappearances.

Warp technology.

Almost eighty of the missing individuals—human, Vulcan, Betazoid, and Tellarite—were involved in some way with the study of multiphysics and the ongoing refinement of warp propulsion.

Their areas of warp expertise varied. Only a few were involved in cutting-edge research. The missing archaeologist had written a paper thirteen years before about the early development of warp theory on Bajor; there were no secrets there.

But, as Kirk knew, the *Monitor* had disappeared on a mission to test a prototype transwarp drive, based, in part, on recovered Borg technology.

Janeway concluded with a summation of Starfleet Intelligence's best estimate of the threat they were facing: "An enemy or enemies unknown appear to be launching a series of covert strikes against Fleet and Federation assets, with the purpose of diminishing our ability to make further developments in warp technology."

Kirk thought it was an elegant, even logical summation.

Except for one detail.

It was wrong.

"What about Spock?" Kirk asked.

"Admittedly," Janeway confessed, "his disappearance doesn't have a strong connection to the pattern identified by Intelligence."

"It doesn't have any connection," Scott said bluntly.

Janeway sighed as if in resignation. Kirk's interest sharpened. If the admiral had been hoping to at least keep back some details about the investigation, she seemed closer to surrender. He needed to learn something he didn't already know.

Janeway closed in on the crux of the mystery. "Starfleet Intelligence put forward the question: Who would benefit from slowing down our ongoing development of warp technology? Already our ships are capable of staggering velocities. In terms of conflict or space battle, we're well beyond the threshold velocities at which it's even practical to engage in offensive maneuvers. So Intelligence looked into the *defensive* aspects of warp technology, and that's where the link to Spock comes in."

Kirk saw it at once.

"Norinda," he said.

Janeway nodded. "The entire *Jolan* Movement."

McCoy coughed. "At my age, I expect to be confused about most things. But this time I'm really lost."

Kirk laid it out for his friend. "Norinda wanted to incite a civil war between Romulus and Remus. The first strike was going to be simultaneous attacks on three Reman cities, carried out by warbirds traveling at warp velocities . . . simply crashing into them."

McCoy looked troubled.

So did Scott. "Kilo for kilo, the energy release would be greater than a matter-antimatter reaction."

"Obviously," Janeway said, "if hypervelocity warp weapons are on the horizon, Starfleet *needs* to build a defense."

"Admiral, there's no shield ye can make that'll stop something with th' mass of a warbird traveling at warp."

"No shield that we know of," Janeway conceded. "But they used to think it was impossible to travel faster than light."

"Technically, it still is," Scott said with his characteristic passion for all things technical. "Y'see, the warp field alters the dimensions of space-time so that our relativistic framework remains unchanged and we never actually move at a velocity greater than . . ." His voice trailed off as he registered the impatient looks on the others' faces. Basic warp theory, like calculus, was taught in the earliest grades, and no one on this bridge needed a refresher course. "Sorry," he said. "You were saying . . ."

Janeway turned her attention back to Kirk. "Norinda wanted to use warp ships as weapons.

Norinda disappeared. When she disappeared, Spock disappeared, as well. *That's* the connection Starfleet Intelligence is pursuing."

"You think that creature is still out there," McCoy said, "determined to strike again."

"At least one working group in Intelligence believes that's possible. Whatever her species, Norinda is a fanatic. She's been talking about bringing 'love' to the galaxy for more than a century."

Kirk looked away from Janeway, to study the surface of Vulcan as it moved steadily across the trio of screens at the fore of the bridge.

"Captain Kirk . . . ?" Janeway said. "You don't seem convinced."

Kirk wasn't. He was certain that whatever Norinda's true motives were, they still hadn't been fully revealed. But before Janeway could question him about his doubts, her combadge chirped.

She touched it. "Janeway."

"Admiral, we've received a priority-one message from Starfleet Command, your eyes only. We need to beam you back at once."

Janeway shot an apologetic look at Kirk. "An enthusiastic exec," she explained. "He's not familiar with what your ship can do." She touched her combadge again. "Mister Nas, the *Belle Rêve* is capable of receiving encrypted Starfleet transmissions. Please forward the message to me here."

After what Kirk considered to be a long pause, Janeway's executive officer replied, not quite as enthusiastically. *"Aye, aye, Admiral. Transmitting now."*

Janeway looked at Kirk questioningly. Kirk pointed

to a battered communications console. Paint was flaking from its side.

"Joseph," Kirk prompted.

"You've gotta see this, Admiral," Joseph said to Janeway as she followed him to the console. He pressed his thumb on a small control that looked like anything but a biometric reader, then he tapped a code into an out-of-date keypad. A moment later, a back panel on the console opened to reveal a translucent control surface of the latest Starfleet design.

"Enter your code here," Joseph said grandly, "and the message will come up here." He pointed to another panel as it slid sideways and a small viewscreen rotated up from the new opening.

Janeway thanked him; then, at his father's beckoning, Joseph joined Kirk, McCoy, and Scott as they gathered by the turbolift doors at the back of the bridge, to allow the admiral her privacy.

The message Janeway received took her less than two minutes to read. She returned to Kirk, cheeks flushed, skin pale. Her summation was succinct. "The Cochrane Institute has been attacked. Completely leveled. Starfleet's top engineers were there for a critical test. Authorities aren't certain if there're any survivors."

Even Joseph picked up on how serious this development was, just from the adults' reaction.

Janeway held her hand to her combadge. "There's nothing covert about what's happened, Captain. The Federation is at war."

She tapped her badge. Kirk understood. The admiral's mind was already elsewhere. Her body would be as soon as she could beam it there.

"Janeway to *Sovereign*. Tell conn to prepare for immediate departure. One to beam back. . . ."

Kirk nodded to Janeway as she quickly faded into the golden glow of the transporter effect. It felt odd not to be heading to the center of the action. But he still had a mission of his own. Spock.

Kirk's friends shared his conviction. Once, they, too, had been indivisible from whatever concerned the Federation. But they were individuals, now. Others had taken, and would continue to take, their places on the front lines.

McCoy found a new station to sit at. "They're doing it again: telling us too little, too late," he grumbled.

"D'ye actually think it's possible they're on to something?" Scott asked. "Could they really help us find Spock?"

Kirk considered the question as he watched Joseph hurry to the conn station and adjust the visual sensors.

"More than a hundred people have disappeared . . . there's got to be something to that," Kirk said. He just didn't know if that something was what Janeway and Starfleet Intelligence said it was.

On the three-part screen, the impressive silhouette of Janeway's flagship appeared—the *U.S.S. Sovereign*, the original vessel that had given rise to the class that now included Jean-Luc's *Enterprise*-E.

"They're powering up," Joseph reported.

Kirk looked over at his son—his child. As most children did, Joseph was going through a stage in which he was utterly consumed by starships. He could recite the statistics for almost half the Fleet.

"They're establishing their warp field. . . ."

Joseph was also an avid student of the *Belle Rêve*'s sensors and scanners. A Starfleet career wasn't out of the question, though Kirk was determined not to force any decisions on him until the child's own interests had had more time to develop.

"Standard power curve," Joseph announced, correctly interpreting the tactical screens at his station.

Kirk saw Scott grinning.

"Takes after his father," Kirk said.

Scott frowned. "I was thinkin' he took after his Uncle Scotty."

Kirk's laugh was lost as the bridge filled with light.

The three viewscreens flared with the silent destructive explosion that struck the *U.S.S. Sovereign.*

Janeway's ship was torn apart.

The war had come to Vulcan.

6

Before the destruction of the *Sovereign* had even registered in his conscious thoughts, Kirk dove to the tactical console to raise shields.

There are few safer places for a spacecraft to be than in orbit of Vulcan, so shields for most ships are routinely set to the lowest navigational settings—enough to deal with any errant orbital detritus that has escaped detection by Vulcan Space Central.

But a seven-hundred-meter-long starship exploding within a kilometer of the *Belle Rêve* would produce debris of a different magnitude.

The bridge of the small ship vibrated as her power plants ramped up from standby to full output. In those few seconds, Kirk stared at the terrible image on his main screens: Janeway's starship was so large, it appeared to disintegrate in slow motion.

The explosion had begun in the lower engineering hull, almost in line with the wide, winglike pylons that anchored the nacelles.

That location instantly told Kirk that something had gone wrong with the *Sovereign*'s warp drive.

Kirk could only watch as secondary detonations raced along the pylons, twisting them and the nacelles they supported. The port nacelle cracked open as streams of antimatter vented through its blue Cerenkov emitters, triggering multiple explosions wherever the hypervelocity clouds of antiprotons made contact with the physical structure of the ship. A glowing haze began to form around the nacelles as the antimatter continued to react with the great ship's lost atmosphere.

For the first few moments of destruction, the main saucer remained intact. Kirk saw a string of smaller explosions—evenly spaced bright pinpoint flashes—stitch across the saucer attachment points.

That meant automatic separation had been triggered—a desperate maneuver under the conditions Kirk saw. There would have been no time to warn the crew. Whoever was in the corridors or turbolifts when the separation charges detonated would already be dead, blown into space the instant the saucer detached.

In just those few seconds that time seemed to slow, Kirk felt the ship's death as if it were his own. He knew what he had to do. So did his friends.

Kirk's hands worked the flight controls to move the *Belle Rêve* in through the expanding vortex of tumbling debris.

Scott was at his engineering station, bringing the sensors and tractor beam online.

"I'll be in sickbay," McCoy said, no quaver in his voice, no hint of complaint.

Kirk kept his eyes on his controls, addressed his son. "Joseph, get to the transporter. Whoever Scotty beams in, you take him to Bones."

Kirk heard a hoarse "Yessir." Then the turbolift doors puffed shut and it was just the captain and the engineer. Their mission: to save whomever they could from a crew of more than one thousand.

Over six hundred died that day.

In two hours of rescue operations, the *Belle Rêve* beamed in twelve survivors.

Kirk located one in space and Scott beamed her aboard in time. She'd managed to get partially into an environmental suit, sealing her helmet, but having no time to don her gloves. Registering the loss of atmosphere from her open sleeves, her suit remained pressurized by inflating emergency cuffs around her forearms. Exposed to vacuum, the soft tissue of her hands had swollen grotesquely to twice its normal size.

Two more were discovered located in an intact compartment, once part of the hangar deck. The pressure door had slammed shut the instant the separation charges blew. No hope existed for their friends who'd been on the wrong side of the door.

The other nine were transported out of sealed rooms in the *Sovereign*'s saucer. They'd been in the lower decks where the connecting corridors had been opened to space and the emergency containment shields had failed.

Of the twelve, most had suffered only minor burns. Remarkably, McCoy reported, even the crew member with the cruelly distended hands could be expected to recover within a few weeks.

By the time the last survivor was safely on board Kirk's ship, Vulcan Space Central was in full control, completing a well-coordinated rescue operation with typical Vulcan efficiency. Small hunter-seeker craft darted among the debris, scanning for life signs, sending their results to *T'Karath*-class hospital ships equipped with multiple transporter stations.

During the extraction of survivors, emergency salvage vessels used tractor beams to stabilize the largest intact sections of the ship and any debris large enough to survive entry into the Vulcan atmosphere.

To Kirk, the intense two-hour rescue passed as if only minutes. But the moment the Vulcans informed him that all life signs had been accounted for and asked him to withdraw, Kirk immediately headed down to sickbay.

He had to know.

"Admiral Janeway," Kirk said as he entered the crowded medical compartment where McCoy tended to the lucky twelve.

Joseph was working at McCoy's side, bringing him the medkits he needed, cleaning up beside him.

A part of Kirk noted his son's actions, pleased, but his concern for the admiral overwhelmed any parental pride. "Does anyone know what happened to her?"

No one from the *Sovereign* did.

They recalled an announcement from the exec telling the crew to prepare for immediate departure. Less than a minute later, they'd felt the explosion— about the time, Kirk knew, it had taken for the warp engines to come online in the standard run-up to operational power.

The main lights had flickered out then. Gravity failed next. More explosions followed.

The darkness and confusion had vanished suddenly for the twelve survivors as they rematerialized on Kirk's ship.

That was the extent of their knowledge. None of them knew Janeway's fate.

Disappointed, Kirk collected the survivors' identification codes, to transmit them to the Starfleet Joint Operations Center, Vulcan. Returning to his bridge, he discovered that Scott had already been making inquiries.

Kathryn Janeway's official status was "missing." She had not been rescued; neither had her body been found. The Vulcans calculated that it could take days before all the salvaged debris could be examined and scanned. From the force of the explosions that had torn through the starship, they also stated that it was possible not all bodies would be recovered.

Given what Janeway had told him about the investigation into the unexplained disappearances, Kirk couldn't help but wonder if some of the missing might have vanished not by explosion but by whatever phenomenon had claimed Spock.

Inexorably caught by the mysteries wheeling within

mysteries, Kirk flew his vessel to a Vulcan ship of the line, the *Soval*. Docking was not required. The Vulcans beamed the *Sovereign* survivors directly from the *Belle Rêve*'s small sickbay and the adjacent corridor where McCoy had set out cots.

It was over.

Kirk felt the unreality of the moment. No doubt within the corridors of Starfleet Operations on Vulcan an investigation was already under way. Encrypted communiqués were flashing back and forth between Vulcan and Earth. Starfleet vessels throughout the quadrants were being issued new orders.

War plans were being made.

But Kirk and his crew, his friends, were isolated from the action. Mere spectators, if that.

Kirk bridled at the thought. But then, wasn't that what he had wanted? To go his own way, and not be subjected to the whims of Starfleet?

"What now, Captain?"

Kirk looked over to Scott at his engineering station, and for one of the few times in his life, didn't have an immediate answer.

I'm losing my command edge, Kirk thought. That was one of the characteristics shared by all great leaders: the ability to make quick decisions. Provided it was accompanied by the wisdom to change course when new facts came to light.

"Lay in a course to Earth," Kirk said at last. He'd make contact with Starfleet Intelligence, see what he could find out about their efforts to find a pattern to the disappearances. He'd follow any trail that might lead him to Spock.

The turbolift doors opened and McCoy and Joseph came onto the bridge.

Kirk turned in his chair. "How well do you remember Earth?" he asked his son. Joseph had been much younger the last time they had visited.

Joseph brightened. "I remember the horses." They'd gone to a ranch resort in Iowa near the site of the Kirk family farm, on the outskirts of Riverside. But the land was now a world heritage park, and not even the foundations of the house or the barn remained. Kirk recalled that, in an earlier time, there'd even been a statue of himself nearby. But that was gone, too. The old saying was true: Fame *was* fleeting. Nor could it compare with the simple joy of riding with his child.

Kirk dismissed his reverie, gestured at the container Joseph carried. "What's that?"

"Dunno," Joseph said as he looked to McCoy for assistance.

"The *Soval* beamed over medical supplies to replace what we used," McCoy said. "This came with them."

Joseph held the container out to Kirk. "It's addressed to you, Dad."

Kirk took it, curious. It was a basic shipping package, large enough for a few books, perhaps a pair of boots. But it was light, almost as if it were empty.

He tapped the container's label and it switched on, displaying his name and his ship, but giving no indication of the sender.

"The Vulcans beamed this on board?" Kirk asked.

McCoy nodded. "Whatever it is, that means it's at least safe."

Kirk looked for the tab pull, gave it a tug, and the molecular seal that ringed the container flashed once, dividing the package into top and bottom.

Kirk slipped off the top, looked inside, then carefully removed the object that was in the container, held it up and to the side.

It was a triangle of smooth metal, unidentifiable in terms of function or planet of origin. But Kirk had seen it often enough to know exactly what it was.

His ship had a visitor.

"You're on my bridge," Kirk said to the object, "and only my crew is present."

At that, he felt the object slip from his fingers as it became fully active, and after a few moments in which the air around it wavered and grew optically dense, a holographic duplicate of Doctor Lewis Zimmerman took shape on the bridge. The figure was clothed in a Starfleet uniform to which the triangular object—a highly advanced holographic emitter—was now attached on the upper left arm, just below the shoulder.

"Captain Kirk, I presume," the Emergency Medical Hologram said. "We meet again."

"Doctor." This wasn't just *a* holographic duplicate of Doctor Zimmerman, it was *the* duplicate—the EMH from the *Starship Voyager*, who had developed self-awareness and sentience on that vessel's perilous journey. "I'm glad you survived."

"So am I," the hologram replied. Then he beamed at McCoy and Joseph. "Doctor McCoy, always a pleasure. And Joseph. The admiral was right, you *have* grown."

It took Kirk but an instant to process the Doctor's seemingly innocuous observation. *If the Doctor had had time to speak to Admiral Janeway about Joseph, then—*

"Janeway survived?"

The hologram's mood became serious. "Barely. She's on the *Soval*, having her lungs resurfaced." He glanced around at his audience, which now included Scott, who had joined the others by Kirk's chair. "That information, of course, is classified."

Kirk's sense of isolation deepened as he studied the hologram. As sophisticated as the Doctor's illusion of life was, it was impossible to see any of the almost imperceptible tics and other body signals that could be used to judge someone's intent and veracity. "May I ask why?"

"As soon as the admiral beamed aboard, she was called to engineering. There was something wrong with the warp core. She gave orders to shut it down, but the controls didn't respond."

"It was just powering up," Scott said sharply. "It doesn't make sense that ye'd get a runaway reaction that quickly."

"She was in a turbolift car when the core breached."

"That was no core breach," Scott said.

The Doctor corrected himself, and at least this time Kirk could see it wasn't something the hologram did often.

"When disaster struck," the Doctor amended.

"That's what saved her?" McCoy asked.

"The car was blown free, leaking badly, but it held its atmospheric integrity long enough for the admiral to be beamed to a rescue vessel."

"You still haven't explained why Janeway's survival is classified," Kirk said.

"The admiral believes that she was on her way to becoming one of the 'disappeared.'" The Doctor regarded Kirk with interest. "She told me you'd understand."

"I think I do," Kirk said, deliberately offering no further explanation. "But did she explain why she felt that way?"

The hologram hesitated, frowning as if he weren't convinced of the accuracy of what he was about to say. "Apparently, just before the breach—" He looked at Scott before the engineer could interrupt. "—the disaster, the admiral claims to have seen a 'black tendril' emerge from the turbolift control panel. She said it happened just as she was using her communicator to speak to engineering, as if . . . as if the tendril had been searching for her, and found her only when she transmitted."

Kirk immediately tried to fit Janeway into the pattern that linked at least some of the missing. "Doctor, is the admiral involved in any project having to do with warp research?"

The holographic physician gave Kirk a questioning look. "At present, she's the acting director of Starfleet Intelligence."

Kirk's eyes widened in genuine surprise. "She never said . . . never told me . . ."

The hologram shrugged as if to say that whatever Janeway had told Kirk in the past was no longer important.

"Suffice it to say that conditions have changed,"

he said briskly. "The admiral is on her way back to Earth and prefers to let our enemy believe she's dead."

Kirk stood up, too agitated to remain sitting, passive. As director of Starfleet Intelligence, Janeway had known far more than she had ever admitted to him. The implication was blatantly clear. Once again he'd been used by Starfleet, even more thoroughly than he had attempted to use them. He was in no mood to appreciate the irony of the situation.

"Then the *Belle Rêve* is going to Earth, too. I need to speak to Janeway."

The holographic doctor followed Kirk to the conn station, his illusion of reality so perfect that his boot heels clacked across the deck.

"The admiral has other orders for you."

"She'll have to give them to me in person."

The hologram smiled broadly. "She told me you'd say that."

"I've never doubted her ability to judge character." Kirk called up the navigational controls. Plotting a standard course from Vulcan to Earth would take less than a minute.

"Before you do anything rash," the hologram said, "wouldn't you like to hear what her orders are?"

Kirk was about to tell the hologram what he could do with Janeway's orders when he caught a glimpse of Joseph watching him.

His son was rebellious enough without seeing that behavior modeled by his father. Kirk reluctantly decided against open confrontation.

"All right," he conceded, "tell me."

77

"Admiral Janeway orders you to find Ambassador Spock—on Vulcan."

Kirk felt instant anger and excitement. Anger that Janeway had obviously been holding information back from him. Excitement that he was about to learn something that might lead him closer to Spock.

In as even a tone as he could manage, he asked if Janeway had reason to believe Spock was on Vulcan.

"No one knows," the Doctor said, and Kirk could almost hear a tinge of sympathy in the hologram's tone. "But our enemy surely is."

7

The first face Riker saw was Jean-Luc Picard's, and the first thought he had was *So Jean-Luc's dead, too. . . .*

Then he heard a voice as familiar to him as his former captain's face.

"He's coming round. . . ." It was Beverly Crusher.

"I can see that," Picard said. He was smiling. "Do you know where you are, Will?"

Riker suddenly became aware of sharp pain at the back of his head and a throbbing in his left arm. "I'd be afraid to guess . . ." he said with difficulty. His mouth felt as if he'd been gargling sand.

"You're on the *Enterprise*." Picard's tone was as warm and welcoming as Riker could ever remember hearing it.

But the name of that ship—the wrong ship—startled him to greater alertness. "The *Titan* . . . ?"

"Shaken about," Picard said, "but still in one piece. As is your crew."

"Deanna . . ."

"Unlike you, she had the good sense to be sitting down when the concussion hit. Not a bruise. She's on your ship with Geordi."

Riker shook his head and instantly regretted doing so. Suppressing nausea, he looked past Picard, recognized a standard Starfleet sickbay. "How long?" he asked.

Doctor Crusher stepped beside Picard, medical tricorder in hand. "It's been ten days since the supernova, Will. I've kept you in a coma for the past eight, ever since we arrived."

Riker tried to sit up, but his body didn't move. The flood of fear was instantaneous.

Crusher was prompt to answer his unspoken question.

"You broke your back, almost completely severed your spinal cord, skull fractures . . . only two other of your crew were in worse shape, but they pulled through just fine."

Before Riker could respond, she added quickly, "I promise you everything's going to work again, but you're here for another three days, at least, while the nerve fibers reconnect. And every time you try to sit up, I'm adding another day to your sentence." The doctor flashed her winning smile, snapped shut her tricorder, then walked away.

Riker looked at Picard. "I need to know what happened."

"Quite a bit, it turns out. Most of it in the past week."

For all the information Riker wanted at that moment, his crew came first. "How much radiation did we take?"

"Very little."

Riker was startled. "The shields held?"

Picard took a moment before answering, and Riker knew him well enough to realize bad news was coming. But if his ship, his crew, and Deanna were all right, how bad could it . . .

Then he knew.

"The Araldii?"

"They saved your life, Will. Your crew and your ship."

Riker didn't understand. "How . . . ?"

Picard sighed. "They placed themselves between you and the radiation front, and the instant the front hit them, they went to warp. We think they were trying to take a large volume of the radiation into warp with them, to create an empty pocket in the radiation blast that was heading for the *Titan*."

"Their ship exploded," Riker said slowly, remembering those last awful moments.

Picard's gaze met his squarely. "But their tactic worked. The Araldii cut the intensity of the radiation hitting the *Titan* by more than sixty percent. Your . . . shall we say, 'audacious' maneuver with the quantum torpedoes created a counter pressure wave that deflected another ten to fifteen percent. What was left, your shields handled easily. By the time the charged particles and stellar gas reached the *Titan*, your engineering crew had full impulse restored and were able to outrun them."

Riker felt simultaneously proud of his crew, and distraught over the loss of Fortral's ship and crew. But one detail remained unexplained.

"Did the engineers install the *Titan*'s backup warp core?"

Riker saw in Picard's eyes that that was a detail he'd deliberately withheld.

"No," Picard admitted. "Under orders from Command."

Riker instantly made the only logical connection.

"The cores were sabotaged?"

"I wish it were that easy." Picard sighed again, and tugged his shirt in a needless attempt to straighten its perfection. "The reality is that no one knows what's happened over the past ten days. Warp cores are malfunctioning, running critical, even breaching, across both quadrants."

Riker stared at his former captain. He didn't even know where to begin asking questions.

"For now," Picard continued, "the best theory is that our section of the galaxy is passing through a region of space-time with altered subspace properties. Starfleet thinks it might be related to the subspace instabilities that build up over well-traveled shipping lanes."

"But we corrected that problem years ago," Riker said, struggling with disbelief. "Modified our engines, and . . ."

Picard didn't let him finish. "Whatever it is, it's a

different phenomenon. On the plus side, Starfleet hasn't lost many ships because of our automated warp-core ejection procedures. But dozens of freighters have been lost. Hundreds of private ships. Vulcan shipping is at a standstill. Officially, the Klingons aren't admitting to anything out of the ordinary, but our listening posts have picked up scores of distress calls."

"So the Araldii ship . . . ?"

"I'm sure they didn't intend to sacrifice themselves for you. But whatever happened to the *Titan*'s warp core also happened to theirs, and they weren't able to eject it."

Riker stared up at the sickbay's overhead, trying to comprehend the implications of all that Picard had told him. But gradually he became aware of another familiar sensation: the heartbeat of the ship he used to serve on.

"The *Enterprise* is at warp," Riker said. "I can feel the generators."

Picard nodded, unperturbed. "Certain types of cores appear to be unaffected. Older ones, especially."

"This ship isn't old."

"Our last refit, after our collision with Shinzon's vessel . . . there weren't enough warp cores to go around. We had a Block Five installed, and I've had to listen to Geordi complain about it ever since."

Riker tried to ignore the pounding in his head and failed. "The *Titan* has a Block Seven."

"Not once we get back to Mars."

"A refit? Already?"

"Starfleet's replacing warp systems on all affected

ships. The program's likely to take years. *Sovereign*-, *Forrest*-, and *Luna*-class ships have priority."

"Years?" Riker repeated.

Picard's next words were even more disturbing. "We've lost more than ships and installations powered by static warp-field generators. We've lost virtually every major warp-core research and manufacturing facility. Including the Cochrane Institute."

Riker stared at Picard. "On New Montana?"

"Death toll in the hundreds. Most of them warp specialists."

Riker's astonishment quickly changed to suspicion. Warp travel was the lifeblood of the Federation. It was what allowed Starfleet to exist. The fact that warp technology was being denied to both entities, and that the scientists and engineers responsible for creating and improving it had been killed, also led to a single, logical conclusion—but one that Picard had already denied.

"Starfleet's certain this isn't deliberate?"

Picard shook his head. "I had my doubts, too. But this is so widespread, across thousands of light-years . . . what kind of an enemy could strike us like that? By changing the fundamental characteristics of subspace?"

"The most dangerous enemies are those we can't predict."

Picard patted the arm of his former first officer. "Nature's unpredictable, but I'm not willing to call it our enemy yet."

But Riker wasn't willing to rule out any enemy.

Not even a force of nature.

8

Entering this desert was little different from stepping into a blast furnace, but to Kirk, the searing wind carried treasured memories and the promise of home.

That's what Vulcan was to him now: a second home, his brother's home.

He pulled back the hood of his cooling cloak to feel the force of that wind and catch the faint, ozone scent of distant sandfire storms.

"Is that wise?"

The holographic doctor stood with Kirk and Joseph on the viewing platform that was carved into an immense formation of wind-eroded rock. Far below was the haphazard community of low, round, sand-colored hostels and hotels that huddled together at the desert's edge—their apparently random distribution unusual for Vulcan, a sign of the age of this place, pre-Surak and logic.

Tradition held that from the Gateway, Surak had begun his journey of enlightenment through the desert known as the Forge. From that crossing, taken more than two thousand years ago, the Vulcan pursuit of logic had arisen.

Though the holographic doctor didn't require it, like Kirk and Joseph he also wore a cooling cloak of red-orange cloth over his projection of civilian clothes, the better to blend in with pilgrims and tourists. In the Doctor's case, the sophisticated heat exchangers that were woven invisibly through the cloak's coarse fabric were not switched on.

"Solar radiation levels are considerably higher than on Earth," the hologram warned.

Kirk knew the Doctor meant well and forgave his concerns. Caution was undoubtedly part of his medical programming; inevitable, given his origins. After the first time they had met, Kirk had reviewed the Doctor's design specifications. The hologram was a composite expert system incorporating the life experiences of at least forty-seven medical specialists.

"I've spent enough time here," Kirk said. "I know when to go indoors." He could have but didn't add that it sometimes felt as if he'd spent lifetimes on this world—the residue, he knew, of mind-melds with Sarek and Spock that had left him with the echoes of memories from generations of Vulcans.

"Dad, can I try?"

His son was looking up at him through tinted eye-shields, his hands already on the edges of his own cooling cloak. Surprisingly, one of the few Vulcan physiological traits Joseph did not seem to have inherited was a protective inner eyelid.

Kirk nodded.

Joseph pulled back his hood and, just as Kirk had done, took a deep breath of the hot dry wind.

Kirk felt a pang of mortality when he saw his son duplicate his actions so precisely. It was another reminder that Joseph would be his living legacy, a reflection of all that he had been long after his own time had ended. Knowing that, Kirk had done all he could to ensure that Joseph would be exposed only to the good in him, to carry only that part forward. But sometimes he worried he hadn't done enough. Joseph was a sponge for all that his father was, good and bad.

Fortunately, his son had other role models to emulate: Scott and McCoy and, until last year, Spock. Kirk could only trust that his friends' guidance and examples would help balance those times when he himself hadn't been at his best.

Joseph took another deep breath, frowned almost comically. "It smells like . . . engineering."

Kirk understood the familiar scent that his son had detected. "Energy discharges," he explained. He pointed out to the horizon. It shimmered with heat where the red of the sky smeared into the red of the land. "There's a region out there where the planet's magnetic field was distorted a long time ago."

Kirk saw no need to tell his son the story of Vulcan's ancient atomic wars right now, and how they had devastated this world. There'd be time enough to share those dark shadows of Vulcan's history when he was older.

"It's almost like a third magnetic pole. Disrupts most electrical and transtator current in the area, lets the absorbed energy leak out into the wind. Creates spectacular lightning displays in billowing clouds of sand."

Kirk caught Joseph's glance and remembered looking at his own father that way, wondering if there was anything the man didn't know.

But for Kirk, hero worship was not required. He only wanted to be a father to his son. "I read all that in the guide padd. You should look at it tonight. Scotty could probably give you a hand with the equations for the energy interactions and . . ."

Joseph turned away with a familiar expression of impatience bordering on rudeness. Kirk leaned closer to him, dropped his voice so Joseph wouldn't think he was being chastised in front of the doctor.

"You know our deal. Most children have to spend time in school. But as long as you're on the *Belle Rêve*, you—"

"You don't have to turn everything into a lesson."

Kirk saw the holographic doctor looking in the opposite direction, as if there was suddenly something utterly fascinating on the horizon.

"Joseph . . . what have I said about using that tone of voice?"

Joseph pressed his lips together, and Kirk could see he was determined not to admit any guilt. The boy's features bore little actual resemblance to those of his father, but for a moment, seeing that defiant attitude in his son, Kirk might as well have been looking into a mirror.

"We can drop the subject for now," Kirk said, falling back on a strategy that had worked before— sometimes, "as long as you agree we'll discuss it tonight."

Joseph hesitated for a moment, then conceded. "Yeah."

Kirk moved to reward his limited success. He pulled a hotel voucher padd from his belt, tapped in a spending limit, then handed it to his son. "Why don't you go get a *jumja*." There was a confectionery stand at the base of the wide, carved stone stairway leading up to the platform. Vulcans didn't have much of an appetite for sugar, but the stand did brisk business with offworlders.

Joseph's struggle with pride was brief. He took the padd with a glimmer of a smile. "Thanks, Dad." He looked past Kirk. "Doctor, would you like . . ." Joseph paused, awkward, as he remembered exactly what the Doctor was.

The Doctor smiled at the boy. "No, but thank you for asking."

"Come right back," Kirk said, and with that Joseph shot off in escape, expertly weaving through the crowd, cloak flapping behind him like a cape.

"You must find it an interesting experience," the Doctor said.

"I can think of a few other adjectives that'd fit, but 'interesting' works, too."

"Are thee Kirk?"

Kirk turned abruptly at the sound of his name,

spoken with the soft, archaic accent of a Vulcan schooled in one of the planet's ancient scholar's dialects.

The Vulcan standing before him was female, clothed in a simple dark brown robe with a tan over-vest. Most notably, though, her head was shaved. Kirk recognized the significance of both her clothing and appearance. They revealed that she was a Surakian. The school of logic to which she belonged was one of the most demanding in Vulcan tradition. Its adherents attained the *Kolinahr* through the strictest interpretation of Surak's teachings. And that included the rejection of all personal possessions, all ornamentation, everything that was not necessary for the pursuit of knowledge.

Kirk also knew who she was. He bowed his head in respect. "Scholar T'Vrel. Thank you for seeing me."

T'Vrel ignored Kirk's statement, looked closely at the Doctor. "What are thee?"

"Like yourself, madam, I am a healer."

T'Vrel's neutral expression did not change, and Kirk realized that he couldn't tell if she was fifty years old, or, instead, one or two centuries.

"Thou are not real," T'Vrel said.

"I assure you, I am very much real," the Doctor insisted. "My physical form is generated holographically, but—"

T'Vrel turned to Kirk as if the Doctor were no longer there. "Ask thy questions, Kirk," she said.

"Is this the best place for our conversation?" Kirk replied. The message he'd received in response to his query to one of Spock's ambassadorial apprentices had told him to meet T'Vrel on this platform. But meeting in such an exposed location and talking here were two different matters.

"There are many outworlders here. It is not unusual for Vulcans to be seen talking with them."

Kirk decided that if T'Vrel was comfortable here, then so was he.

"I've been told you worked with Spock on Romulus," he said.

T'Vrel did not respond.

Kirk had seen this form of Vulcan logic at work before. She would say something only to correct him, or to answer a question. He continued, unperturbed.

"You were with him when he was abducted by the Remans working for Norinda."

"That name is not familiar."

"She was the leader of the *Jolan* Movement on Remus."

Again T'Vrel gave no response.

"I believe Norinda is also responsible for Spock's disappearance."

"Explain."

Kirk tried his best to comply. "Despite appearances, she wasn't . . . humanoid. I saw her dissolve into black dust . . . black smoke . . . black sand . . . something . . . a substance or phenomenon that then captured Spock and absorbed him into it."

Though T'Vrel remained impassive, Kirk sensed the time she had allotted to him was rapidly diminishing.

"I also believe Spock's not the only one who met that fate."

"I have no time for what thee 'believe.' I meet with

thee because thou are Spock's friend. Ask a question, or end the conversation."

"You asked me to explain."

"Yet thee do not."

"I *believe* Spock is still alive, and I *believe* the way to find him is to find Norinda." Kirk felt secure in that statement, knowing Janeway had also reached the same conclusion.

T'Vrel angled her head by millimeters, and considering her lack of reaction thus far, to Kirk it was as if she had applauded in enthusiastic agreement. "Logical," she said.

Hoping that T'Vrel's response was acceptance of his explanation, Kirk finally asked his question.

"I've been given reason to suspect that Norinda, or others acting on her behalf, might be on Vulcan, attempting to do here what she attempted on Romulus and Remus. Are you aware of any political, philosophical, or academic movement on Vulcan that fits that profile?"

For the first time, T'Vrel took her attention away from Kirk and glanced around at the other Vulcans and aliens on the viewing platform. When she looked back at Kirk, she gave no indication of what she was thinking, yet from her next words, Kirk could guess.

"Come with me to my *s'url*."

Kirk recognized the Vulcan word. T'Vrel had invited him to her school—the closest thing a Surakian had to a home.

"Of course. I'll get my son," Kirk said.

"This is not a matter for children."

Kirk looked at the Doctor.

"I'll be happy to take Joseph back to the ship," the hologram said.

Kirk and the Doctor walked with T'Vrel toward the staircase. "I'll just tell my son where I'm going."

T'Vrel said nothing. Again, Kirk took her silence as acceptance.

At ground level, a noisy, grunting group of Tellarites jostled around the confectionery stand. While T'Vrel waited by an ornately carved stone baluster at the base of the staircase, Kirk and the Doctor squeezed past the Tellarites.

Kirk sighed. There was no sign of Joseph at the counter. He scanned the small plaza ringed by restaurants, shops, and hotel entrances.

"I don't see him," the Doctor said at Kirk's side.

"He has a voucher padd," Kirk said with a parent's wisdom. "He's probably in one of the shops."

Kirk reached inside his cooling cloak and tapped the combadge pinned to his shirt. To all outward appearances, it was a plain silver disk with a manufacturer's symbol embossed in its center, no different from any other civilian model. Inside, though, it had the latest Starfleet circuitry and could operate through subspace at ranges approaching several light-days. "Kirk to Joseph," Kirk said.

He waited a few seconds, in no mood for his son's games. Annoyed, he tapped the combadge again. "Kirk to *Belle Rêve*."

This time the reply was almost instantaneous. *"Scott here, Captain."*

"Scotty, lock on to my signal and Joseph's and tell me where he is."

Kirk heard the engineer's knowing laugh. *"Up t' his old tricks, is he?"*

Kirk didn't have time to explain. He didn't know how long T'Vrel would wait. "Just stand by to beam him up along with the Doctor."

"Aye . . . I've got him. Five meters south of your position."

"Five meters . . ." Kirk said. He looked south.

The confectionery stand.

Kirk checked that T'Vrel hadn't left, then quickly walked back to the stand, certain Joseph was hiding behind it. The Doctor helpfully skirted the Tellarites and went around the other side.

They met at the back. No Joseph.

Kirk tapped his combadge again. "Scotty, where'd he go?"

"Och, he hasn't moved. You're within two meters of him."

Kirk looked around, truly puzzled, his frustration at Joseph's timing tempered by his admiration for his son's renowned skill at hiding.

He looked at the back of the confectionery stand. "He's got to be inside."

The Doctor pulled back the fabric drape concealing the gap between the stand's sloped roof and its waist-high wooden wall.

Almost at once, the stand's indignant Ferengi proprietor grabbed the drape away from the Doctor. "Customer service at the counter!"

The Doctor ignored the protest, tugged the drape open again, leaned over the wall to examine the stand.

Kirk saw the Ferengi draw back, then shove his hand forcefully at the Doctor's shoulder to push him away. But the Doctor adjusted his holographic density so that the Ferengi's hand passed *through* him.

Having attempted to shove a ghost, the Ferengi shrank back, squealing in fright. The Doctor ignored him, turned back to Kirk, shook his head.

Kirk didn't understand. The only other thing back here was—

With a sudden surge of alarm, Kirk rushed to the waste container—a drum-shaped barrel a meter tall.

Kirk ripped the cover from it, looked down, felt true fear as he saw the hood of a cooling cloak.

"Joseph!" Kirk pulled up on the cloak, terrified of what might be beneath it.

But all he revealed was a sticky mound of confectionery wrappers and *jumja* sticks.

Kirk ran his hands down the empty cloak, felt Joseph's combadge pinned to it, and nothing else.

His child was gone.

9

U.S.S. ENTERPRISE
STARDATE 58562.5

Had it been any other time, any other occasion, Picard would already have begun to feel restless. This close to home, he always was.

Earth and her solar system had been tamed generations ago. Each planet, moon, and major asteroid mapped to resolutions that banished all mysteries. The domed cities of the moon allowed families to picnic by Earthlight. Mars had green fields and blue oceans, fresh clean air, skiing at the poles, and soon, according to the environmental engineers, burgeoning rain forests would arise in the equatorial lowlands.

Even the vast, underground data repositories and museums of Pluto had stripped the romance from that distant world, still considered a planet by tradition, if not by astronomers.

In fairness, Picard couldn't complain about humanity's imprint on nearspace—the sectors that surrounded his homeworld and home system. Those were the first his species had visited in the great wave of exploration that followed in Cochrane's wake.

But he didn't have to like it. And he didn't.

This close to home, his heart remained on the frontier.

In his soul, he was an explorer, and he feared for the day when humanity's descendants would place their footprints on the last world at the galaxy's edge. Where would the human spirit turn to then? Would there be new frontiers to delve into? Or was he part of a dying breed? Just a point on the graph from Cochrane and Archer and Kirk to a future that had a definite end?

"Captain . . . ?"

Troi's gentle inquiry broke through Picard's introspection. He saw her standing beside his chair on the bridge, concern and curiosity in her large dark eyes.

"Is coming home really that bad?" she asked.

Picard smiled. He had forgotten the ease Troi had brought to his ship, and to his command. A Betazoid counselor who could sense his emotional state tended to keep him focused and aware of the present. And he rarely had to explain himself to her. With the *Titan* in tow and Riker still in Doctor Crusher's sickbay, Picard was pleased that Troi had chosen to take up guest quarters on the *Enterprise* for the journey back to Earth. Especially since the *Enterprise*'s new counselor, T'Lana, was on leave to attend a negotiation workshop on Babel.

"Under the circumstances," Picard said, "not really. We're needed here. Exploration can wait for now."

Troi's smile was warm and kind and let him know that she saw right through him. "You've never believed that, Captain. But like all of us, you put duty first."

Picard returned the smile. "I've missed you, Counselor."

"I know."

Their conversation was interrupted by Lieutenant Leybenzon, the ship's security officer. The taciturn human had earned a field commission during the Dominion War, and his martial expertise had proven his worth many times over, both in war and in peace.

"Captain, we're receiving a transmission from Jupiter Outpost Ninety-two."

Picard was familiar with that security station. It was part of Sector 001's deep-space tracking and communications network, built into and onto the ninety-second moon of Jupiter. That particular moon was a rock scarcely larger than the *Enterprise*.

Picard straightened his jacket. "Onscreen."

At once, a man in unusual black clothing appeared on the viewscreen. To Picard, the outfit seemed more like a uniform than civilian garb, though he could see no insignia. In the background, among nested banks of operations consoles, uniformed Starfleet personnel rushed back and forth, or conferred in close conversation. The mood seemed tense, the activity almost erratic. But the man, whoever he was, whatever his function, clearly belonged at the station he occupied.

"Captain Picard," the man said, "please drop from warp at Kuiper Five-seven-five. We have tugs waiting to bring the *Enterprise* and the *Titan* to Jupiter Station."

Picard bristled at the thought of letting smaller craft guide his ship. Even more disturbing was that Kuiper 575 was an icy planetesimal, twice the size of Pluto and half again as distant from the sun. As far as he was aware, it was a Fleet deuterium refueling depot for freighters. The *Enterprise* had no business there, especially when the *Titan* needed urgent repairs at the Utopia shipyards.

"May I ask why? Our destination is Mars."

"We're operating under emergency conditions, Captain. You'll receive further orders when you report to Kuiper Five-seven-five."

The man in black moved to touch a control, no doubt to break the connection, Picard assumed. But Picard wasn't finished with him.

"I'm sorry, but I don't know you and I'd prefer to get changes to my orders from Starfleet personnel. May I—"

The viewscreen flashed back to a visual sensor image of Earth's sun, the brightest star in the galactic swath, still several light-years distant. Closer stars smeared past at warp on the edges of the screen.

Picard stared at the stars, puzzled and annoyed. Then, as if no time had passed since she had last served as counselor on his ship, he turned to Troi.

"Impressions?"

"Whoever he is," the Betazoid said thoughtfully, "he's not used to being questioned. And he was at a high level of alert. I have no doubt he feels he's operating under emergency conditions, as he said."

Picard made his decision, looked over at the tactical station. "Mister Leybenzon, open a channel to Starfleet Command."

The chief of security efficiently called up the main com controls on his board, sent the automated sequence.

A moment later, the viewscreen flashed again.

It was the man in black. "Captain Picard, is there a problem?"

Picard stood. Something wasn't right. "My communications request was sent to Starfleet Command."

"That's what you've reached. Starfleet's Jupiter facilities are now provisional Fleet headquarters."

"Since when?"

"Since Starfleet Headquarters in San Francisco closed down two days ago. Now change course to Kuiper Five-seven-five."

Picard's mind raced. How could headquarters be relocated without the news spreading over the subspace net? "I've received no notification."

"And you won't until you've passed through engrammatic identity verification at Kuiper Five-seven-five. Now change course immediately, or I *will* declare you a hostile vessel."

Picard looked to Troi, mouthed the words "Identity verification?"

"Whatever it is, he means it," the counselor quietly replied.

Picard turned back to the screen, weighing the possibilities that might explain what he was facing. But whatever was going on, he refused to concede his command authority without good reason. The stakes were too high.

"Under the circumstances, I need to receive orders from a source I recognize," Picard stated.

The man's jaw clenched and Picard didn't need a Betazoid to tell him he was witnessing a sudden burst of anger.

"Captain Picard—*if* that's who you are—drop out of warp now, disable your weapons, and wait to be taken in tow. If you continue to approach this system, you will be fired upon, and you will be destroyed. Starfleet Command, *out.*"

Once more the stars returned to the viewscreen.

"Strong suspicion," Troi said, clearly startled by the man's hostility. "He truly doubts your identity. He's frustrated. And disappointed."

"Disappointed?" Picard asked.

Troi shook her head as if there was something about the man that was just out of her grasp. "I think, when you first spoke to him, it was almost as if he was hoping you could help him."

"Help him with what?" Picard momentarily appreciated the irony that just a few minutes ago he had been thinking that his home system held no mysteries. But now . . .

"Mister Leybenzon," Picard said, "do you detect any vessels heading to intercept us?"

"Negative, Captain."

"Can you pick up any standard communications traffic from Command, San Francisco?"

"A lot of subspace static . . . unusual. If there are

standard transmissions, under these conditions they'd be undetectable."

Picard knew he needed more time to sort out what was happening. "Conn, change course to Kuiper Five-seven-five."

Ensign Choyce replied with a brisk "Aye, sir," and almost at once the starfield on the viewscreen began to shift as the ship's heading changed.

Now Picard stepped behind his operations officer at her station. Lieutenant Commander Miranda Kadohata had been trained by Data on the *Enterprise-*D before transferring to other vessels, and Picard had welcomed her return to his ship. "Commander, have the science department heads prepare a report on that interference. But first ask Commander Worf to report to the bridge at once."

Picard walked back to Troi. "I can only surmise that the current situation is somehow related to the warp-core failures."

He could see that Troi sensed what underlay his conclusion.

"You're beginning to think it's not a natural phenomenon after all."

"If headquarters *has* been relocated, perhaps it's because they fear what happened at the Cochrane Institute could happen there. And as to doubting my identity . . . that's reminiscent of the Dominion War, when anyone could be a Changeling."

Troi smiled at Picard. "Not within range of a Betazoid, sir."

Picard appreciated Troi's assurance, but he was also aware of how someone else might see the situation. "Unless the Betazoid was a Changeling as well."

Troi's nod showed she conceded the point.

A turbolift door opened and Worf emerged, instantly making the bridge feel smaller.

Picard was not the only one who stared at Worf as he strode to the chair that had once been Will Riker's. Picard's new first officer wore the full uniform of a Klingon battlegroup commander, and his metal-clad boots rang out as he crossed the deck.

Worf returned Picard's stare. "I was relaxing. On the holodeck. Your summons did say, 'At once.'"

Picard nodded. "The uniform suits you." He gestured to the back of the bridge. "Let's adjourn to the ready room." He included Troi in his invitation. "Counselor, I would very much appreciate your input."

"Certainly, sir."

But before any of the officers had reached the ready room door, Lieutenant Commander Kadohata changed their plans.

"Captain—the subspace interference around Earth is intensifying."

Picard turned back to the bridge. "Can you tell what's causing it?"

Kadohata's hands expertly played over her console as she brought up the science sensor readings being used by department heads throughout the ship.

"Multiple subspace distortions . . ." She looked back at her captain. "Sir, the energy signatures are consistent with warp-core explosions."

Picard felt his stomach tighten. "Raise Command again."

The viewscreen showed stars. Only stars.

"Command is not responding," Kadohata said.

"Find any channel," Picard ordered. "Focus on Jupiter, any signal."

At last the stars disappeared, replaced by a visual sensor image.

Picard focused his attention on the image, saw that it originated from a navigational beacon near Jupiter Station, one of the largest research platforms in the system. The station supported a permanent population of almost ten thousand.

In the upper right quadrant of the viewscreen, an oasis of lights was clearly visible against the deep black of Jupiter's nightside clouds. The station itself spread out like a snowflake with each branch five kilometers long.

Many of the lights were moving away from the main structure, as if the snowflake were breaking apart at the edges.

"What's happening?" Troi asked.

Worf had the answer. "The ships docked to the station . . . they're withdrawing."

"There shouldn't be so many doing it at the same time," Kadohata said. "Regulations prohibit—" She gasped.

One of the small points of light moving from the station suddenly flared like a nova.

Then another.

"Their warp cores . . ." Picard said, barely believing the disaster unfolding before him.

The time for reasoned, thoughtful consideration of options had passed. Picard issued his new orders crisply.

"Conn, set a course for Jupiter Station. Mister Ley-benzon, release the *Titan* from the tractor beams." Picard looked to the hidden com system in the bridge's overhead. "Picard to engineering."

"La Forge here, Captain."

"Geordi, I want maximum warp right now. Consider this a priority emergency."

The veteran engineer knew better than to ask questions. Within seconds, Picard could feel the deep thrum of his ship's warp coil as it ramped up to maximum output. The *Enterprise* waited on his command, and he gave it.

"Engage."

10

It took twenty-three minutes for the *Enterprise* to arrive in orbit of Jupiter. In that same time, thousands died.

Even those ships that remained intact offered little in the way of protection for their crew and passengers. As close to Jupiter as the major research platforms were, the planet's radiation field was lethal within minutes of exposure. When the ships lost their warp cores, they invariably lost their shields until auxiliary generators or batteries could come online. That delay was fatal.

The *Enterprise* swept her sensors over ship after ship tumbling in erratic orbits. While many had survived—their warp cores safely ejected before disaster struck—their shields had clearly faltered. Even now, though shields had recovered and were once again working perfectly, on dozens of vessels they protected only corpses.

Other ships were prowling the primary orbital planes—impulse-powered transports for the most part, spared from whatever phenomenon wreaked such havoc on warp technology.

One hour after the wave of core detonations had devastated the Jupiter installations, the *Enterprise* was the de facto command focus of the rescue efforts. Lieutenant Leybenzon and a relief crew coordinated the efforts of more than eighty smaller vessels from the *Enterprise*'s battle bridge—in Picard's estimation, a much worthier use of that particular backup facility than the one for which it was intended.

But on the main bridge, it was Picard who spearheaded the most critical phase of the recovery operations—saving Jupiter Station itself.

The vast orbital platform had taken damage when docked ships had been destroyed. Though its shields were holding, the station's thrusters were inoperative, and almost at once it had begun its slow fall to the bottomless clouds of the system's largest planet.

There were too many crew and workers and visitors on board the falling station to be beamed off or evacuated by shuttle or escape pod. The only way to save the lives of almost ten thousand was to save the station, though not even the *Enterprise*'s tractor beams could move such a mass.

But that didn't stop Picard from trying.

He had La Forge operate the tractor beams from engineering, using technical readouts of the station's superstructure to find those points that could take the strain of a beam's contact. With no time to describe the problem to the ship's computers, La Forge worked mostly by intuition, applying a beam here, a beam there, grabbing hold at an anchor point just long enough for some of the station's momentum to bleed back over the beam to be absorbed and compensated for by the *Enterprise.*

Picard could hear his ship creak, feel it tremble as its structural-integrity field was taxed to its limit. But gradually, over the course of another hour, Jupiter Station did cease its slow roll and errant tumble. It was still falling toward Jupiter in a decaying orbit, but it was stable again.

For what Picard planned to do next, that stability was essential.

It was a maneuver only a student of history could conceive of—something that stretched back to the dawn of the space age, when nations applied all their resources and humans risked their lives just to reach low Earth orbit.

Picard himself took the conn for what had to be done now. He could not, would not, shift the burden of the risky attempt to any of his crew.

Gracefully, Picard's ship banked above the clouds of Jupiter, to settle into an orbit only tens of meters lower than the station. Then, at a velocity of no more than a few meters per minute, the *Enterprise* rose, coming up beneath the station until the ship's main hull was directly beneath the station's center of mass.

Worf handled the shield settings for the maneuver, aware that they had to be tuned to provide full protection from radiation and any fast-moving orbital debris, yet still allow low-velocity objects to pass and make contact with the ship's hull.

Low-velocity objects such as Jupiter Station.

"Five meters . . . four point five . . ." The Klingon's deep voice was calm and steady, reflecting the trust he had in his captain.

Picard eased his hands along the navigation and propulsion controls. Impulse engines were on standby; he was flying his ship strictly by its docking thrusters.

"Two meters . . ." Worf said.

Picard kept his attention on the conn readouts. He didn't risk more than a quick glance at the viewscreen where the ventral surface of the station's key node took the entire field of view. Engineering codes and safety labels were clearly legible.

"One meter . . ."

"All hands, brace for impact," Picard said quietly.

Then a low-pitched metallic clang reverberated through the bridge as the *Enterprise* swayed, almost as if the starship were a sailing vessel on a becalmed sea.

"Contact," Worf announced.

Picard knew that it would have been an easier maneuver had he chosen to bring the *Enterprise* to one of the station's docking ports; then the computers could have handled it on automatic. But in order to take his ship into what was essentially a collision course, he had had to override the computers.

"Are we stable?" Picard asked.

Beside him, his ops officer checked her readings. "No drift," Kadohata confirmed. "We're in solid contact."

"Then here we go," Picard said, and once again he

adjusted the thruster controls to apply gentle pressure, slowly forcing the *Enterprise* up against the station.

It had to be gradual, otherwise the ship might punch through the key node, snapping off the station's six arms, turning them into unpowered and doomed spacecraft of their own.

Metallic scrapes and clangs, stuttering vibrations from the structural-integrity field in constant reset mode, the pulse of the artificial-gravity generators as they fruitlessly tried to propagate their pseudo-inertial field through the immense volume of the station above . . . to Picard, all these sensations brought his ship to life for him, like horseback riding: a magnificent steed so in synch, so responsive, that there was no distinction between horse and rider.

Bonded even as he was with his ship, Picard still endured twenty minutes of uncertainty before Commander Kadohata called out what he'd hoped to hear.

"Captain, our orbit is changing."

Picard felt the rush of relief. Just as primitive chemical-powered spacecraft had once been used to raise the orbits of Earth's first pioneering space stations, the *Enterprise* now carried Jupiter Station on her hull, lifting it from certain destruction. With momentum begun, he switched to impulse propulsion.

The station rose like a phoenix, untouched by what would have been its fiery fate, leaving the planetwide storms of Jupiter's endless clouds below.

After four hours of slow but constant acceleration, La Forge reported that the main impulse manifolds were in danger of overheating. But in this new orbit, he also confirmed that the station would be safe for months, ample time for new thrusters to be installed and repairs undertaken.

Picard throttled back the impulse engines, and so gently that he did not feel the change, Jupiter Station moved up from the *Enterprise*, safe in its own orbit.

Only then did Picard take his hands from the controls, and almost at once he realized that his shoulders and back were knotted painfully. He had been hunched over, unmoving, for hours.

He stood up carefully, arched his back. "Ensign Choyce . . . take the conn."

As Picard stepped away from the station, Choyce slipped into his place.

"We'll need to take all the survivors we've brought on board to medical facilities," Picard said. "The Denobulan Center on the moon might be best."

Instead of complying though, or announcing that he was laying in a course, the ensign simply looked up at Picard with a nervous expression, then moved his eyes meaningfully aft.

Perplexed, Picard followed the ensign's gaze, and saw that his ship had a visitor.

"Admiral Janeway," Picard said, startled. "A welcome surprise."

The admiral sat in Picard's command chair, one finger lightly tapping the arm. There was no telling how long she had been there, but Picard appreciated that his crew had chosen not to disturb him.

"We'll see how long you think that," Janeway said. "We're going to Mercury. At impulse."

Picard looked to Worf and to Troi, but saw no sign of comprehension from either of them.

"Clearly, there's more going on here than I know," Picard said carefully.

Janeway sighed, but made no move to get out of his chair. Picard noticed her eyes were shadowed, skin pale. She was an admiral who hadn't slept for days—never a good sign.

"Jean-Luc, for the past year, an enemy has made preparations to invade the Federation. In all likelihood, they've been at it even longer than what we've been able to uncover."

Picard forgot about his aching muscles. "I assure you we are ready to meet any invader."

Janeway shook her head. "It's too late for that. The invasion's already taken place, and we still don't know who we're fighting."

11

"There is no crime on Vulcan," Prefect Vorrel said calmly.

Trying to remember all that Spock had taught him, Kirk matched the young Vulcan bureaucrat's emotionless tone. "Yet my son's been kidnapped."

"That is not a logical conclusion, Mister Kirk."

Vorrel might have thought he was keeping his emotions in check, but Kirk had no trouble detecting the condescension in his voice. Still, Kirk wouldn't give the prefect the pleasure of seeing him react like the Vulcan stereotype of an emotional outworlder.

"It's the *only* logical explanation," Kirk said evenly. "Perhaps I should talk with an official with a more certain grasp of the facts."

It was just a subtle sign, the momentary lifting of one eyebrow a millimeter higher than the other, but

Kirk could see that his insult had had its desired effect.

Vorrel made a show of checking his evidence padd—the only object on his polished wooden desk. The rest of his office was equally bare. A single carved stone IDIC broke the monotony of the smooth, rust red plaster walls and dark wooden beams. Even the dust in the air, caught in the daylight seeping in through sand-frosted glass, was still and unmoving.

"You admit you argued with your child," Vorrel stated.

"I understand that fathers and sons have been known to argue even on Vulcan."

The prefect folded his hands on his desk, angled his head in a show of confidence, as if Kirk had just passed control of the conversation to him. "But on Vulcan, neither individual gives in to an emotional response to that argument."

It was all Kirk could do to remain seated. His son had been missing for almost an entire Vulcan day. He needed access to public surveillance records, satellite monitoring, all the public safety systems that this smug prefect claimed Vulcan didn't have or need because there was no crime here.

"I know my son, Prefect. If he gets mad at me, he sulks in his quarters, he pretends he can't hear me, he spends time with his Uncle Scotty in the engine room. But he does *not* run away from me on an alien planet. He knows the rules I've set and he follows them."

The Vulcan's infuriatingly placid attitude didn't change. "One reason why Vulcan parents and children argue is that children often conclude that the rules governing their behavior must change before the parent agrees. Am I correct in thinking that situation can logically be applied to humans, as well?"

With rising despair, Kirk understood that this Vulcan would do anything in his power to demonstrate that alien emotions were to blame for Joseph's disappearance. There was nothing wrong with Vulcan—only with the aliens who visited the world.

The realization gave Kirk the strategy he needed.

"Then prove me wrong," he challenged the prefect. "Check the public surveillance records for images of my son taking off his own cooling cloak and running away by himself. Use satellite sensors to locate him so he can confirm your conclusion."

Vorrel leaned back slightly, just enough of a change in posture for Kirk to see the prefect suspected a trap. "The Bureau of Public Safety does not maintain surveillance records on Vulcans in public venues."

"On Vulcans, no," Kirk agreed. "I agree. That wouldn't be logical. But the Gateway attracts visitors from dozens of worlds. Are you saying that you don't monitor hundreds of emotional aliens who might disrupt the public order?"

The prefect took several moments to reply.

I've got you, Kirk thought. But he kept his own expression as impassive as Vorrel's.

"There are no public surveillance records for the viewing platform," the prefect admitted.

Kirk saw his opening. Unless they had a strong motive, Vulcans as a rule would not lie. But that tradition didn't prevent them from withholding information when it suited them.

"I wasn't talking about the platform. I found Joseph's cloak behind the confectionery stand at the base of the platform. Are there records for the plaza?"

The prefect tapped a finger once on his desktop, obviously agitated at having lost this round to the human. "I see. Your request was not precise. I believe there might be a visual sensor in that area. To monitor . . . alien activities."

Kirk refrained from gloating. He slid a small padd across the desk. Its display held an image of Joseph recorded just last week. "He's quite distinctive."

Vorrel glanced at the padd, raised an eyebrow without attempting to hide his reaction to Joseph's multispecies appearance. "Indeed" was his only comment.

Then he pressed a hidden control, and a larger datascreen folded out from the side of his desk, while an input panel glowed up from the wooden surface. Until the moment it was activated, it had been completely hidden.

Vorrel input several commands and the datascreen lit up. He checked his notes on the evidence padd, entered more information. "You sent him for candy at the fourth ode, past noon?"

"About that time," Kirk confirmed, struggling not to appear impatient. He was familiar with Vulcan timekeeping.

The prefect placed Kirk's padd beside his control panel in order to transfer Joseph's image into the main computer system.

It took less than a second to run the search. Even that brief time seemed too long to Kirk.

"And there we have him."

Vorrel turned the screen on its support arm so Kirk could see the frozen image displayed on it.

It might as well have been a phaser set to stun.

In one instant, Kirk felt relief. There was Joseph in the plaza by the carved stone staircase, cooling hood back, Romulan ears, Klingon head ridges, Trill-like dappling . . .

And then came the next instant.

The figure he had taken for Joseph was too tall, almost Kirk's height.

The breeze had made the cooling cloak cling to the figure's body.

It was a female.

A female of Joseph's species.

But Joseph was unique, born of the combined genetic heritage of Kirk and Teilani, herself a product of Klingons and Romulans and Vulcans and humans.

How could there be another?

"Run the image," Kirk said.

The prefect hesitated, reached out to swing the screen back.

But Kirk didn't care about protocol anymore. He stood up abruptly from his chair, swung the screen back to keep it in sight. "Run the image! That's not my son!"

Keeping his attention completely on Kirk, as if Kirk were a wild animal about to lunge at him with glistening fangs, Vorrel hit the proper control without looking.

On the screen, the surveillance image came to life; tourists and pilgrims, aliens and Vulcans, all began to move about the plaza.

Except for the female.

She remained at the base of the stairway, occasionally looking around the immediate area, but spending most of her time looking up the stairs, as if waiting for someone.

Expecting someone.

Kirk's attention was riveted to the screen. He didn't blink as seconds turned to minutes, marked by the Vulcan timecodes that wove themselves around the dialectic staff at the side of the screen, resembling musical notation.

And then, on the stair at the topmost part of the screen, a familiar pair of boots appeared. The image was silent, but Kirk knew the thunder of those small feet—he had heard them so many times on the *Belle Rêve*.

"There he is . . ." Kirk said, his voice unexpectedly tight.

On the screen, Joseph raced down the stairs, almost comically changed direction, holding his voucher padd high as he ran for the confectionery stand.

He didn't even notice the female as he passed within a meter of her.

But she had noticed him.

She turned toward the stand.

She took a step forward.

The image dissolved into a blur of static.

"What happened?" Kirk asked.

Instead of attempting to turn the screen away from him again, Vorrel got up from behind his desk to look at it from Kirk's side.

"Unusual," he said. Kirk was unable to read any emotion into the statement.

The prefect leaned across his desk, entered more commands.

The static shifted, then the image from the plaza appeared again, running in reverse as Joseph ran backward up the stairs.

"What's wrong with the recording?" Kirk demanded.

Vorrel tried other commands, but to no effect.

"The record has been erased," he said.

Kirk's fears soared. This couldn't be a coincidence. Not on Vulcan.

Joseph's disappearance was no random crime. It had been planned.

"Who has the authority to erase that record?" Kirk demanded.

"Records can't be erased," Vorrel said. "There's ample storage available. Future sociologists could find—"

"Then how did this happen?!"

Kirk had nothing more to lose. If Vorrel wanted to think of him as a typical, emotional human, then Kirk wouldn't disappoint him.

The prefect moved warily back to the other side of the desk, as if intending to shield himself behind it. "I . . . I will have to conduct an investigation."

"I want access to satellite surveillance records. Joseph has a unique biosign."

"This is a municipal center, Mister Kirk. What you ask is outside my authority."

"Then find me someone who *does* have the authority, *now.*"

The Vulcan jumped at Kirk's raised voice.

"Sir, becoming irrational will not help matters."

"My son has been kidnapped from a region under your jurisdiction. If I find out you're in any way responsible for this atrocious breach of security . . . you have not begun to see me get 'irrational.'" Kirk pointed to the control panel.

Vorrel changed the control configuration to a communications system.

A Vulcan voice answered at once. *"Proceed."*

The prefect cleared his throat, studiously avoiding looking at Kirk. "I am Prefect Vorrel, Gateway Region. A crime has been committed against an outworlder. I require the assistance of the Ministry of Planetary Defense."

"State the nature of the crime."

Kirk heard every word the prefect said in reply as a knife wound in his heart. "A child has been abducted."

"A state of emergency is in effect. That crime does not warrant the involvement of the ministry at this time."

Enraged, Kirk charged around the desk to shout at the Vulcan on the screen. "That is unacceptable! My son is missing and Vulcan security records have been altered to hide the crime!"

The figure on the screen wore the red uniform of Vulcan's Planetary Defense Force. She glanced away from the visual sensor transmitting her image, appeared to read something of interest.

"Voiceprint analysis identifies you as the human, James T. Kirk."

"I am," Kirk confirmed. Though he was usually reluctant to trade on any notoriety he had earned during his Starfleet career, under these circumstances, he'd use any advantage that might help him get the cooperation of Vulcan authorities.

"That is fortunate," the Vulcan said. *"We have been looking for you."*

And before Kirk could even ask why, he felt the familiar cool rush of the transporter effect as Prefect Vorrel's office dissolved into light around him.

They have me, was his last thought before dissolution. *Just like my son.*

12

Picard staggered from the transporter pad. It had been an unusually rough beam-in. He felt disoriented.

A Starfleet medical technician was there to take his arm, steady him.

"Sir—do you know where you are?" the medic asked. He had raised his voice, as if he expected Picard to be unable to hear him.

Picard was puzzled by the question—not because he didn't know the answer, but by the fact it was asked at all.

"Sir?" the medic prompted again.

Picard saw another medic a few meters away in the undersized transport chamber, aiming a medical tricorder in his direction. There was no one else present, not even a transporter technician.

"Vostok Academy," Picard answered. The venerable

outpost, deep beneath the surface of Mercury, was one of the oldest planetary research facilities in Earth's home system.

"Do you know what stardate it is?"

Irritated now, Picard yanked his arm from the medic's grip. "Fifty-eight five sixty-three. What's this about?" He glanced back at the pad. It was still glowing, as if about to accept another beam-in. "Is something wrong with the transporter?"

"No, sir. But you were in the buffer for about ten minutes, and that can sometimes—"

"What?"

"Identity confirmation," the medic beside Picard said. He looked to the medic with the tricorder. "Match?"

The second medic nodded. Only then did Picard notice that she carried a phaser at her side. The first medic had one, too.

"What is going on here?" Picard demanded.

The first medic ushered Picard toward a closed door. "You're scheduled for a briefing, sir. That should answer all your questions."

Then the doors opened and Picard felt himself propelled forward by a firm hand in the small of his back. The light gravity of Mercury, only a third of Earth's, made him stumble again until his reflexes adjusted.

The corridor outside the transporter chamber was empty. It smelled damp and musty to Picard. The white walls were dingy, the light from the overhead panels decidedly blue. Combined with the absence of artificial gravity, the whole effect was one of age and neglect. Picard decided this must be part of the original outpost, which he thought had been abandoned as new extensions had been constructed.

A voice came from an unseen speaker in the wall, not his combadge.

"Captain Picard, please follow the corridor to your left."

"Who are you?" Picard snapped. "Where's Admiral Janeway?" The admiral had beamed down with Picard after the *Enterprise* had established standard orbit of the planet. He had expected that they'd arrive together.

"The admiral has already been processed. Please follow the corridor."

"Processed?"

"Please, Captain, you're delaying the next arrival."

Picard suppressed his questions and temper with difficulty.

Proceeding along the corridor to his left, he stopped before an emergency pressure door. Paint flaked from it in sections, revealing thick coats that had built up one over another, giving the impression of a topographic model. To Picard's eye, the door appeared to be an antique, dating from a time before forcefields, when atmospheric containment had to be accomplished solely by physical means.

"Stand close to the door, please."

As Picard did so, he heard mechanical hums and clanks from the corridor ceiling; then a second thick door suddenly dropped down behind him.

His ears popped as pressure equalized in the small volume of air between the two doors.

An emergency airlock. Picard tabled the realization

as the wheel-like locking mechanism of the first door rotated noisily. The moment it stopped, he felt a vibration in the floor, and the door slid open to reveal more of the corridor, and a Starfleet security team.

The commander of the team was a Betazoid, his large dark eyes unreadable as he approached. Behind him, waiting impassively, each with a hand on the phaser he or she carried, were four large humans, heavily muscled, as if they had been born on high-gravity colony worlds.

"Captain Picard, welcome to Mercury. Your right hand please."

The Betazoid held a white device that Picard recognized as a modified medical monitor designed to be fastened around a patient's wrist. It was old technology, not often seen on a starship, where sensors could monitor anyone in sickbay from a distance.

"I'm not ill," Picard said.

The Betazoid held the monitor out to Picard, open like a manacle. "We know. While you were in the transporter buffer, your entire genetic and cellular structures were thoroughly analyzed. This monitor will enable us to maintain somatic continuity."

"Somatic continuity?" Picard asked.

The Betazoid held up his right wrist. He wore a monitor.

Picard looked over at the security team. Each of them had a monitor, as well.

The Betazoid's professional smile faded. "We need to know that the person who emerges from the transporter remains the same person while he's stationed here."

Picard held out his right hand.

The Betazoid fastened the monitor around his wrist, then used a welder's plaser to seal it.

Picard tried to adjust the position of the monitor, twisting it back and forth. Molecularly sealed, it wasn't coming off, and it felt uncomfortably tight.

"I sense your resistance," the Betazoid said. He was checking the display on the tricorder he aimed at the monitor. "Understandable. But not, perhaps, the best attitude to have at this time." His smile was perfunctory, somehow false.

"The monitor's operational, Captain. If it should ever stop working, or the sensor web reports difficulty in receiving its signal, you'll hear an announcement. At that time, you will stop whatever you're doing and remain in place and in view of the nearest visual sensor until a security detail can reach you."

Picard made a last attempt to penetrate the officiousness of the Betazoid. "Has there been an incident that these procedures protect us against?"

"You'll be briefed," the Betazoid said.

The statement was obviously intended as a dismissal.

The pressure door behind Picard slid shut.

"We have other arrivees to process," the Betazoid said. He gestured down the corridor, past the security team. "You want the blue door. Thank you, Captain."

Picard made the decision not to protest his treatment. Until he knew what had happened to cause Starfleet to establish this level of security, it was clear that questioning the procedure would be useless.

The blue door was several hundred meters along

the curving corridor. Picard passed only two other people on the walk there, both civilians, both wearing medical monitors like his. Neither spoke to him, acknowledged him only with a nod.

A hand-lettered sign had been placed on the blue door. All it said was BRIEFING.

As Picard looked for a control panel, the door opened to reveal a large balcony of slatted metal looking into a cavern large enough to hold the entire Federation Council chamber. The stale, moist air that rushed out told him why the corridor smelled as it did.

The balcony was bolted to the cavern wall as if it were part of some long-abandoned mining operation. It was thick with worn paint, like the pressure doors in the corridor, and starkly lit by what appeared to be temporary emergency lights clamped to the railing every few meters. They marked the way to a wide staircase, also of slatted metal, leading down to the cavern's floor, supported by improbably thin posts.

Looking ahead, Picard could see several islands of light in the cavern, created by pole-mounted fixtures. Some areas were stacked with cargo containers. One held a row of portable toilets. Still another appeared to be a field kitchen. Starfleet personnel and civilian workers were busy everywhere, carrying supplies from the containers, assembling portable equipment. . . . The whole effect was one of hurried preparation, like an army on the run.

The idea of a Starfleet installation having been driven underground, so quickly and so readily, was unsettling.

Picard descended the stairs, grim. One oasis of light contained a black conference table set up on a low platform to provide a level floor. The table was surrounded by enough chairs for about fifty participants, but only twelve people were present, Admiral Janeway among them. Of the other eleven, as Picard came closer, he recognized Fleet Admiral Robur Burnett, currently the number-three officer at Starfleet Command, and two civilian politicians: President Wheeler of Mars, and Jeroba Tak Fong of Alpha Centauri. Councillor Jeroba was New Montana's representative on the Federation Council and chairman of the Starfleet Oversight Committee.

The others in attendance were a mixture of Fleet personnel and civilians, all human and all unfamiliar to Picard.

They, however, recognized him, and as soon as he stepped from the rough cavern floor onto the platform, everyone turned toward him. As yet, no one addressed him, and Picard followed suit, maintaining silence.

It was Janeway who directed him with a gesture to a chair beside hers. She saw him look at her medical monitor. Each person gathered around the table was wearing one.

Picard decided it was time to speak.

"Are these truly necessary?" he asked as he took his seat beside the admiral.

"Yes," she answered quietly, but didn't elaborate. Again, Picard followed her example and said nothing more.

Then Admiral Burnett stood up, a holographic

screen forming behind him, blocking out a looming dark rock wall a dozen meters beyond. On the screen, Picard identified a standard fleet-deployment map of the Alpha and Beta quadrants, though with many fewer assets inscribed on it than usual.

Burnett cleared his throat and began the briefing. He wasted no time with pleasantries. His voice sounded weak, swallowed by the enormity of the cavern, but what he had to say produced enormous impact.

"In the past eleven days, Starfleet has lost approximately two-thirds of its warp-capable fleet."

Picard was stunned, and so, he could see, were most of the others at the table. Janeway, surprisingly, was not.

"Fewer than five percent of the affected vessels have been outright destroyed. In most cases, safety systems performed as designed and warp cores were ejected."

A civilian blurted out a question. "Is every loss related to a warp-core malfunction?"

"Every loss," Burnett confirmed. "Of our remaining warp-capable assets—" He gestured to Picard. "—such as the *Enterprise*, most of them are equipped with older-model cores or are on station with orders not to go to warp."

Another civilian interjected with alarm. "Admiral, are these 'malfunctions' a direct attack on the Federation?"

Burnett glanced at Councillor Jeroba as if they had already had that conversation. "Not just on the Federation. Though the Klingon Empire hasn't officially commented on any unusual shipping losses, unofficially our contacts with the Imperial Fleet suggest they have lost more than half their warp vessels. Communications intercepts from the Romulan Star Empire indicate their losses are much less, but still significant. Apparently, their larger vessels that use nanoscale singularities to enable warp have not been affected. But their civilian fleet has been almost totally wiped out.

"Even more disquieting is that Deep Space Nine reports no warp vessel, scheduled or otherwise, has emerged from the Bajoran wormhole in the past eight days. That strongly suggests that the malfunctions are occurring in the Gamma Quadrant, as well."

Picard had to interrupt at that. He raised his hand to signal Burnett, disturbed again by the unfamiliar weight of the monitor on his wrist.

"Jean-Luc," the fleet admiral said.

"Admiral, if the malfunctions are indeed occurring throughout the galaxy, then why are we certain they're the result of a deliberate attack and not some new natural phenomenon?"

Burnett held up his own medical monitor. It gleamed in the harsh light surrounding the table. "Why these, you mean."

Picard waited for an answer.

"In a number of cases," Burnett said, "the malfunctions appear to be associated with acts of infiltration."

That was a new revelation to Picard and most of the others. A buzz of reactions grew around the table.

"Can you characterize the nature of the infiltration?" Picard asked.

Again, Burnett held up his monitor. "Shapeshifters. Far more sophisticated than the Founders, or, for that matter, any other polymorphic species known to us. Hence the need to bring all of you here by transporter, so your identities could be confirmed by comparison with earlier transporter records. More serious is that these shapeshifters, in the guise of specific Starfleet personnel, have been sighted on dozens of affected vessels, spread across thousands of light-years, all within days of each other.

"And most serious," Burnett concluded, "after the time and effort these beings have expended in infiltrating our vessels and installations, they appear to be all too willing to die in the malfunctions they create."

There the fleet admiral paused as several heated conversations began.

For all the questions that Picard wanted answered, one was critical. He had little doubt that all other answers would flow from it.

"Admiral," Picard said, cutting through the background clamor of other speakers, "why have *we* been brought here?"

Burnett grimaced, and Picard did not need the abilities of a Betazoid to sense the weight of defeat the admiral felt.

"For the moment," Burnett said, "all of us at this table *are* Starfleet Command."

The room fell silent.

"What about Admiral Mueller?" Picard asked in bewilderment. Eric Mueller was the commander-in-chief of Starfleet, only a few months into his posting.

"He's presumed lost. The *Erebus* was en route from Vulcan six days ago. The warp core breached so suddenly, it couldn't be ejected. No survivors."

Picard understood that he was no longer in the company of strangers. Everyone present was now his colleague and he theirs. The *U.S.S. Erebus* was a *Sovereign*-class starship, as was the *Enterprise*. Admiral Mueller's fate, and the fate of all those on his ship, could also have been the fate of Picard and his crew— if not for his encounter with Shinzon and the subsequent installation of an old-model warp core.

"Are we to presume other personnel losses have brought us to this?" Picard asked.

"A combination of factors," Burnett said tersely. "Some members of Command are known to have perished. Others are known to be stranded in interstellar space, awaiting transport by warp-capable rescue vessels. So many, though, that it could take months for all of them to be returned to Mercury. Others are simply missing. Admiral Janeway will brief us on that aspect of what we're facing, later."

Picard had no idea what Janeway could have to say about missing personnel, but one other detail of what Burnett had just said needed clarification.

"Why Mercury?"

The admiral gestured to a gaunt, bearded man at his right. Like Burnett and most of the others present, he appeared to have gone several days without sleep. "I'll leave that to Doctor Muirhead."

Though they had never met, Picard recognized the engineer's name. He was the chief administrator of Starfleet's Propulsion Technologies Division.

Muirhead stood as Burnett sat. He was equally plain-spoken.

"We don't know what's causing the rash of core malfunctions. In the beginning, only certain models were affected. However, we do have detailed engineering logs from a handful of incidents and they appear to indicate that in almost all cases the cores failed during power-up."

"What about the other cases?" someone at the table called out. Picard couldn't see who the questioner was.

"Location also appears to play a part in the malfunctions," Muirhead answered. "Vessels, even those with susceptible cores, that went to warp deep within the gravity well of a star or other massive object were not affected. This suggests to us that whatever technique is being used to trigger warp-core failures involves the distortion of ordinary space-time. Where a particular volume of space-time is already distorted by a strong gravity source, the technique is not effective. This could also account for why the larger Romulan vessels, powered as they are by miniature black holes, have not experienced the same failure rate."

Now Picard understood why Starfleet Command had been relocated to Mercury. That planet was so close to Earth's sun that even five hundred years ago, in the infancy of multiphysics, the sun's relativistic effects on Mercury's orbit had been noted by astronomers.

"However," Muirhead continued, "what little protection a gravity well provides is likely going to be temporary." He picked up a small padd from the table, input some commands, and the holographic screen changed its display to show a three-dimensional graph. The primary values being charted on it progressed to zero over time.

"As you see, the characteristics of the affected warp cores are following a diminishing energy curve. Our most powerful designs were affected first, beginning eleven days ago with the devastating breach at the Cochrane Institute. Since that time, however, less powerful cores are being affected. If the pattern continues, as shown on this chart, within ten more days, Cochrane-based warp travel will be . . . impossible."

Shocked silence greeted that revelation.

Muirhead sat. Burnett folded his hands on the table and the weariness he felt, and his despair, were evident in his heavy tone. "In other words, what we are faced with is the end of interstellar trade, interstellar traffic, interstellar culture . . ."

Burnett looked around the table, as if making sure everyone understood exactly what their position was.

"In ten days, the United Federation of Planets will cease to exist."

13

Kirk resolved from the transporter effect determined he had had enough of Vulcan obstructionism.

But even as he prepared to logically register his objections to being beamed against his will, he realized he was facing not a Vulcan, but a human.

A compellingly attractive, dark-haired woman in a Starfleet captain's uniform.

"Mister Kirk, I'm Captain Blakely. Sorry for the abrupt—"

"No apologies," Kirk said. He wanted no wasted words. "My son's been kidnapped. The sensor records of the Vulcan authorities have been compromised. I need a starship with a full sensor suite and I need it now."

The captain was unperturbed, as if she had anticipated Kirk's defiance. "I am sorry about your child. I had no—"

"I'm not interested in 'sorry.'" Kirk pushed past Blakely, heading for a viewport. From the steady lights of the stars he could see through it, it was obvious he was in space. Even more obvious, from the idealized painting of Mount Selaya on the far bulkhead, he was on a Vulcan facility. He needed to know if it was a vessel or a space station.

"What ship are you from?" Kirk asked sharply.

Blakely stepped beside him as if they were having no more than a casual conversation. "The *Magellan*."

Kirk wasn't familiar with it. He took a guess. "A science vessel."

"Yes," she said, inexplicably smiling, "but that's not the point."

"No, it's not," Kirk agreed. He peered out the viewport, saw from the nested cylindrical projections that he was on a space station. Judging from the size of Vulcan far below, the station was in a geostationary orbit. Not good enough for a full planetary sensor sweep. He needed to be able to scan the entire planet. "Where is it?"

Blakely studied him with curiosity as if he, not she, were out of line.

"Your ship, Captain Blakely. The *Magellan*."

The captain finally found her voice. "It no longer exists, Mister Kirk. That's why I'm commandeering the *Belle Rêve*."

"No. You're not."

Blakely held up a small Starfleet padd, showed its screen to Kirk.

"These are my orders," she said. "The *Belle Rêve* is one of the last Starfleet vessels in the Vulcan system cleared for warp. I'm to take it to Earth at once."

Kirk didn't bother reading the orders. He gently but firmly pushed the padd aside.

"*I'm* under orders from Admiral Janeway. And she wants me on Vulcan."

For the first time, Kirk saw Blakely's expression falter. "Admiral Janeway was killed on the *Sovereign* . . ."

Kirk hid his surprise. He'd just let slip information he'd assumed a Starfleet officer would already have. He tried to cover. "She gave me the orders before she returned to the *Sovereign.*"

"Then the admiral wasn't aware of the difficulties we've encountered with our warp drives." Blakely put her hand on Kirk's shoulder, a strangely familiar gesture. "I think we can safely say the admiral would change her orders in light of the current situation."

Kirk knew that was not the case, but didn't want to jeopardize Janeway's plans to keep her survival a secret from whatever enemy Starfleet faced.

"I need to speak to your commander," Kirk said.

"My commander's dead."

Kirk wondered if the woman had taken too many stress tabs. "Where did your orders come from?"

Blakely smiled again as if Kirk were an old friend. "I need the *Belle Rêve.*"

Kirk had no intention of giving up his ship.

"So do I."

Blakely placed her hand on Kirk's chest, more the touch of a lover than a Starfleet officer determined to put a civilian in his place.

"I need *you*," she said. Then she grabbed the back of Kirk's head and forced him forward, kissing him.

Kirk instantly pushed at her, to make her step away, but her strength was—

Inhuman.

"No!" Kirk twisted his face away from her but could not escape her grip.

"James, please. . . ."

His eyes widened in horror. He *knew* that voice.

That voice still whispered to him in his dreams.

The voice of a woman who had died five years ago at Halkan.

Teilani . . .

It was his beloved wife, mother of Joseph, who embraced him now. The Starfleet uniform of Captain Blakely evaporated like mist, leaving this creature unclothed, unthreatening, incredibly desirable in his arms.

"I love you, James. . . ."

Kirk pushed and struggled but her arms drew him closer. Fingers like duranium talons twisted the back of his head, forcing him to gaze into eyes he'd known so well.

He saw his own face, distorted in fear, reflected there.

"And I know you love me. . . ."

Millimeter by millimeter, the creature with Teilani's form, Teilani's voice, Teilani's scent, forced his head forward to her lips.

"Accept. . . ." she whispered, and her intoxicating breath was warm and sweet and stirring.

"Norinda!" Kirk shouted, struggling to break the creature's spell.

Then he gasped as Teilani's face webbed with a mesh of fine dark lines and her skin fissured along those lines into cubes and he felt the hand at the back of his neck flatten and spread.

"Be loved," the creature said.

Kirk gasped for air as that face smothered him in a wave of choking darkness.

And then there was a flash of light.

The sting of heat.

A familiar numbing of his fingers, arms, and legs.

He felt himself fly backward to land jarringly on the deck.

His face was suddenly clear. But he swatted and rubbed to get rid of the sensation the darkness had left on him, as if he had walked through a spider's silk.

Then he saw the darkness, separate and distinct.

A mound of it, cubes of different sizes, slowly folding into themselves and shrinking as if melting into the deck, as phaser beams splashed over it, causing the shadows that textured it to jump and flash.

With great effort, Kirk turned his head away from the abomination that had tried to claim him, to see a Vulcan security detail in the doorway, three of them firing phasers, a fourth rushing to his side.

"James Kirk?" the fourth Vulcan asked. He was in a red uniform, the color of the Vulcan desert. He helped Kirk to his feet.

"I am," Kirk said. He could still feel his heart racing.

The dark mound was now a powdery stain, all traces of it slowly fading.

"How did you get here?" the Vulcan asked.

"You beamed me in," Kirk said indignantly.

The Vulcan shook his head. "This is a restricted defense installation. Your beam-in was unauthorized."

Kirk would not accept that. "Is this installation protected by shields?"

The Vulcan was about to answer, then stopped as he realized what Kirk was implying. "Logical" was all he said. Obviously, if Kirk had been transported aboard the space station, someone with authority had adjusted the shields to let the beam through.

"I'll start at the beginning," Kirk said, then rapidly filled the Vulcan in on everything he had done since Joseph had vanished. When he reached the point at which Prefect Vorrel had contacted the Ministry of Planetary Defense, the Vulcan security officer blinked, signaling disturbance.

"That's when," Kirk concluded, "I was beamed here."

"A moment," the officer said. He walked over to his three companions who were continuing to take handheld sensor readings of the now unmarked deck where the dark residue had vanished.

Kirk was not inclined to wait until the Vulcans had reached a consensus. He tapped his communicator pin. "Kirk to *Belle Rêve*."

Scott responded at once. *"Captain, where are ye?"*

"On a Planetary Defense space station, geostationary orbit." Kirk didn't like the sound of the engineer's voice. "What's happened, Scotty?"

"The prefecture office was just bombed. We thought ye were in it."

Kirk felt off-balance. He wondered if the bomb had been meant for him. But then, why had he been allowed to be beamed out of the building?

The answer came to him.

Norinda wanted him alive.

Norinda had just attempted to do to him what she had done to Spock. And if that act of dissolution *was* fatal, then there was no sense in allowing him to escape the bombing. She could have killed him in the prefecture office much more easily.

That confirmed it for Kirk.

That meant Spock *was* alive.

The commander of the Vulcan security team returned to Kirk.

Renewed with hope for Joseph and Spock, Kirk tapped his communicator again. "Stand by, Mister Scott."

The Vulcan's face was unreadable, even for Kirk. "Your story is troubling. It implies that the security of our planetary defense and local peacekeeping organizations has been compromised."

"I agree," Kirk said.

The Vulcan glanced back at the deck. "And the phenomenon that we have witnessed . . ."

"Is known to Starfleet," Kirk said. "And I have no doubt it's got something to do with the kidnapping of my child."

The Vulcan considered his next words, and the longer the silence lasted, the more Kirk knew he wasn't going to like what the Vulcan had to say.

"As a civilian, you cannot remain on this station."

"I understand," Kirk said. "If you beam me back to the Gateway, I—"

"No," the Vulcan interrupted. "You cannot return to Vulcan, either."

"Why not?"

"A state of emergency exists. As an alien, you must apply for a landing visa through your embassy."

Kirk felt his face flush with anger. "My son is on Vulcan. I will not leave without him."

The Vulcan raised a finger and the other three members of his team were instantly at his side.

"Mister Kirk, given the capabilities of my world's peacekeeping agencies, it is not logical for a criminal organization to keep a kidnapping victim on Vulcan. Therefore, your son is not on Vulcan."

For a few moments, Kirk's mind raced as he weighed what he would need to do to get past the security team. But just as quickly he decided that the effort wouldn't be worth it. Even if he managed to drop all four Vulcans, there would be more in the corridors outside the transporter depot.

The wiser course was to return to the *Belle Rêve* and, from there, to make his way back to the planet below.

If Norinda wanted him to return to Earth, then more than ever, Kirk knew, for Joseph's sake he must remain on Vulcan.

He felt certain even Spock would approve of his logic.

14

It took less than twelve hours for Kirk to return to Vulcan.

The *Belle Rêve* maintained a full data library of Starfleet's most secure codes, including those required for high-level communications with Vulcan authorities. It also carried a simple device that, when worn like a combadge, overwrote the individual Starfleet ID code that was transmitted with each personnel transport.

Kirk applied for a landing visa under the name of Lieutenant Roger Ramey of the *Starship Sovereign*, and the *Belle Rêve*'s computers were able to surreptitiously upload Lieutenant Ramey's service record into the memory banks of Vulcan's Joint Operations Center.

Kirk doubted any Vulcan would personally review his application—the entire system was automated and, under present circumstances, operating at the limits of its capacity. He beamed from his ship to an orbital hotel where some of the survivors from the *Sovereign* and other stricken vessels were being quartered. From there, with Lieutenant Ramey's ID, he had his request to beam to Vulcan approved without comment.

Kirk had been tempted to try to arrange for a second visa, so that Janeway's Emergency Medical Hologram could accompany him. But the Doctor's holographic emitter would likely be flagged as suspect technology during transport, and Kirk was determined not to do anything that might attract attention. Instead, the Doctor remained on the *Belle Rêve* with Scott and McCoy, standing by to retrieve Kirk the moment Kirk felt retrieval was necessary.

Thus, alone, Kirk beamed into the central transport hub at the Gateway, and at once made his way to the only local contact he believed he could trust not to report his presence.

Scholar T'Vrel.

As Kirk had expected, T'Vrel's *s'url* was a simple compound, completely unremarkable, except for its location in the oldest part of the ancient desert community. Supposedly, several of its buildings had existed in Surak's day, though Kirk doubted any structure from that time had survived the battles that had raged in this location.

Wide stone steps, heavily worn by centuries of grit and dust and the sandals of thousands of pilgrims, led up from the street to an unornamented portico of stone blocks. The blocks were deep desert red, a peaceful color to Vulcans, Kirk knew. It spoke to them of the stunning vistas of their desert regions, and of the absence of blood.

Kirk walked up the center of the steps, his coarse-woven cloak wrapped about him, his hood pulled forward, not for cooling, only for anonymity.

As he reached the top step, he looked into a wide courtyard of wind-smoothed stone slabs, ringed by a series of single-story buildings, each with a wide sheltered walkway serving as a porch, and as a way to move from one building to another in shade. But for now, it was nearing sunset, and the orange Vulcan sun cast long shadows from the horizon. Shade wasn't necessary.

A solitary Vulcan, dressed in brown and tan robes identical to those T'Vrel had worn, swept the sand from a few stone slabs with precise, methodical movements. The impossibility of ever completing that task across the entire courtyard made Kirk think the exercise was more one of meditation than of groundskeeping.

The soft glow of candlelight flickered through many of the open windows of the surrounding buildings. Kirk paused, trying to see if one building seemed more likely than another to be a main hall where he could inquire after T'Vrel.

In those few moments, one of the nearest doors opened and a second Surakian walked out, not slowly, not rushing, but with purpose.

The Surakian lifted her hooded head as she neared Kirk and, from what little Kirk could see, she was young, no more than twenty standard years. It is only after Vulcans reach full adulthood that their chronological ages become difficult to reconcile with their appearance.

Because the young Vulcan's robes were colored with a single shade of brown, and not two like T'Vrel's, Kirk judged she was a novice. Still, she might know where T'Vrel could be found.

"Good evening," Kirk said as the young woman came within speaking distance.

Her eyes met Kirk's with surprising intensity, and in a soft whisper, she said, "You're not safe here—follow me at once."

There was no time for Kirk to reason his way through to a decision. No chance to apply logic to an assessment of how likely a trap might be. Instead, acting solely on instinct, he changed direction in midstride and followed the novice back down the stone steps, into the sunset shadows of the street.

The cloaked figure didn't look back to see if Kirk followed. Kirk understood; her Vulcan ears would have answered that question upon hearing Kirk's footsteps stay close.

For fifteen minutes they proceeded on a circuitous route that Kirk assumed was designed to expose anyone who might be following them. It was little defense against orbital scans or even a distant pursuer with a tricorder, but Kirk guessed the young woman was employing other defenses against those techniques. Simply ignoring them wouldn't be logical.

At last, night fell and the Vulcan stars came out, much fewer than seen in the desert skies of Earth due to the brightness of the two small companions to this world's primary star. Eridani B and C, so distant they were little more than points of light, still were bright enough and close enough together this time of year to cast faint double shadows between the widely spaced streetglows illuminating the empty thoroughfares.

Eventually, the young woman turned in to an alleyway, and when Kirk followed, he found her waiting for him, her face still half obscured by her hood.

"Did T'Vrel send you?" Kirk asked.

Her answer surprised him.

"No. She expected you. But so did others. There was concern you would be captured and we had no clear plan to prevent it."

"Captured by whom?" Kirk asked.

"I think you know." She turned toward an unmarked door in the side of what appeared to be a warehouse. "In here."

Beyond the door was a narrow corridor. At the end of the corridor, another door. As to what lay beyond that, on any other occasion Kirk might have laughed at the incongruous and very un-Vulcan scene before him.

It was a bar, old and run-down. Mostly for alien visitors, it seemed, but with many Vulcans, both as customers and staff.

The light level was low. Most illumination came from phosphorescent channels in the floor, evoking the living lights of Vulcan's T'Kallaron caves.

The sound in the bar was a gentle rush of a dozen alien tongues, too many for the universal translator in Kirk's combadge to make sense of all at once.

But most notable of all, there was a faint scent to

the air that brought back an intense memory for Kirk. A mixture of burnt cinnamon and an Andorian spice like anise, blended with the sweat of a dozen other species and the smoke from an open grill that burned Vulcan stonewood.

The first time Kirk had experienced that tantalizing mélange from far-off worlds had been in San Francisco, lifetimes ago, before he had entered the Academy.

Kirk closed his eyes, captured the moment and the memory, recalled his dream.

Do I have your attention?

He was getting closer to Spock. He could feel it.

"This way," the Surakian prompted. The young woman's words thrust Kirk back into the present.

He followed the novice to a small table in a corner, apart from the others.

Two battered wooden chairs were leaning against the table, telling Kirk that it had been set aside for them. From under the protective shadow of his hood, Kirk glanced around but saw no one paying any attention to either him or his guide.

They sat down. The young woman pulled off her hood.

Kirk was surprised that her head wasn't shaved.

Even more surprising, she wasn't even Vulcan.

She read the question in Kirk's eyes.

"Correct," she said. "I'm Romulan. But as far as deception goes, you're not Lieutenant Ramey. So we're even."

Kirk was both impressed and concerned by the woman's knowledge.

"My name's Marinta," the Romulan said.

"I take it you know who I am."

Marinta nodded once. "And I know both reasons why you're here. To find your son. And Ambassador Spock."

Again, Kirk looked around the dimly lit bar but caught no one paying particular attention to the two robed figures in the corner.

"What else?" Kirk asked. He knew he was being cautious, perhaps overly so. But there was still a chance that Marinta had led him into a trap rather than away from one.

She reached into her robes, brought out a small padd. At least, Kirk thought it was a padd, though it had no display screen.

Marinta slipped a slender transparent cylinder from the device, handed it to Kirk.

"Place this on your eyes."

Kirk saw a small indentation on the cylinder, held it to the bridge of his nose.

The cylinder remained in place, a narrow tube of clear material poised before both eyes like impossibly thin spectacles.

"You're aware of what happened at Starbase Four-ninety-nine." Marinta didn't make it a question.

Kirk recalled what Janeway had told him of that disaster. When the facility's static-warp-field power generator had failed, the entire base had been destroyed. In all likelihood, it was the first case of whatever phenomenon was now affecting warp cores throughout the galaxy. It also had been the incident that had brought Starfleet Intelligence into the investigation of the missing multiphysicists and warp specialists, including Spock.

"I am," Kirk said.

"The entire staff was lost, including several prominent visitors."

Janeway had told Kirk that, as well. Six admirals, four starship captains and their science officers, and three civilians. The fact that civilians were present suggested they represented Starfleet Intelligence, or some other organization that worked in the shadows.

"Starbase Four-ninety-nine was little more than a subspace relay station," Marinta said. "Six admirals. Four starship captains. Why were they there?"

Kirk wasn't certain what Marinta was suggesting. "As far as I know, they were investigating the disappearance of the *Monitor*."

"Correct."

Kirk removed the transparent cylinder so he could study Marinta more closely. There was only one reason why the Romulan had brought up the *Monitor*'s disappearance.

"You think everything's connected," Kirk said.

"I know everything's connected," Marinta replied.

Kirk sought more details. "I understand the similarity between the destruction of the starbase and the warp-core malfunctions. But the *Monitor* vanished six years ago. How's that related to what's happening now? And what could it have to do with my son?"

Marinta indicated the unusual padd. "Access the viewer and see for yourself."

Kirk studied the cylinder for a moment, then placed it back in position before his eyes.

Marinta slid open a panel on the small device, pressed a control.

Instantly, the sights and sounds of the bar dissolved around Kirk, and all he could see was a shimmering wall of holographic static.

"It's not working," Kirk said.

"Focus," Marinta told him.

Then the images began, and Kirk witnessed the death of the *Starship Monitor*.

15

THE GATEWAY, VULCAN
STARDATE 58563.6

The images projected onto Kirk's retinas seethed with static, and were sometimes barely recognizable.

The sounds transmitted directly to his ears drifted in and out of comprehension, ghostlike, mournful, offering up fragments of words, a sudden insight from the tone of a voice, a murmured prayer as the end neared.

The recording lasted seven minutes.

At an earlier time in his career, Kirk would have discounted its story. It was that fantastic. That unbelievable.

But now, he'd experienced enough of life's mysteries to understand that the universe held an inexhaustible trove of secrets to discover. Just because his mind couldn't immediately grasp all of what this recording seemed to represent, Kirk knew, was no reason to disbelieve it.

However, there was every reason to question it.

"How did you get this?" he demanded.

Marinta didn't answer. Instead, she looked past Kirk toward the entrance of the bar and in an unhurried movement tugged her hood back into place. "We should go," she said. She palmed the small player padd as she stood up from her chair.

Kirk had no choice; she knew this outpost better than he did. He got to his feet, pulling his own hood into place.

As he followed her to the back, where the light was even dimmer, he glanced over his shoulder to see two Vulcans in red uniforms talking to the server behind the bar.

Marinta opened another door, motioned to Kirk to step past her into the corridor beyond. Then, as she quietly closed the door behind them, she removed a second device from her robes. It was an IDIC pin, a plain, inexpensive version like those sold to tourists in the town square.

Marinta attached the pin to Kirk's cloak, made an adjustment to it.

"It'll disguise your biosignature," she said. "It's only effective against general sensor sweeps, but at least to a security tricorder you'll appear to be Vulcan."

"What about you?" Kirk asked.

Marinta turned back a fold of her robe to show she had her own IDIC pin. "Our intelligence was correct. They didn't find you at the *s'url*, so they've begun a search."

Kirk could see that Marinta wanted to hurry along

this new narrow wooden corridor, but his suspicion regarding her motives was undiminished.

He held up the transparent viewing cylinder. "Convenient that the authorities arrived just as we were going to discuss this."

Marinta didn't bother to hide her annoyance. "The recording you saw was an intercepted transmission. We obtained it eighteen months ago from a Tellarite freighter." She gestured down the corridor, urgent. "We have to go."

She started to walk quickly. Kirk made no further protest, kept pace.

"Wherever you got it from, the recording's been altered."

Kirk had seen enough visual sensor logs to recognize the cruder forms of forgery. Years ago, he had been victim of that kind of fraud himself.

"Not altered," Marinta said. "Enhanced. The original subspace signal was severely degraded. It traveled three hundred and fifty thousand light-years."

"Which is, of course, impossible."

Marinta stopped by another wooden door—this one distinguished by carved Vulcan script and an ornamental inlay of oxidized copper.

"On the face of it, yes. And yet, you've seen the recording for yourself. You recognized Captain Lewinski?"

She tapped a fist against a section of the dirt-stained wall, and a hidden panel opened, revealing a palm scanner. Marinta placed her hand against it and the scanner bed glowed green.

Taking one last look back along the corridor, Kirk

confirmed that he had indeed recognized the captain in the images he had seen. Nine years ago, Lewinski, Kirk, and Jean-Luc Picard had undertaken a joint mission on the *Monitor*. At the time, Lewinski had done Kirk and Picard the honor of changing the name of his vessel from *Monitor* to *Enterprise.*

The heavy carved door swung open to reveal a narrow wooden staircase leading up into total darkness.

Marinta stepped back, indicating for Kirk to go first. With some misgivings, Kirk complied.

Marinta continued her efforts to convince him as they climbed. "And you're familiar with the trajectory and the capabilities of the Kelvan Expeditionary Return Probes?"

Again, the Romulan was correct. Kirk himself was responsible for that audacious mission.

More than a century earlier, a generational ship from the Kelvan Empire in the Andromeda Galaxy survived passage through the galactic energy barrier only to crash in Federation space. Though the Kelvans on that ship had intended to lay the groundwork for conquering the Federation's own galaxy, they were in fact refugees from what they described as a natural disaster affecting Andromeda—a rise in radiation levels that would make all of their home galaxy uninhabitable.

Within two years of this first contact with the Kelvan scouts, the Federation launched three high-speed robotic probes to the Kelvan Empire in order to relay the Federation's offer of planets suitable for Kelvan colonization. Even with the probes' use of advanced

Kelvan warp technology, the Federation's leaders of today knew the spacecraft would still require two more centuries to reach their destination. Presumably it would be an additional three centuries until the Federation bureaucrats of the twenty-ninth century could look forward to handling the disposition of the Kelvan evacuation armada.

"I'm very familiar with the probes," Kirk said. He saw no reason to offer further detail.

The staircase shook slightly as the wooden door at its base closed solidly.

Kirk wheeled around, suddenly certain he had heard running footsteps an instant before.

"Did you hear something?" Kirk asked.

Marinta shook her head, pushed him forward. "We need to get to a place of safety, where they won't be able to scan us individually."

Kirk kept climbing the stairs, picking up his pace in response to Marinta's increasing insistence.

She paused at the top of the stairs, producing a small sensor padd. In the dim light from its screen, Kirk could see a narrow metal door only a meter ahead.

"What now?" he asked. He hated being at this woman's mercy. He couldn't be sure whether they were being followed. He couldn't be sure whether she was merely leading him on.

Marinta kept her attention focused on the sensor padd's screen. "We have to wait," she said.

"For what?"

She looked at Kirk, changed the topic. "In addition to the Kelvan probes, do you recall the unusual colony world that some call Mudd?"

"I know it, but I don't see the relevance."

"Two hundred thousand synthetic humanoids," Marinta prompted, undeterred. She stared past Kirk, down the stairs into darkness. "Robotic survivors of a scientific outpost established by another Andromedan species. Unlike the Kelvans, they claimed they were escaping their sun's destruction."

"I remember the world, and the humanoids," Kirk said. The planet had been the site of his second run-in with the exasperating Harcourt Fenton Mudd. "But how does it tie in with the *Monitor* transmission and the Kelvan probes?" He peered into the darkness, too. But saw nothing. Heard nothing.

"Consider the distance the makers of those synthetics traveled," Marinta said. She'd dropped her voice to a cautious whisper. "Surely if it were only a single star's death they faced, there were other safe havens more readily available in their own galaxy."

That simple fact was all it took for the answer to crystallize for Kirk. "Something else is happening in Andromeda," he said.

"The signs have been there for decades," Marinta agreed. "But no one put the details together. The synthetic beings, the Kelvans . . ."

Kirk didn't need her to continue. "It's not a natural disaster. It's not dying stars or rising levels of radiation. They were all escaping the Totality."

Marinta snapped the sensor padd closed. "Now!" she said, then pressed her shoulder against the metal door.

It creaked open onto a deserted street, illuminated only by the pale light of the planet's companion stars.

Kirk hesitated, about to demand that Marinta provide a full explanation of what she was implying before he took another step.

Then he heard the low-power hum of a phaser and the crack of wood splintering.

Flashes of light flickered at the bottom of the stairwell, spiking through the suddenly shattered door.

Marinta hissed, "Keep moving!" She dragged Kirk onto the street by the sleeve of his cloak.

Kirk ran beside her until they rounded a corner and found themselves on a more crowded street.

Shops were open and light spilled from them onto the sand-covered walkways.

Marinta settled into a purposeful walk, lowered her head as if she were nothing more than a novice.

Kirk did the same at her side, all the while listening intently for the sound of running footsteps behind them.

As if they weren't in danger, as if they weren't being pursued, Marinta continued their conversation. "Whatever the Totality is," she said quietly, "we must conclude its conquest of Andromeda is complete." She glanced at Kirk from the recesses of her hood and he saw her dark Romulan eyes flash at him. "And now it's invaded our galaxy, to do the same."

Kirk kept walking, weaving through the crowd of pilgrims and tourists, almost overcome by the chilling pattern that was coalescing in his mind.

From a strategic perspective, everything the Totality had attempted to date fit perfectly with a plan for military conquest.

Even for a life-form that could, as the *Monitor*

transmission implied, construct transwarp passage-ways between *galaxies*, the logistics of projecting enough force and combatants from Andromeda to this galaxy had to be an enormous undertaking. So what better way to conquer this new island universe than by turning its own inhabitants against each other—utilizing the resources already in place?

Kirk thought back to his own first meeting with Norinda, when she herself had claimed to be a refugee from the Totality. Though he'd only realized it now, her game plan had been revealed from the beginning: all the starship captains who had come to her aid, she had pitted against one another. But that competition hadn't been a game as she had de-scribed it—and as Kirk had accepted it. It was a care-fully calculated ploy to determine which of the species inhabiting this quadrant would be the easiest to turn into a weapon to be used against the others.

At the time, he'd been surprised when Norinda had awarded victory to an unknown species with an undetectable vessel. Only in hindsight had Starfleet realized the Romulans had won Norinda's contest.

Thus the Romulan Star Empire had become the in-cubator for Norinda and her plans to sow dissension.

Until her second encounter with Kirk.

When Spock had staged what appeared to have been his assassination on Romulus, Kirk had investi-gated, arriving just as Norinda's plan to foment civil war between Romulus and Remus had been set to proceed.

Kirk's arrival had not been a coincidence. Spock's desperate action had been triggered by the inexplicable resistance his unification movement encountered. Spock had suspected there was an unknown group spreading dissension, but hadn't know it was Norinda and her followers in the *Jolan* Movement.

But Kirk had exposed Norinda's manipulation of Romulan politics. With Picard and with Spock, with the *Belle Rêve* and the holographic doctor, and even with the help of Joseph, Kirk had revealed the true nature of Norinda and maintained the stability of the Romulan Empire.

Norinda's plan had failed.

But in confronting an intelligence with the capacity to conquer entire galaxies, Kirk knew, it was the height of arrogance to think that there would not be a second plan.

"They couldn't force us into a war," Kirk whispered to Marinta, "so now they're working to keep us confined by destroying our ability to travel between the stars."

"Trapped," Marinta agreed. "So they can systematically eliminate us, world by world. Their logic is unassailable."

The Romulan's cool summation triggered a flash of anger in Kirk. "You think we should give up?"

Marinta turned toward him, and with an extremely familiar expression, raised an eyebrow at the question.

"On the contrary. The reason I've contacted you is because you've shown a consistent ability to succeed in the face of logic."

There was something familiar about those words, something unusual about this Romulan, but Kirk was unable to define either characteristic in words. He only felt them.

"Who else knows about the recording?"

Marinta and he had stopped to talk, and Kirk could see she was uncomfortable with remaining still. Now she scanned the crowded market street. "Other than the specialists who died at Starbase Four-ninety-nine, only a handful."

Kirk's suspicion grew. "Why haven't you shown it to more people?"

Marinta turned, the movement sharp and sudden, and for the first time Kirk saw her Romulan passion rise above what he took to be her Vulcan training.

"The people at the starbase *died*, Captain. Everyone who gets the recording and tries to study it *dies*."

Kirk stared at the young woman, and not because of her display of emotion.

Marinta appeared to sense something had changed.

"What is it?" she asked.

Kirk didn't know where his next words would lead, but had to find out. "You called me 'Captain.' There're not too many people who do that these days."

Marinta closed her eyes as if realizing an error. But she didn't try to bluff.

She met Kirk's gaze, let him see she had nothing to hide. "I spent a great deal of time with Ambassador Spock. I worked with him on Romulus. A year ago . . . that night in Primedian, at the coliseum . . ."

"When he staged his assassination," Kirk said.

Marinta didn't argue. "I was with him. I was . . . part of the plan."

"Why wouldn't you tell me that from the beginning?" Kirk asked.

Marinta's nerves won the battle and she turned on her heel, began walking quickly.

Kirk caught up with her. "Why didn't you tell me?" he asked again.

"I was concerned you'd hold it against me. That you'd doubt the veracity of the *Monitor* transmission."

Kirk had the feeling that he was missing something, that Marinta hadn't fully explained what she wanted.

"I don't understand what's so important," Kirk told her. "Even if the recording's real, all it does is explain what happened to the *Monitor*."

"It's more than that, Captain Kirk." Marinta stopped again, and with a display of anger that did not fit her Vulcan robes, pressed the padd player into Kirk's hand. "This recording could tell us how to defeat the Totality."

Kirk made no move to slip the padd into his own cloak. "Not in what I saw."

Marinta's eyes swept the street like a soldier's on patrol. "There's more to the transmission than seven minutes of visual-sensor recordings. Captain Lewinski compressed three years' worth of research into the signal. Everything he and his crew had been able to learn about the Totality's subspace conduit, the way one of the Kelvan probes had been destroyed, the nature of what Lewinski and his crew called 'the Distortion' that was coming after them. It's all in that recording. All you need to do is separate the data from the noise."

162

"Why me?" Kirk asked. "Why not the authorities?"

Marinta looked up at Kirk as if he had heard nothing she'd told him. "The Totality can be *anywhere*, be *anyone*. . . . Captain Kirk, *there are no more authorities.* There's no one we can trust."

Kirk could understand Marinta's argument, but he needed one more piece of reassurance.

"How do you know you can trust me?" he asked her.

With an expression of angry defiance, Marinta tugged back her hood, grabbed Kirk's right hand, placed it on her face as she positioned her own hand on Kirk's *katra* points.

There in the street, surrounded by shoppers, watched by gawkers, she gave the ancient incantation.

"My mind to your mind . . . my thoughts to your thoughts . . ."

Kirk felt the familiar onslaught of telepathic contact. "But you're Romulan . . ." he gasped.

"Our minds are one," Marinta intoned.

And then Kirk felt his thoughts and her thoughts entwine and blend and both participants shared the presence of Spock in their lives and their minds.

He was the common ground that bound them together.

The common ground that let Marinta know she could trust Kirk, that let Kirk know he could trust her—a Romulan who believed in the unification of her people and Vulcans, who had worked for that cause, worked for Spock, trained in the Vulcan disciplines, and found within her mind the ancient talents that reached back through time to when Romulans and Vulcans had been one and the same.

Kirk broke the contact. He had seen and sensed just enough, and felt no need to progress to greater depths of intimacy.

But one clear emotion rang loud and true as he took his hand from Marinta's face.

"You loved him. . . ."

She didn't deny it.

And then a spotlight blasted down on them from overhead and Kirk heard amplified voices bellow: "Outworlders, remain where you are. You are under detention."

The authorities had arrived.

Authorities who could not be trusted.

16

They all wore medical monitors now. No one was allowed to move through the *Enterprise* unescorted. By
order of Provisional Starfleet Command, Mercury,
three crew must be present at all times. Anyone found
alone or with only one other companion was subject
to be stunned on sight.

In the awkward silence of the turbolift, Riker
voiced his disapproval. "This is unacceptable."

Picard kept his eyes straight ahead. "I agree." He
sighed. "But given that we're dealing with shapeshifters, can you think of any other way to ensure our
security?"

Riker shook his head. Troi placed her hand on his
arm.

He knew she meant it to be comforting, but the

gesture did the opposite. All Riker could see was the white manacle his wife wore on her wrist. They were all captives. What made it worse was that they were captives by their own choice.

The turbolift doors swept open onto the bridge of the *Enterprise.* Picard nodded to the three security personnel stationed between the turbolift alcoves, and Riker was appalled at how easily and automatically he and Picard and Troi raised their right wrists to show that their monitors were still in place, establishing their somatic continuity.

"We're going to the ready room," Picard told the lieutenant leading the security detail.

The lieutenant nodded as if giving permission.

Riker knew it was useless to object, or even comment.

In the ready room, La Forge, Crusher, and Worf were waiting.

There was an empty chair beside them and it brought Riker a pang of loss as he thought of Data. The android's absence was deeply felt. The knowledge that he had sacrificed his existence to save Picard's life gave some solace, but not enough.

La Forge stood to greet Riker with a handshake. "You're looking well, Captain."

"A new spinal cord will do that," Riker said. He turned to his Klingon friend, now in a regulation Starfleet uniform. "Worf."

"Captain."

The two men had exchanged a wealth of emotion with those two words, both pleased to see each other again. Both glad that whatever the overwhelming menace facing the Federation in these dark days, at least they were confronting it together.

Then Riker gave a small smile to Doctor Crusher as he saw the medical tricorder in her hand. "Shouldn't you be off duty?" he asked. "You pronounced me cured six hours ago."

Crusher shut the tricorder. "It never hurts to be cautious."

Picard took his seat behind his desk. The others recognized that as a sign Picard's meeting had started, and found chairs.

"To begin," Picard said, "any questions regarding our orders?"

"*Are* we allowed to question them?" La Forge asked. He said it as if making a joke, but Riker knew there was truth in those words.

Picard clearly recognized that truth as well. He treated La Forge's comment seriously.

"Geordi, Starfleet has never faced such an overwhelming threat. The enemy doesn't have a fleet we can attack, no homeworld we can isolate. We don't even know how they move from one location to another. They have no weapons systems we can target, or even create defenses against. Fighting them is . . . like fighting smoke."

Riker understood all that. He was certain everyone in the room did. But prosecuting a war wasn't his objective right now. Neither was it Starfleet's.

"My concern," Riker said, "is that I don't believe our current orders are sustainable."

"Probably not," Picard agreed. "Not in the long run. But we do need to secure ourselves."

"With a systemwide *embargo*?" Riker asked in frustration. "Isn't that the obvious purpose of these attacks? To shut down interstellar traffic?"

"And in that they have been successful," Picard said.

"Then aren't we simply helping the enemy achieve what they set out to do?" Riker asked. "I'm reluctant to take a course of action that's been dictated by whoever's attacking us."

Picard didn't offer an argument, which made Riker guess his mentor didn't have one.

Instead, Picard asked a question of his own. "What would you suggest, Will?"

Riker had to consciously shake off his reluctance to confront his old friend as an equal. He had been Picard's executive officer for more than a decade, and old habits died hard. But now they were two starship captains, face to face.

Riker spoke his mind.

"The first thing I suggest is that we don't give up. We don't do what the enemy wants us to do. Ending interstellar travel . . . putting a shipping embargo around every system . . . that's the same as cowering in a cave."

Riker paused to give Picard a chance to respond, but Picard kept his silence.

Riker continued.

"To start with, according to Doctor Muirhead's analysis, we have at our disposal dozens of ships with outmoded warp cores that presumably won't be affected by whatever's causing the malfunctions for at least a week. Let's use them to make the enemy attack at a time and place of *our* choosing, so we can fully analyze their tactics and technology."

Riker paused again and this time Picard did have a question.

"How do you propose we invite such an attack?"

"Use the *Titan* as bait," Riker said. "Install a new-model warp core, ferry her out to interstellar space, then we'll power it up while surrounded by other ships, sensors at full resolution."

Picard dismissed the idea. "We've lost too many ships already. Even with only impulse propulsion, the *Titan* is crucial to maintaining the embargo around this system."

"The *Titan* won't be in danger, Jean-Luc. We already know her core-ejection system works. At worst, we lose another core. At best, we figure out how the enemy manages to attack."

"And then what?" Picard asked.

Riker looked at his other friends in the room, saw no signs of support or of disapproval. Everyone, even Troi, appeared willing to let the two captains have their discussion uninterrupted.

Riker proceeded with his explanation. "If we learn something from the attack, then we have a starting point for developing a defense."

"And if we learn nothing more than what we've already learned from eyewitness accounts and sensor logs from hundreds of other attacks, what happens then, Will?"

Riker had seen this sharpness in Picard before, but never directed at him.

Picard answered his own question. "There's a

strong possibility that by the time your plan could be put into effect, the escort vessels with their outmoded warp cores will finally have become vulnerable. In which case, we'll have another handful of ships lost to us, stranded between the stars, needing years if not decades to reach port at slower-than-light velocities.

"And each ship we lose like that is one ship fewer to defend this system. To defend Earth."

"Defend against what?" Riker asked, and he instantly regretted raising his voice.

Picard's response was swift.

"Romulan warbirds are *not* affected. The theorists believe that the transwarp conduits used by the Borg are *not* affected. Those are *two* enemies of the Federation that'll be able to travel faster than light, and we can't discount the possibility that there are others— either those responsible for the attacks, or those eager to exploit our new weakness."

Riker didn't want to argue. He only wanted a discussion of the facts. Careful to keep his tone calm and reasonable, he began again.

"All right, Jean-Luc, let's see where Command's plan leads us. We set up an embargo around the system, ostensibly to keep the enemy from reaching us. We have the *Titan*, the *Enterprise*, a hundred other ships, all take up stations in the Oort Cloud, ready to intercept and check every vessel that comes our way."

Picard nodded, confirming what Riker knew: The scenario matched the general idea of Starfleet's strategy.

"If we do that," Riker said evenly, "Romulan warbirds will drop out of warp at the orbit of Mars and attack Earth while our ships are still light-hours away. Is Command really willing to risk that possibility?"

Picard responded with the same measured calculation, appearing equally reluctant to argue with his former officer, as if he, too, regretted the momentary tension that had flared between them.

"You're forgetting that other ships are on picket duty at every major facility in the system. If the Romulans do decide to attack, Starfleet Intelligence believes it could take them months to organize. We'll use those months to build our own singularity-drive vessels."

Picard paused as if considering how much more to reveal, then added, "A crash program to perfect warp-conduit drive is also under way. Command is confident that within two years, we'll have regained interstellar capability."

"Two years of hiding," Riker said. It was hard to keep the disappointment from his voice. "Leaving ourselves open to whatever the next step is that the enemy has planned."

Picard regarded him sternly, offered his own interpretation. "Two years to rebuild our fleet so we can face the enemy on more equal terms."

The two captains studied each other in silence for a few moments. Picard glanced at the others in the room. "Feel free to add your thoughts to the debate."

Worf didn't hesitate. "Captain Riker is correct. The only way to meet this attack is with a counterattack, while we still have the resources to do so."

La Forge sounded almost apologetic. "I think we should attempt to draw out the enemy, too. Two years is way too optimistic for thinking we'll be able to duplicate the Romulan drive. We don't even know how they contain their nanoscale singularities. And there's speculation that they don't manufacture the singularities, they *capture* them. That means we'll have to have a different form of interstellar propulsion to go hunting for singularities in order to develop the Romulan version." La Forge shrugged. "From an engineering standpoint, I think we're looking at anywhere from ten to twenty years to achieve that goal."

"However long it takes," Doctor Crusher added, "at least we'll be safe."

Everyone looked at her, waiting for her to explain her statement.

"All the enemy has done is take away our ability to travel at warp. Even in those systems where no warp capability at all exists, we haven't heard of any follow-on attacks. So maybe that's all the enemy wants. They've achieved it. And now they'll leave us alone."

Riker couldn't blame Crusher for preferring a strategy that might lead to lower casualties, but he knew she was wrong. "I'm sorry, Doctor, but I think that's a naïve assumption."

Then Riker heard Troi take a deep breath and knew what was coming. She did that in preparation for all the times she disagreed with him.

"On the contrary," Troi said, "I think Starfleet's taken the correct approach." She spoke directly to Riker—not as his wife, but as a Starfleet officer. "I understand your frustration." She turned to Worf. "And I understand the need to feel as if we're doing something, striking back." She looked to La Forge. "And I know that Starfleet's schedule for developing a totally new system of faster-than-light propulsion is based as much on optimism as on reality.

"But Captain Picard's right. We *don't* have the resources to embark on a risky plan that, in addition to just not working, might result in losing more ships."

She saved her summation for Riker. "The enemy's intent seems to have been to keep us out of interstellar space. As hard as it is to admit it, they succeeded. But as Beverly reminded us, there's no indication of any follow-on attacks on individual worlds. So let's bide our time, rebuild our fleet, and strike back when we're fully prepared—from a position of strength, and not desperation."

Riker knew there was no point in continuing. Picard might have been swayed if those present had been in agreement. But a three-three tie among people Picard knew and trusted, with strong arguments on both sides, was a recipe for staying with the original plan.

He nodded at Doctor Crusher, repeated the same words she had said to him when he had entered the ready room. "It never hurts to be cautious."

Worf grunted, letting the others know exactly what he thought of that particular sentiment.

Picard laid the subject to rest. "I promise you, Will—if the malfunctions stop spreading to the older cores, leaving us with at least some warp capability, I'll present your plan to Command. We should know in two weeks or so."

In the end, Riker knew, he and Picard weren't

equals. Picard was part of the Provisional Starfleet Command. Riker wasn't.

"Thank you," Riker said.

He gave Troi a smile of resignation, saw the questioning look in her eyes, and not for the first time was relieved that though his Betazoid wife could sense his emotions, she couldn't read his mind.

17

For Kirk, this was not a question of mere survival.

It didn't matter if Marinta had been claimed by paranoia and the arriving Vulcan authorities were legitimate. It didn't matter if every word she'd spoken was true. Either way, Kirk knew that if he allowed himself to be captured here and now, Joseph would be lost to him.

So his goal was simple.

He would *not* be captured.

He held one hand to his forehead to shield his eyes from the glare of the overhead spotlight, scanned the confused onlookers who dropped back unprotesting as the Vulcan security officers moved forward, encircling their prey. There was no break in that circle. No logical escape.

Which meant only the illogical was left.

Kirk grabbed Marinta by the arm to keep her by his side, then rushed the closest officer, shouting at him to *Move! Move! Move!*

The Vulcan hesitated, startled by Kirk's unpredictable response. That momentary lapse, only a heartbeat in length, gave Kirk his advantage. He swung up his elbow and clipped the surprised Vulcan's helmet, sending him spinning.

Maintaining their momentum, Kirk propelled Marinta through the shop door in front of him, and at once they were enveloped in the cloying scents of ripe fruit and animal droppings.

They were halfway down the first aisle of counters displaying local sandberries when Kirk heard the first hum of a phaser beam. Its warbling pitch told Kirk it was set to stun.

Instantly, he dove to the side, pulling Marinta with him, both of them sliding behind a teetering stack of net crates kept upright by a battered antigrav cargo loader.

More phaser beams buzzed through the air and now Kirk could hear cries of confusion in languages other than Vulcan as customers scattered for cover.

A small explosion flashed on the other side of the sprawling shop and instantly the overhead glow fixtures went out. Kirk decided that another phaser blast must have hit a power node.

Now the only light came through the doorway and window slats facing the outdoor marketplace, reducing the Vulcan security officers to ominous silhouettes against the pale orange illumination of the filtered streetglows. The officers were in constant motion, attempting to intercept and check each escaping customer.

Kirk touched Marinta's arm, signaling to her to move with him deeper into the shop, behind another row of display tables.

From their new hiding place, Kirk looked up to see thin shafts of blue light spike through the loose boards of the ceiling. The shafts were slowly changing their angle as whatever flying craft they originated from took station over the shop. From the movements of the light, it was clear the craft was positioning itself to hover directly over them. Somehow, they were being scanned.

It was time for a new strategy. Then the sound of mewling startled Kirk. It came from somewhere near the shopkeeper's desk. He glanced back to see two Tiburons huddled there, their pale, bald heads glistening. Behind them, a wall of small cages held hungry, insistent domestic sehlat cubs, each no larger than an Earth puppy. This was a pet distribution outlet; the fruit was animal feed.

The new strategy came to Kirk at once. He held out his hand to Marinta, whispered urgently, "Your IDIC."

Whatever training she'd received, Vulcan or not, Kirk appreciated that it had been thorough. Without hesitation, Marinta handed him the simple metal trinket that was in reality a sophisticated biosign generator.

Kirk only had time to nod toward the back of the shop as he unclipped his own IDIC. But Marinta understood.

Kirk sprang out of his crouch, sprinted toward the shopkeeper's desk, Marinta right behind him.

Another phaser beam flashed in the darkness, but it was too late. Kirk and Marinta were already beside the trembling Tiburons.

"It's all right," Kirk whispered. "They're after us, not you." He waved the shopkeepers up. "Get out of here. You'll be all right."

The humanoids' webbed earflaps quivered in fear. In the Alpha Quadrant, Vulcan—like Earth—was a world renowned for having banished all criminal behavior.

"Go!" Marinta hissed.

As if electrified, the Tiburons leapt to their feet and ran toward the front door.

Kirk counted to three before phasers fired again and both Tiburons thudded to the floor, heavily stunned.

Then slow and deliberate footsteps advanced into the shop.

Kirk needed no further proof that Marinta was correct. Vulcans did not shoot first and check their targets second. Whoever the security officers were, they weren't Vulcan.

But that realization did nothing to alter the next step of Kirk's plan.

Swiftly and silently, he and Marinta unlocked and opened all the sehlat cages they could reach.

Though only a few months old, bristling with short fur and still without fangs, the sehlat cubs growled and spit as they broke for freedom.

Kirk swept two up and clipped an IDIC to each of

their collars, then just as quickly dropped them, but not before their tiny claws had slashed him. As soon as the snarling sehlats hit the floor, they disappeared under the counters and displays, their short stubby legs keeping them low to the ground.

"They're getting away!" a security officer shouted.

Kirk peered out from behind the table and saw several of his pursuers aiming tracking tricorders toward the other side of the shop. As he'd anticipated, the officers had set their devices to scan for the false biosignatures generated by the IDICs.

Running footsteps, the crash of crates, the squeal of sehlats.

A perfect diversion.

Kirk and Marinta ran for the curtained doorway at the back of the shop. But before they reached it, an officer sprang at them from the shadows.

An iron hand closed on Kirk's throat.

Kirk twisted, struggled, but the grip was unbreakable.

He could see the officer's Vulcan features in the pale orange glow of the marketplace light. The officer opened his mouth, began to shout: "They're here!"

But before the last syllable left the officer's lips, Marinta's knuckles slammed into his throat, left him gasping.

His grip on Kirk failed. Kirk spun to confront his attacker. But Marinta's hand was already inside the neck of the man's uniform, her fingers seeking contact with the unprotected flesh of his shoulder.

Kirk knew what she was doing but was still amazed—a Vulcan nerve pinch delivered by a Romulan.

The man collapsed with a strangled moan, his attempted cry of warning unheard in the noisy confusion of the ongoing search of customers, enhanced by the snarls of fleeing sehlats.

Kirk and Marinta rushed through the curtained doorway, escaped the shop.

The small alley behind the row of shops offered no place to hide.

Kirk paused to get his bearings.

Marinta studied the dark canopy of sky, agitated. "When they realize they've been fooled by false biosignatures, they'll start scanning again. Probably from orbit."

Kirk guessed what she was about to propose, didn't agree. "It's too dangerous to split up."

"Captain, they'll be scanning for two individuals traveling together—human and Vulcan. From orbit, that's how I'll appear to them." She handed him the message player. "You have to get this to someone with the ability to extract all possible information. Someone you can trust."

Kirk hefted the player in his hand, judging the weight of it—not mass, but the power it might have to stop the Totality. "There's no one on Vulcan who can be trusted," he said.

"You're a starship captain. You have a ship. Use it."

The air trembled. Something big and dark was moving through the sky. Kirk recognized the glow of an aerial searchlight approaching as whatever vehicle hovered over the shop began to change position.

"My child is on Vulcan," Kirk said quietly. "I won't leave him."

Marinta pulled her hood up, hiding her features, preparing for flight. "You have to! The only way you can save Joseph and Spock is to defeat the Totality. The answer's in that message. If you stay on Vulcan, you'll lose it."

Marinta suddenly reached up to touch Kirk's face as if she meant to meld with him again. "I felt the echo of Spock in you. You know what he'd want you to do. You know what you have to do. Not just for your son and your friend, but for all life in this galaxy."

Kirk pulled back from her. In his mind he knew she was right, but his heart couldn't accept it.

"Joseph's my child. . . ."

"And if you save Joseph and lose the galaxy, what will you have gained? What legacy will you have left him?"

A sudden wind blew through the alley. A blinding spotlight stabbed the rough paving stones just ahead of them.

"You *know* what you have to do," Marinta said. And then she turned and ran into the spotlight, rushed through it, kept moving.

The flying craft above the alley, its silhouette indistinct against the Vulcan stars, rotated as it banked to change direction, its spotlight sweeping forward, following Marinta.

Kirk forced himself to turn away from her, to run down the alley in the opposite direction. He wouldn't leave Vulcan. He wouldn't abandon his son.

And then he saw the shadows of the alley peel away from the walls and the trash bins and empty crates, rising into the air before him, knit together like living tentacles.

Kirk stumbled to a stop.

From some far distance behind him, he heard a woman scream, knew instantly it was Marinta.

He wheeled to see only a flare of blue reflected from the twisted alley walls and the belly of the craft that hung in the air like a storm cloud.

Kirk turned back to see that the tentacles of darkness were gone. In their place, a woman.

A creature.

"James . . ." Norinda said. Her voice was Teilani's, tearing at his heart.

She moved toward him and with every step he saw her more clearly as the glow of the searchlight came closer.

The wind quickened.

She was almost within reach.

"You know you want me," Teilani whispered.

She was right, Kirk knew. But what he wanted, and what he had to do, were not the same.

Kirk reached into his robe for his combadge. He felt as if he were moving through heavy water.

Teilani's arms stretched out for him, elongating, slithering, becoming tentacles again.

"Accept," she pleaded. "Embrace. . . ."

Kirk's heart ached for his lost wife and he knew how easy, how blissful, it would be to fall into her embrace once more, no matter how false the sweet illusion.

"Kirk to *Belle Rêve*," Kirk said, stepping back from paradise. The hoarseness of his voice unnerved him.

He couldn't leave Vulcan. He couldn't abandon his son. Teilani's son.

"Scott here, Captain. . . ."

The tendrils were almost touching him.

"Now, Scotty," Kirk gasped. "Now!"

"James, no! Don't leave me!" Teilani cried.

She rose up like a giant cobra, expanding to swallow him as the wind pushed him toward her.

But the glow of the searchlight was already merged with the shifting light of the transporter beam.

An agonizing moment—lifetime—later, Kirk bolted from the transporter pad on the *Belle Rêve*, still moving as if to fend off the suffocating tendrils that had sought to claim him.

He halted, breathing hard, squinting in the brightness of the transporter room. The harsh light was almost painful after the dark Vulcan alley.

He hit his combadge again. "Scotty—full shields! Get us out of here now!"

The engineer's response was exactly what Kirk had come to depend on.

At once he heard the thrum of the matter-antimatter reactor power up as the vessel's shields went from standby navigational mode to battle strength.

By the time he reached the corridor, he could feel the characteristic lurch of the artificial gravity that indicated his ship had gone to warp. By the time he reached the ladder that ran up to the bridge, he felt the shudder and heard the surge of the shields as the *Belle Rêve* was struck by enemy fire.

Twice on his climb to the bridge, Kirk almost lost his grip as the ship's violent maneuvers strained the inertial dampers and threw him side to side. He counted three more hits, but the shields were holding. He felt certain that given the size of the *Belle Rêve* and her apparent condition, his pursuers were more than likely surprised by his ship's unexpected defenses.

On the bridge at last, Kirk jumped from the ladder and made straight for the navigation console, where Scott piloted the ship.

On the center screen, Kirk saw stars streak past at warp. On the left-hand screen, he saw three Vulcan cruisers in pursuit. On the right, a readout of the *Belle Rêve*'s key systems showed all in the green.

One of the cruisers flashed with a pulse of green light.

"Torpedo closing," Scott said calmly. "Doctors, if ye wouldn't mind . . ."

Kirk looked over at the tactical consoles. The Emergency Medical Hologram expertly operated the weapons controls. Beside him, a surly Doctor McCoy watched over the shield settings.

"Deflecting," the hologram said brightly, as if he was thoroughly enjoying his duties.

The left screen suddenly flared with golden light, though Kirk noted no other effect on the ship.

"Shields unchanged at ninety-seven percent," McCoy reported.

Scott gave Kirk a smug smile. "They cannae keep up with us. Another five minutes and we'll be out of range."

Kirk patted his engineer's shoulder. "Good work, Scotty."

"Is there any particular heading ye'd like us to take once we've left them in our wake?"

Kirk touched the message player secure in a pocket in his cooling robe.

If there was no one in authority he could trust on Vulcan, then at least he could go to someone he could understand. Someone who could bend the rules as he did. Someone with the assets to extract every last bit of data from the *Monitor* transmission.

And someone no one would ever expect him to turn to for help, so that no trap could be set.

There was only one person who met that description.

Kirk gave his orders.

18

Sleeping was the worst.

Each night, Picard and Beverly Crusher were locked into the captain's cabin under visual sensor surveillance as three guards stood watch in the corridor. Each officer assigned to this mission was required to follow the same routine.

The enlisted crew slept on bunks in the hangar bay, using the emergency supplies the *Enterprise* carried for humanitarian aid and mass evacuations. There could be no privacy, not even in the heads and showers.

Despite the forced company everyone on board had to endure, Picard was not the only one to note how empty his ship seemed to be.

Worf, La Forge, Beverly—they all had commented on the eerie sense of abandonment they felt.

Even with the need for trios of security guards, the crew complement was less than half its normal number. There were no non-Starfleet family members on board. The science departments had been closed and all staff reassigned to Mercury. In engineering, La Forge had kept only enough specialists for three skeleton shifts. With the warp core shut down, there was no need for warp engineers.

That, more than anything else, Picard decided, was what made his ship feel so lifeless: the constant, almost subliminal vibration of the warp engines was gone, as if the *Enterprise* had lost her pulse, her heart.

She was no longer a starship, just another spacecraft.

Lying quietly in the darkness of his quarters, Picard felt as if a part of himself had withered along with his ship, and he feared that soon the Federation would follow in this slow descent into helplessness. Not even the comforting presence of Beverly beside him could dispel his apprehension and his growing sense of vulnerability.

At 0300 ship's time, it was those dark thoughts and not Picard's sleep that was disturbed when Worf called him from the bridge.

Picard felt Beverly stir, turned his head to look at the com screen by his bunk, no need to open his eyes. "Go ahead, Mister Worf. I'm awake."

"Captain, there is a ship approaching our coordinates at high warp. It's on course for Earth. It will reach our position in thirty-three minutes."

Picard sat up, eyes now open, staring at the image of his first officer on the bridge. Beverly got out of bed, used to the hours of a ship's captain, little different from those of a chief medical officer.

After three days on picket duty in the Oort Cloud surrounding Earth's solar system, the *Enterprise* hadn't encountered a single warp vessel. The other ships enforcing the embargo of Sector 001 had reported only a handful of vessels requesting entry. All available information indicated the inexplicable warp-core malfunctions had continued to propagate as Doctor Muirhead had predicted. Older and less powerful cores were being affected now, stranding even more ships in interstellar space, a new diaspora.

"Is it a Starfleet vessel?" Picard asked.

"Technically, yes."

" 'Technically'?"

"It is a Q-ship. A Starfleet vessel with civilian registry. The *Belle Rêve*."

Picard knew the name well.

"That's Kirk's ship," Beverly said.

"So he claims," Worf replied.

Picard headed for his private lavatory as Beverly stood by the cabin's small replicator, ordering Earl Grey and coffee. He understood Worf's skepticism. Under the current rules of engagement, no Starfleet vessel was to accept the identity of the crew or passengers of an approaching ship until genetic identity had been confirmed and somatic continuity had been established.

The lavatory door slipped open as Picard approached. "I'll be on the bridge in a few minutes. Tell Captain Kirk I look forward to his arrival."

"I don't think he is planning on rendezvousing with us."

Picard paused in the doorway, looked back at the com screen.

"Kirk *does* understand the current situation, does he?"

Picard couldn't see Worf on the screen, but he heard his barely constrained frustration. Apparently, he had had a conversation with Kirk. "He was not . . . forthcoming. I believe you will have to discuss the matter with him yourself."

"Understood. Ten minutes."

Picard set the sonics for a quick, bracing shower.

He had a feeling he'd need to be on his toes.

When it came to James T. Kirk, nothing was ever easy.

The *Belle Rêve* sped for Earth at battle stations.

Kirk had spent four days focused solely on events at Vulcan. Nothing had intruded on his quest to find Spock and to rescue his child.

And in that time, the Federation had been brought to the brink of collapse.

The details Kirk had received during his conversation with Worf had left him stunned. The situation seemed unreal. And yet Marinta's words came back to him, giving him perspective, as if she had known the full scope of the threat they faced when he had seen only the personal.

"If you save Joseph and lose the galaxy, what will you have gained? What legacy will you have left him?"

The Federation in danger. The interaction of the entire galactic culture at an end.

The Totality was not just *his* enemy. It was everyone's.

But even knowing that was not enough to change his plan.

"Jim, are you sure about this?" McCoy asked.

Kirk was at the navigation console on the bridge of his ship. Scott was back in engineering; the warp engines would likely need some adjustments in the next hour.

The Emergency Medical Hologram was at tactical. Doctor McCoy, who was one of the medical experts whose personality and knowledge had been used to help create the EMH, stood at Kirk's side.

"If what Worf said is true," Kirk explained, "then the *Belle Rêve* could be the only warp vessel within twenty light-years of Earth. If we rendezvous with the *Enterprise* . . . as soon as we stop, we're a target."

McCoy frowned. "That's assuming the *Enterprise* has been compromised or taken over. You don't have any evidence of that."

As far as Kirk was concerned, he had all the evidence he needed and was surprised McCoy didn't understand. "Then where's Jean-Luc? You saw the bridge crew when Worf hailed us—other than him, did you recognize anyone?"

"It's ship's night," McCoy argued. "Worf said Picard's on his way to the bridge."

"Then when he arrives, I'll reconsider. In the meantime, Bones, I want you and the Doctor to stand by on shields and weapons."

The hologram spoke up from the tactical console. "I, for one, would feel more comfortable changing course to avoid the *Enterprise* altogether." He shrugged at Kirk. "I will not direct lethal fire at a fellow Starfleet vessel."

"Understood," Kirk said. They had already had that conversation. If the need should arise, Kirk would take over the weapons, shooting only to disable.

"Then why ask for a confrontation?" the hologram persisted.

Kirk called up a tactical display on the right-hand screen. It showed the Oort Cloud—a spherical shell of icy material left over from the formation of Earth's solar system, fully three light-years across. But it was the interior boundary of the cloud, stretching between thirty to fifty astronomical units from the sun, that Kirk was concerned with.

There, the collection of primordial material was the densest. Thousands of bodies, many larger than Pluto, and which would have qualified as planets in their own right had they been closer to the sun, moved in vast, slow orbits. It was from this shell that the majority of the system's comets originated. Since the Romulan War, centuries earlier, it was considered Sector 001's first line of defense against invasion.

After his initial brief conversation with Picard's first officer, Kirk had used the *Belle Rêve*'s powerful sensors to scan that interior shell of cosmic debris. Though it would take days and a much closer position to assemble a complete picture of the current structure of the shell, it was instantly obvious to Kirk that Starfleet hadn't changed its tactics.

Sensors identified approximately eighty vessels positioned in the cloud, each about the same distance from the others, establishing a defensive network. And if Kirk could see eighty ships with a preliminary, long-distance sensor sweep, he suspected that meant hundreds of others were also in position, carefully hidden among the planetoids and smaller orbital debris.

Even a warp vessel attempting to pass through the Oort Cloud to enter the system could find itself under fire from those ships. And if that vessel stopped, as Worf had instructed Kirk to do, it would quickly be englobed—surrounded in three dimensions. Escape from such a trap was possible, Kirk knew, but could be costly.

The end result of the tactical situation was that, contrary to the holographic doctor's wishes, it would not be possible to avoid confrontation. So, in his search for advantage, Kirk decided to maintain course toward the *Enterprise*, if only because a few members on that ship's crew, like Worf, might still remember him, and that memory might result in a few seconds of doubt and delay before hostilities began. Battles and the fates of empires had been decided by less.

"I'm not *asking* for a confrontation," Kirk said reassuringly to the hologram. "It's just that of all the ships defending the system, the *Enterprise* is the one least likely to fire on us."

"You mean, as long as Picard's still in command," McCoy added. He sounded unconvinced.

Kirk wasn't open to debate. "Bones, I didn't abandon Joseph on Vulcan to come here and waste time. We're not stopping till we get to Earth."

"Well, don't waste time telling me," McCoy said crossly. "Tell them."

On the center screen, the sensors finally were in range to create the subspace image of the ship they bore down on.

At the edge of a cluster of tumbling ice and rock that in battle could be used to confuse sensors, the enemy waited.

The *U.S.S. Enterprise.*

19

"He is not slowing," Worf growled as he moved from the center chair.

Picard remained standing, studying the viewscreen. The *Belle Rêve* was twelve minutes out but little more than a smudge of white on the screen, even at maximum enlargement. Tactical sensors showed it closing at warp nine point two. He wasn't certain what kind of engine could produce that factor in such a small ship. But then, that was the idea behind its unique design: surprise and misdirection.

Picard glanced over at Lieutenant Leybenzon at tactical. "Hail the *Belle Rêve.*"

The young officer acknowledged the order with military crispness, and a moment later the viewscreen switched to an interior view of the small starship's bridge.

In the center of the image, on a blocky, black command chair that to Picard looked antique, sat James T. Kirk. He wore civilian clothing, but for the calm assurance he projected, it might as well have been a Starfleet uniform.

"Jean-Luc," Kirk said in greeting.

"Jim," Picard answered.

Kirk smiled. "We have to stop meeting like this."

Picard momentarily looked to the side as he heard turbolift doors open. Deanna Troi hurried out, escorted by three guards. She had agreed to Picard's request to return to his crew for the duration of the current emergency; as the flagship for the embargo mission, the *Enterprise* was in need of the most experienced counselor in the system. Picard knew he was lucky to have her.

"Like what?" Picard asked.

"With the odds against us and the situation grim."

Picard returned Kirk's smile, remembering their first face-to-face meeting, ten years ago at Veridian. Kirk had said the same words then as now.

But Picard knew Kirk wasn't making idle conversation, nor was it Kirk's nature to dwell in the past. He had chosen his words carefully and deliberately to let Picard know that he *was* Jim Kirk.

Unfortunately, in a universe where telepathy was a given, Starfleet demanded more than shared knowledge to confirm identity.

"Jim," Picard said, "Worf tells me he briefed you on the current state of emergency that Starfleet's declared."

"Shapechangers."

"Exactly," Picard confirmed, pleased. Kirk was never one to talk around a subject. "The nature of the enemy we're facing is such that a new series of identification protocols has been established."

"Understandable," Kirk said. "I've seen what these creatures are capable of."

That revelation took Picard by surprise.

"You've encountered them?"

"I believe Vulcan is now under their control."

Reflexively, Picard looked to Troi, tapped the audio control on the arm of his chair to prevent what she might say from being transmitted.

She looked stricken, almost fearful. "He's telling the truth as he believes it. And at his core, he's troubled."

Picard turned his attention back to the screen, enabled audio again. "Clearly, we have a great deal to discuss."

Again, Kirk got to the point. "Not today, Jean-Luc. I'm not stopping until I get to Earth."

Picard knew there was nothing to be gained by confronting Kirk so quickly. The *Belle Rêve* was still eight minutes out.

"May I ask why?" Picard inquired.

Kirk stretched back in his chair, looked thoughtful. "Let's just say the concerns you have about me not being who I appear to be . . . it works both ways."

Picard understood. He raised his hand to show Kirk his wrist monitor. "That's why we wear these," he explained. "When our ships rendezvous, we'll beam you over. That'll enable us to compare your cellular and genetic structure with our identification files. Once that's done, you'll receive a monitor like this that can be scanned continuously, establishing what they call somatic continuity, so we can't be replaced by a shapechanger."

Kirk remained noncommittal. "Sounds complicated enough to be a Starfleet plan."

Picard heard Troi speak softly, telling him what he already knew. "He's not convinced."

Picard tried another tack. "Jim, if you can't be certain that *I'm* who I say I am, why do you think it'll be easier on Earth? If the *Enterprise* has been taken over by shapechangers, why not all of Starfleet Command?"

"It's easier to take over a ship than a planet." Kirk glanced to the side. "My sensors show your warp drive is offline, so to be where you are now, you've been away from Earth for two or three days at least. A lot can happen in that time."

Picard was again surprised that the little ship's sensors could detect the condition of the *Enterprise*'s warp drive at its current distance. He cut the audio, looked over at the tactical station.

"Lieutenant, call up the specifications for the *Belle Rêve*."

The security officer didn't look up from his console. "Aye, sir."

Picard turned back to the screen, enabled audio again. "Jim, two years ago, you remember that vacation we tried to take?"

"We'll have to do it again, sometime."

"In the desert, we spoke about risk."

Kirk's benign expression changed as his eyes narrowed. Picard hoped he was thinking back to their adventure on Bajor.

After a few moments, Kirk nodded thoughtfully. "I remember."

"By now you've scanned the system's defensive perimeter. You know what you're facing. And even in the *Belle Rêve*, you have no chance of getting through. What you're going to attempt, that's *my* definition of risk, Jim. It's not worth the gamble."

Kirk tapped a control on his chair arm, and the image on the viewscreen changed from one of Kirk to a wide-angle view of the entire bridge.

"Since we're both being paranoid," Kirk said, "and can't be sure who else might be listening, here's my entire crew. Do you see who's missing?"

Picard recognized Montgomery Scott and Leonard McCoy, exactly as he would expect to find on any ship Kirk commanded. But he was puzzled to also see an Emergency Medical Hologram at the tactical console.

As for who was missing, Picard didn't know. Ambassador Spock had disappeared a year ago and, in any event, was never a member of the *Belle Rêve*'s crew.

"I'm afraid I don't," Picard confessed.

"Remember little Melis," Kirk said evenly.

"He's doubting your identity," Troi whispered.

Picard tried to place the name . . . Melis . . . Melis . . . "The little girl." He remembered her now. A Bajoran child afflicted with F'relorn's disease. It was caused by environmental toxins left by the Cardassian Occupation. But why was Kirk invoking her memory now?

"I had a difference of agreement with the Prophets," Kirk said.

"Captain," Troi said quietly, "he's not interested in your memories of the past. He's probing how you think."

Picard understood at once. It was entirely possible that the shapechangers attacking the Federation had the ability to extract information from the beings they impersonated, so they could answer any question about that being's past, know every secret.

But *how* a person thought, that was a dynamic function of mind and spirit, and Kirk was attempting to see if the Picard he spoke to was the real captain, and not just a duplicate with all of Picard's memories.

And then Picard had it—what Kirk was trying to tell him.

On Bajor, the mother of the stricken child had believed that the illness was the will of the Prophets, that the child was being punished for her father's transgressions.

The sins of the father . . . Picard thought.

Kirk had somehow cured the child, though he had insisted he had merely delivered her into the hands of the Prophets.

But the story was enough for Picard to understand Kirk's question.

"Joseph," Picard said. And in Kirk's eyes he saw the rest of this story, the revelation of what drove Kirk now.

Kirk spoke the terrible words no father should ever be forced to say. "I left him behind."

Picard knew then there was nothing he could say or do to change Kirk's mind.

If Joseph was on Vulcan, the only possible reason Kirk could have for traveling to Earth was because he believed it was the only way to save his son.

"Jim, rendezvous with the *Enterprise*. Let me help."

A haunted expression came to Kirk then, as if something Picard had said meant something other than he had intended.

"I can't."

"I'm under orders, Jim. I'll have to stop you."

Kirk held his hand over a control on his chair.

"You can try."

For a moment, it seemed as if Kirk was about to say something more, but at last, all he added was, "Kirk out."

The viewscreen changed to an image of the *Belle Rêve*, coming closer.

There was nothing more Picard could do.

"Battle stations," he ordered.

20

"Jim, you *have* to reconsider."

"Let Jean-Luc do the reconsidering. He's the one under orders."

Kirk got up from his chair, went to the tactical console. Doctor McCoy stayed at his side.

"Listen to yourself," McCoy said. "You *know* that's Picard on the *Enterprise*. This isn't a trap."

"It's not as simple as that," Kirk said. "On Vulcan, Marinta was exactly who she said she was. But she was also bait for a trap she didn't know about." Kirk checked the readings on the tactical console, frowned at the holographic doctor. "Why aren't the weapons online?"

The Doctor folded his arms across his chest. "As I told you, I will not fire on a Starfleet vessel."

Kirk reached past him to engage the master arming

controls. "No, but you *will* fire on planetesimals, cometary bodies, and other debris that's about to get in our way." The status indicators on the console now glowed green, ready for firing. "Won't you?"

The holographic doctor frowned, but he didn't argue.

Kirk stepped away from the console to find McCoy still staring at him.

"I don't think Jean-Luc Picard will be as easy to fool as a young Romulan ambassadorial attaché," McCoy said.

"Bones, you're right. Jean-Luc is right. Everyone's right. But we still don't know how Norinda and . . . and the Totality, move from point to point. There's no way to know where they might appear next." Kirk knew he owed his old friend a better explanation. "If you were chasing me, had me on the run, who's the first person I'd go to for help?"

Kirk could see that McCoy sensed he was being led into a logical trap, didn't like it.

"With Spock not here," McCoy said, "you'd go to Picard."

"And that's exactly why I *can't* go to him." Kirk started toward Scott at the navigation console. "Norinda has had access to Spock and Teilani . . . two people who know me well. Everything I do now has to be something that I wouldn't normally do, so she can't predict it." Kirk realized he had no choice. He had to reveal the reason why he was determined to get to Earth. "That's why we're going to Earth, to get help from Admiral Janeway and Starfleet Command."

McCoy nodded in reluctant agreement. "You're right about that. You going to *Starfleet* for help these days, that's definitely a tactic no one would expect."

Kirk gave McCoy a tight smile to thank him for his unenthusiastic support, then looked over Scott's shoulder. "How're the engines, Mister Scott?"

"Purrin' like tribbles."

"Very good." Kirk took a breath, knew he was about to commit his ship and his crew to a course of action from which there was no coming back. "Set a rendezvous course for the *Enterprise*—" He ignored Scott's questioning look. "—and start to slow to warp-one-point-five. Make it look as if we're going to do what he wants."

Even as Scott questioned Kirk, he made the necessary course adjustments and began to decrease the power output of the warp engines. "Aye, Cap'n. But why one-point-five?"

Kirk patted his chief engineer on the shoulder. "I don't want anyone to get hurt."

"The *Belle Rêve* is slowing, sir. She's . . . she's on an intercept course."

Picard knew better than to ask if Lieutenant Leybenzon was sure of his readings. Instead, he looked to Troi. "Counselor?"

Troi seemed as puzzled as the security officer. "I didn't sense that Kirk was intending to do anything except go past us." Her expression became grim. "But the fact that his ship is now doing what he said he wouldn't do implies there might have been a change in command."

Picard understood the conclusion, but didn't see how it was possible. "He only had three crew: two retired Starfleet specialists and a hologram. That's not the makings of a mutiny."

Troi frowned. "Three crew that we were permitted to see."

"Good point," Picard acknowledged. He turned back to Leybenzon. "Lieutenant, scan the *Belle Rêve* for life signs. I want confirmation of how many crew Kirk has on board, and where they're positioned."

The security officer brought up the tactical scanner controls on his console at once. But he also replied, "Captain, I've reviewed the specifications of Kirk's ship. With the signal processors and emitters on board, he could have a battle group of Jem'Hadar warriors belowdecks and we wouldn't be able to detect them until we're within docking range."

Worf stepped closer to Picard, dropping his voice. He was always reticent to offer advice to his captain when they were in other than private surroundings. "Captain, it might be better not to scan them. Why give them reason to think we have any suspicions?"

"And that way, we keep the advantage," Picard said, instantly understanding Worf's suggestion. "Lieutenant, belay that last order. Do not scan the *Belle Rêve* until she comes alongside."

"Aye, aye, sir."

Picard saw that Troi was about to object, stopped her. "It's all right, Counselor." He added for Leybenzon, "And if, instead, the *Belle Rêve* does try to bypass us, here are additional orders. . . ."

* * *

"The last thing Jean-Luc will want to do is destroy us," Kirk said. "He knows it's me on board and not a duplicate. But he can't be sure we're not being manipulated, any more than we can be sure he's free of the Totality's influence."

"You think he's bluffing?" McCoy asked. It was clear from the way he asked the question that he thought no such thing.

"Not completely. He's going to try to disable us." Kirk looked past McCoy to his engineer. "Scotty, what's the best way for the *Enterprise* to attack us with maximum damage and minimal chance of casualties?"

Scott didn't have to think about his answer. "Knock out our warp engines with an overload surge. If we have to rely on impulse alone, we'll be outnumbered before we reach the orbit of Neptune."

"Exactly," Kirk said.

"Exactly?" McCoy repeated.

Kirk shrugged. "That's what I'd do in Jean-Luc's position."

"So what's our defense?" McCoy asked.

Kirk watched the center screen, where the *Enterprise* was growing larger, showing more detail as the *Belle Rêve* closed in. "With the shields we have, Bones, there's only one way the *Enterprise* can target our engines without tearing the rest of the ship apart."

Kirk smiled as he saw Scott and the holographic doctor look to him with the same expectant expression McCoy had.

"This is what we're going to do," Kirk said.

* * *

"He's at warp-one-point-eight, and still slowing," Worf reported.

The Klingon had taken Leybenzon's position at the tactical console. The security officer was now at an auxiliary station that had been configured to control the ship's transporters. As soon as the *Belle Rêve*'s shields went down, Kirk and everyone on board his vessel—however many there really were—would be beamed off and held in the buffer while their identities were confirmed. La Forge had set up a separate circuit for the holographic emitter that gave the Emergency Medical Hologram his physical form.

"You're not certain you've covered all contingencies," Troi said quietly.

Picard sighed. She was right, as usual.

"Kirk can dock with us, in which case we can beam him aboard, confirm his identity, and move forward," Picard said. "Or, he can try to speed by us at warp. If he does, I doubt even the *Belle Rêve*'s shields can withstand the onslaught of phaser fire and quantum torpedoes we'll be able to direct at her. Or, he can turn around, in which case we'll have another opportunity to disable his engines and take him in tow. It's difficult to think that he has any other options."

"Yet you're not convinced," Troi said.

"I keep asking myself: What would I do in Kirk's position?"

Lieutenant Leybenzon looked up from his auxiliary console. "Sort of like playing chess against yourself. Impossible to make secret plans."

Picard agreed. "I know Kirk's sitting on his bridge

right now, asking himself what *he* would do in *my* situation."

Worf gave another report from his console. "The *Belle Rêve* has slowed to one-point-five and holding."

Picard looked to Worf. "He's not dropping to impulse?"

"No, sir."

"What is it?" Troi asked, and her concern mirrored the alarm Picard suddenly felt.

"Kirk knows exactly what strategies I'll take against him. . . ." Picard's apprehension escalated as he took the next step and tried to work out Kirk's next move. "So he'll . . ." And then he had it.

He jabbed at his communications controls. "This is the captain . . . all hands brace for collision!"

"You can't be serious," McCoy said.

"Take a seat and brace yourself," Kirk said. "Mister Scott, keep us on course, fifty-meter deviation only."

"They won't know what hit them," Scott said.

But Kirk knew better. "Yes, they will. By now, Jean-Luc knows exactly what I'm going to do."

"Fifteen seconds to impact," Scott said. He sounded as calm and confident as Kirk felt.

"But his ship will be destroyed!" Troi said.

Picard felt anger surge within him. "He won't hit us dead-on. The fact that he's only at one-point-five means he doesn't want to destroy us any more than we want to destroy him."

Worf growled from his station. "May I suggest evasive maneuvers, sir?"

"That's what he wants us to do," Picard said. "It'll give him just enough of a delay to slip past us."

"I don't understand," Troi said. "Why is he doing this?"

Picard tried to hide his admiration for Kirk's tactic, but failed. "With him coming directly at us, we can't hit his engines without shooting through his bridge. And he knows I won't do that."

"We're just going to sit here?" Troi asked.

"It's an old Earth game called 'chicken,'" Picard said. "But I know how to change the rules, too."

"Captain Kirk! The *Enterprise* has dropped her shields!"

Kirk reacted to the holographic doctor's shock with admiration for his foe, and his friend. *That* particular tactic he hadn't anticipated.

"Well done, Jean-Luc," Kirk murmured. "Are all her shields down?"

"Navigational shields only," the Doctor replied. "But they'll only protect her from dust and debris, not us."

"It's all right," Kirk said. "Jean-Luc knows we won't hit him."

"Orders, Captain?" Scott asked.

"Maintain course," Kirk said as he once again put himself in Jean-Luc's position and guessed what his fellow captain's next move would be.

"He's going to try and slow us down with tractor beams."

"Och, but that'll tear us apart!"

"They'll have transporters on standby, ready to save us."

"Should I change course?"

"No," Kirk said. "Power up *our* tractor beam and don't hide the signature. We *don't* have enough transporter capacity to save Jean-Luc's crew, so if he wants to cause damage, he'll have to be sure he can clean up after himself."

"*Their* tractor beams are powering up," Worf said.

Picard grinned—the only one on his bridge who wasn't behaving as if total destruction was only a few seconds away. "Got him."

"What?" Troi asked.

"Anything I can think of," Picard said, "Kirk can think of, too. So the trick is to stay just one step ahead of him, even for a few seconds . . . Mister Worf, stand by on shields . . ."

"Standing by," Worf growled. "Impact in—"

"—five seconds," Scott said. "Four . . ."

Kirk gripped the arms of his chair, and only at three seconds to impact did he finally realize that Picard had outmaneuvered him.

"Scotty!" Kirk shouted. "Hit him dead-on! He's going to—"

21

Like their captains, if the *Belle Rêve* was the irresistible force, the *Enterprise* was the immovable object.

At one second before impact, the *Enterprise*'s shields flared into life at full power, just as Kirk had anticipated.

The *Belle Rêve*'s shields impinged on the *Enterprise*'s in a silent, rippling flare of blue Casimir energy.

But not enough energy to completely dissipate the forces of that collision.

Some bled into warp space as spreading pockets of subspace distortion. Some spread into normal spacetime as cascading gamma radiation that over the course of hours would register on astronomical detectors throughout the inner solar system.

And the barest fraction of one percent was converted into kinetic energy.

Motion.

The *Enterprise* spun around her center of gravity, an enormous, off-center windmill.

Inside her hull, alarms screamed and the structural-integrity field that held her together drew all power from her generators, lowering gravity, blacking out the lights.

The crew not strapped into place at their duty stations were thrown into bulkheads, slid up to the overheads, propelled by centrifugal force.

Sparks erupted from overloaded systems.

Smoke and cries of protest filled air that was no longer being recycled as life-support went offline.

Outside of the mighty ship, streaming trails of vapor marked the futile firings of her chemical reaction-control thrusters, trying to bring her into trim. But too much energy had been imparted to her by the collision, and only her impulse engines could stabilize her again—engines that had no power because of the requirements of the structural-integrity field.

The *Enterprise* spiraled out of control.

The *Belle Rêve,* barely a third the length of the *Enterprise,* was in little better condition. Though it was the energy of the smaller ship's momentum that had been transferred into the *Enterprise,* the *Belle Rêve* was left spinning just as violently. But because she was of lesser mass, her thrusters were able to counteract the unwanted motion more rapidly.

Had this collision happened in interstellar space, Kirk's ship would have recovered well before the *Enterprise* and continued on her way.

But this was the Oort Cloud.

The *Belle Rêve* slammed into a nameless chunk of primordial ice roughly the size of a runabout, ten seconds after the ship had caromed off the shields of the *Enterprise*.

The wildly spinning *Enterprise* collided with another, larger cometary fragment seventeen seconds later.

The chain reaction of ship and smaller debris collisions continued for six minutes.

And in the end, the immovable object and the irresistible force, like their captains, hung dead in space, engulfed by clouds of shattered rocks and ice, both their missions over.

There was so much redundancy built into the *Belle Rêve,* serious damage was the least of Kirk's concerns.

He was with Scott at the environmental station, working to be certain life-support still functioned. With only three people on board requiring those systems, the demands were not great.

The next question was warp capability. Despite the *Belle Rêve*'s advanced shields and weapons, her biggest advantage over the *Enterprise* was speed.

"Warp status?" Kirk asked.

The engineer scanned the diagnostic screens at the navigation console. "Offline but resetting. . . . All the backups are enabled."

"How long?"

"Ten minutes," Scott said.

"Make it five," Kirk told him.

He saw Scotty's sly grin. "I had a feeling you were goin' to say that. Five it is."

Kirk heard an echoing boom thunder through the bridge. The sound originated somewhere below the bridge. He joined the two doctors at the tactical console. "What was that?"

"Debris strike," the hologram said. "Our shields are down and those particular backups are *not* resetting."

Another bang made the bridge shudder. Then Kirk heard what sounded to be a shower of sand rushing overhead.

"We're moving at almost the same speed as the debris, so the impact energy is negligible," the hologram explained.

Kirk didn't need him to finish the thought. "But we can't go to warp without shields."

McCoy frowned at him. "We can't even go to impulse, Jim—not out here."

Kirk called to his engineer. "Scotty—you'll have to get shields up first."

"Then I'll need to get down t' engineering."

"Go," Kirk said. "And let's hope the *Enterprise* is in worse shape."

Scott threw Kirk a skeptical look as he rushed for the turbolift. "Somehow, I doubt it. . . ."

The new restraints on the bridge chairs had kept Picard's key staff in position during the impact and its aftermath, but more than half now succumbed to nausea from the violent spinning.

Picard was one of the few who successfully fought against it, and when the inertial dampers had at last caught up with the spin rate and gravity was restored, he punched out of his restraints and carefully made his way to the tactical console.

Worf had been standing at the time of collision. He was now unconscious on the deck by the ready-room doors, being treated by an ensign who had been stationed at an engineering console.

On the main viewscreen, the stars still spiraled.

"Compensate for the ship's motion on the viewscreen," Picard ordered. "Then find Kirk's ship!"

The ensign at ops modified the viewscreen's output so that the distant stars remained still. Picard was surprised to see that some points of light continued to swirl past, but quickly realized they were part of the ice blizzard the two ships had created.

"Thermal reading on the *Belle Rêve*," the ensign said. "Distance: eighty-three kilometers. Sending to tactical."

On the tactical console, Picard studied the new image of the smaller ship. It had stopped spinning, but seemed locked in a dense cloud of debris. He saw no sign of atmospheric or antimatter venting, so he felt confident the ship was intact.

And if it was intact, it was still a threat.

"Bridge to engineering," Picard said.

La Forge answered at once, coughing, sounding winded.

"How soon will we have propulsion?" Picard asked.

"Captain, we're good to go on one impulse thruster right now. But we won't be able to get a crew in place to reset the others while it's operating."

Picard frowned. With only one thruster, a lunar shuttle could outrun his ship.

"Do we have tractor beams?" Picard asked.

"That I can give you," La Forge answered.

"Power them up," Picard said. "Conn, set a course to the *Belle Rêve.*"

And with the tractor beams as the feint, Picard called up the controls he would need to launch his real attack on Kirk.

"Jim, the *Enterprise* is coming about. . . ."

Kirk looked up from the engineering station, saw Picard's ship on the center screen, literally plowing out of a cloud of cometary ice, heading directly for the smaller ship.

"Scotty . . ." Kirk said into the console communicator.

"Shields or engines, Cap'n—I can't give you both by the time that behemoth reaches us."

Kirk called over to the doctors. "Is he powering up his weapons?"

"All weapons systems appear to be offline," the holographic doctor said.

But beside the EMH, the flesh-and-blood doctor added, "We're picking up fluctuations from their tractor-beam emitters."

Kirk stared at the screen, thinking like Picard. "He can't outrace us, he can't outfight us, so he's going to grab on to us. . . ." He tapped the console communicator again. "Scotty, what's the status of *our* tractor beams?"

"What tractor beams?" the engineer replied. *"All the emitters are fused."*

Kirk knew what Picard was going to attempt. With a tractor beam, he had a chance to counter the move.

Without one . . . Kirk ran through the capabilities of his ship, seeing each system as a potential weapon. But time was almost up.

"Get me shields as soon as you can," Kirk said. "Jean-Luc's trying to misdirect us with those tractor beams, but he's going to come at us with the transporter."

Just as Picard got his transporter locks on Kirk, McCoy, Scott, and the holographic doctor's emitter, the *Belle Rêve*'s navigation shields flashed on and ended his attempt to retrieve the crew.

Without wasting a moment, Picard activated the tractor beams at full power, latching on to Kirk's ship.

He braced himself at the tactical controls, waiting for Kirk to attempt to pull away. But instead, the *Belle Rêve* accelerated toward the *Enterprise* even faster than the tractor beams propelled it.

Picard checked the sensor scans: none of the *Belle Rêve*'s propulsion systems were active.

"What's driving that ship?" Picard asked aloud, again trying to put himself in Kirk's position.

The answer came from La Forge in engineering. *"Captain—they've boosted their artificial-gravity generators! The main field's outside their hull and they're falling toward us!"*

The *Belle Rêve* twisted suddenly in place, and with the combined torque imparted by the *Enterprise*'s tractor beams and the smaller ship's reconfigured gravity field, the *Enterprise* was forced to swing slowly around, directly into a cloud of debris.

But the *Enterprise* had what the other ship did not—a working thruster.

She reversed, skimming the debris cloud, but pulling the *Belle Rêve* into it instead.

The *Belle Rêve* swung out of the cloud, trailing flashes of superheated ice and organic gases that had been old when Earth's sun was new. Her weakened shields were overloading and the *Enterprise*'s transporter beams punched against them, again and again, speeding their failure.

In response, the small ship fired a quantum torpedo past the *Enterprise,* to detonate behind her and send a rush of radiation against her one operational thruster, trying to overheat it.

The *Enterprise* countered by throwing all power to its aft shields and abruptly cutting its tractor beams. As if an elastic cord had been cut, the *Belle Rêve* fell *up* under the attractive power of its own artificial gravity, scraping against the *Enterprise*'s lower hull until it was once again held in place by tractor beams, just in front of the sensor dish. Then the larger ship reestablished its shields with the *Belle Rêve* inside their perimeter.

They were locked together now, both ships evenly matched in a complex equation of capability and battle damage. Both captains masters of their art, equally determined, each with a single, different advantage.

Picard's advantage was that he did not fight alone. Three Starfleet vessels were already under way to lend assistance. The first, the *U.S.S. Tucker,* would arrive within twelve minutes and the *Belle Rêve*'s capture would be complete.

Kirk's advantage was an operational warp drive.
And at this distance, it was a weapon.

"If we go t' warp inside her shields, ye'll tear the
Enterprise apart," Scott exclaimed.

Kirk bounced his fist on the arm of his command
chair, calculating the odds. "No. Jean-Luc won't risk
his ship. When we power up our warp engines, he'll
lower his shields."

Scott didn't look convinced.

McCoy was more vocal. "He won't, Jim. Picard's
under orders to protect his home system. There're
three ships coming to help him right now. And he
knows you're not willing to kill half his crew."

"What if those ships that're on their way are full of
shapechangers, Bones? What if Picard's unwitting bait,
just like Marinta?"

The holographic doctor scowled in disapproval. "I
have never seen a more dispiriting display of obsessive
distrust. Captain Kirk—you and Captain Picard are fellow starship captains . . . friends. Is there no common
ground you can find between the two of you?"

"He's fighting for his home," Kirk said. "I'm fighting for my son."

There could be no common ground.

22

Worf, forehead glistening with newly regenerated skin, reported from his console. "Captain—the enemy vessel is powering up its warp engines."

Worf had identified Kirk as "the enemy." *How has it come to this?* Picard thought.

"Mister Scott's on that ship," he said. "He knows what going to warp inside our shields would do to us."

Troi leaned forward from the chair to his left, spoke urgently. "Captain, I'm certain you were speaking with the real James Kirk. I sensed no duplicity, no indication that he might've been an impostor. But I can't be certain about Scott."

Picard fought succumbing to paranoia. But what choice did any of them have?

"How soon until the *Tucker*'s within range?"

Kadohata spoke from her ops station; she had

arrived on the bridge just a few minutes earlier, along with the rest of the senior crew.

"Nine minutes."

"When will the *Belle Rêve* be ready for warp?"

Worf answered. "Less than a minute."

"Captain . . ." Troi began, and Picard could hear from the counselor's plaintive tone that she sensed what decision he'd made—the only decision he could. He didn't let her finish.

"Number One, reduce our shield perimeter to hold the *Belle Rêve* as close to us as possible. Divert all additional power to our structural integrity field. Have all nonessential crew move to the escape pods."

Worf growled in approval. "Understood, sir. She won't get away."

Picard sat back in his chair as once again his restraints folded into position. "She won't get away because Jim Kirk won't go to warp," he said firmly.

He wished he could believe that.

Kirk didn't need Scott's expertise to interpret the basic data readouts on the left-hand viewscreen. Picard was preparing for the worst.

"I don't think he's bluffing," Scott said.

"Neither do I," Kirk agreed. "Are we going to be able to get through his shields when we go to warp?"

"Aye. But our warp bubble will take most of th' *Enterprise*'s lower decks with us. And that extra mass will put our field so far out of balance, we won't get far before our overload safeties shut us down. Maybe five, ten AUs. After that, we'll be on impulse like every other ship in the system."

Kirk knew Picard was sending him a message. He could read it in the steps Picard was taking to protect the *Enterprise* as best he could. The message was blunt: If you're bluffing, I'm calling.

Kirk decided to raise the stakes.

"Scotty, tune our warp bubble to the smallest possible volume so we'll cause the least damage to the *Enterprise*."

McCoy looked at Kirk in horror. "Jim . . . you can't."

"Bones, Jean-Luc's not giving me a choice. All he has to do to save his ship and his crew is drop his shields."

Kirk felt as if he were about to step out of a shuttle to start an orbital skydive without a ceramic suit. His fingers tightened on the arms of his chair. He took a breath, gave his orders.

"Mister Scott, we need to let the *Enterprise* know what's coming. Begin a thirty-second countdown to warp initialization."

The engineer frowned, but he had no other strategy to offer. "Aye, Captain . . . tuning the field . . . minimum volume . . . and the countdown starts . . . *now*."

"They've started a thirty-second countdown to warp initialization," Worf announced. "They've also reduced their warp-field volume."

"He's trying to minimize the damage he's going to cause," Troi said. "He's going to go through with it."

Picard watched the time display on a console screen mark the seconds remaining. "Mister Worf, will we be able to stop him?"

"No. But the damage we inflict will prevent him from traveling at warp for more than a few seconds. That will put him within range of the other ships before he reaches the outer planets." Worf paused, then added proudly, "We will be making an honorable sacrifice."

Picard's mind spun as he weighed the odds . . . *twenty-two seconds* . . . No matter what he did now, Kirk was going to escape . . . *twenty seconds* . . . But the *Belle Rêve* would be compromised . . . *eighteen seconds* . . . In that situation, could he count on Kirk being stopped before reaching the inner solar system? *sixteen seconds* . . . Was he about to risk his ship and his crew for nothing? *fourteen seconds . . .*

Picard came to the hardest decision of his career, prepared to give his orders to his crew. And then—

"Captain . . . sensors have detected an anomalous surge in his warp generator."

Picard felt electrified. "A malfunction?" Could it be that simple?

"His warp core *is* building toward a breach," Worf added. Without waiting for further orders, the Klingon sounded the collision alarm.

"Sir, we must drop shields to allow him to eject his core, otherwise the explosion *will* destroy both ships."

Picard knew that—but was the breach *real*? Or was this another of Kirk's tricks? Tortured by possibilities, uncertainties, Picard stared at the time display.

Ten seconds . . .

"Scotty . . . ?" Kirk stood from his chair as he saw the warp readings go off the scale. "Is that a breach?"

"No . . . it's somethin' else, but what, I can't tell ye . . ." Scott worked feverishly at his console, called up a visual sensor image of engineering. "Och . . ."

Kirk stared at the screen with alarm. The compact warp core of his ship was half-enveloped in winding tendrils of black sand.

As he watched, they moved, like time-speeded vines. The same black tendrils he had seen claim Spock. The same black tendrils that had grown from Norinda's outstretched arms.

"Shut it down!" Kirk ordered.

"I'm tryin'," Scott answered. "But it's drawin' power from another source!"

"Then shut down every power source on the ship!"

"If we drop our shields," Scott warned, "the *Enterprise*'ll beam us out in nothin' flat."

It was one thing to risk his life for a chance at victory, Kirk knew. But it was folly to invite outright disaster.

"We've lost, Scotty—shut it down!"

The lights flared once, went out. An instant later, the battery-powered emergency fixtures flashed on. In the low light, the bridge was oppressively dark. The color of defeat.

The viewscreen image of engineering also faltered, but stayed onscreen.

Kirk turned to his engineer, surprised; there was no backup power source for the screen.

"Scotty, shut down *every* system."

"Captain, I have. . . ."

McCoy and the Emergency Medical Hologram stood on either side of Kirk, sharing his confusion.

According to the data readouts on the screen, the *Belle Rêve*'s power output was zero. Yet her shields were still up and her warp core remained energized.

Then, on the screen, the dark tendrils peeled off the warp core and wove together into an undulating column like a Martian dust devil that shifted in form and color until it became—

Norinda. In a Starfleet admiral's uniform.

Kirk slammed his fist against the com controls on his chair, opening the channel to engineering.

Norinda smiled warmly into the visual sensor. "James, there's no need for this."

"Get off my ship."

Norinda shook her head, her smile unchanged. "I don't want you to die. I don't want Jean-Luc to die. I don't want anyone to die. There's been too much of death, don't you think?"

"I don't believe you," Kirk said. He moved quickly to Scott's console. "On Remus, you told me you wanted to engulf the galaxy in war, so we'd know what it was to reject 'love' and 'peace' and 'understanding.'"

Kirk touched Scott's arm and pointed to the control set for the warp-generator baffles, indicating that he wanted them opened so the engineering compartment would be flooded with delta radiation.

"Don't do it, James. I'm the only one protecting you."

Kirk gestured to Scott to stand by.

"From whom?" Kirk asked. But almost as the words left his lips, he knew the answer. "From the Totality. . . ."

Norinda nodded, her friendly expression unchanged.

"I thought *you* were the Totality," Kirk said.

"We're *all* the Totality. It's just that you won't accept it."

"You haven't answered my question."

"Answer mine instead," Norinda countered. "What do you want, James? Why do any of you . . . *creatures* want to open yourselves to the ultimate truth of existence?"

Kirk studied her carefully, remembering her in all her deceitful and dangerous incarnations through the years. She had the power to completely cloud his attention through a form of telepathy that could kindle unthinking and inescapable desire—the first manifestation of love she had attempted to offer him when they had first encountered each other. Yet for now, she had chosen not to use that ability. Why?

Kirk had just spent the past hour trying to think like Picard. Now he gave himself a more difficult test: thinking like Norinda.

He didn't like where those thoughts took him.

Though he still had no way of knowing what the Totality's ultimate goal was, what if Norinda wasn't a monster? What if she wasn't driven by conquest and the hunger for victory like the Romulans and the Borg? What if she were genuinely driven to understand the "creatures" she was in conflict with?

What if she truly wanted—*needed*—an answer from him, one that might lead to a peaceful resolution of their conflict?

If that were so, then Kirk saw a possible advantage, took it.

"Return Spock," he said suddenly, gambling that Norinda's need might spur her to make a gesture.

Norinda stared at him from the viewscreen, perplexed. "Return him? From where?"

Kirk spoke calmly. "You took him on Remus, dissolved him into black sand just like you tried to do with me."

Norinda looked even more confused. "James, I gave Spock a gift—*the* gift. I didn't take him. He's not gone."

"The gift . . ." Kirk repeated, puzzled by those words, trying to understand her meaning. And then he saw it. There was a pattern in what Norinda had been saying—now, *and* a year ago on Remus. "Did you give Spock . . . peace?"

Norinda's confusion evaporated and her smile returned, beatific. "Yes, James, yes! The Peace of the Totality! Your friend knows, now. He knows the ultimate truth of existence!"

Spock's words came back to Kirk then, and he knew that they held—had always held—the secret to all that had happened.

"We're life, Jim. But not as they know it."

They, Kirk thought. *The Totality.*

A form of sentience so alien that it shared nothing in common with biological life.

"If Spock *knows* that truth," Kirk began carefully, "if he *knows* the Peace of the Totality, then let him come back to tell us about it."

"But, James, *I've* told you about it."

Kirk tried again.

"We're different from you, Norinda. It's . . . difficult for us to understand each other. But Spock . . . he's experienced both sides. He'll be able to tell us what you need us to know in a way that our form of life will understand."

Norinda remained motionless. Kirk could almost believe that her consciousness had shifted to another realm.

Then her blissful smile broadened. "I understand," she announced. "*Ambassador* Spock. Unification. But on a larger scale. A universal scale. You are right, James. We *do* want the same thing."

Kirk persisted. "Will you return him?"

Norinda shook her head. "You know better than that." Then her form melted into wisps of smoke and the last tendrils of utter blackness on the warp core untwisted swiftly into nothingness, until there was no trace of her left in engineering. Only her voice drifted out from the void.

"He has always been with you."

Something new lay on the deck. A body, sprawled, unconscious, wrapped in the jeweled robes of a Vulcan ambassador.

Spock.

23

The bridge of the *Enterprise* was quiet, charged, tense.

The *Belle Rêve* was still within the *Enterprise*'s shields, held against the larger ship's lower hull. Her warp core had not breached. Sensors showed it was no longer operational. But her shields remained up.

That meant Picard could not beam Kirk, Scott, McCoy, and the holographic doctor off the captured vessel and end this standoff peacefully.

Eighteen minutes had passed since Worf had detected the *Belle Rêve*'s warp core as it built to a breach, then abruptly and inexplicably powered down. La Forge had reviewed the sensor readings and could make no sense of them; the core should have exploded. Why it had not remained a mystery.

But at least, Picard thought with relief, whatever

had happened—or was happening—on the *Belle Rêve*, he was no longer caught in an equal confrontation with Kirk. Two Starfleet vessels had joined the *Enterprise*: the *Tucker* and the *Garneau*. Both ships were *Gagarin*-class: fast, heavily armed and heavily shielded cruiser-escorts built to engage the Dominion's Jem'Hadar.

The two ships held station a dozen kilometers to the port and starboard of the *Enterprise,* their weapons locked on Kirk's ship, ready to disable it the moment it tried to escape. And in less than an hour, the hastily repaired *Titan* would arrive, as well. With the combined tractor beams of four Starfleet vessels, Kirk's ship could finally be taken in tow, no matter how he tried to manipulate his artificial-gravity field. The waiting would be over.

Then Leybenzon reported from his auxiliary console and everything changed once again.

"Captain Picard, it looks like Kirk *was* hiding his full crew complement from us."

Disappointment stung Picard.

"I know," Troi said consolingly, without his having said a word. "You were hoping for the best."

As always, the counselor was right. Picard had anticipated Kirk's being pigheaded and stubborn, but he had not wanted to think that Kirk would deliberately lie. Outright deception was the mark of an adversary.

"How many crew?" he asked.

Leybenzon adjusted the controls on his console. "So far, I've picked up one additional life sign."

"Only one?" Picard didn't understand. He went to

the security officer's console to review the sensor readings himself. "Why use the *Belle Rêve*'s screens and shields to hide just *one* individual?"

"Sensors indicate that Kirk's ship didn't employ any deceptive countermeasures. That tells me that either his real countermeasures are even more sophisticated than the specs we have, or—"

"Or that extra crew member just appeared on the ship in the last few minutes," Picard concluded.

He couldn't imagine how the situation could get worse. Now it didn't matter if Kirk had been lying or not. Somehow, in some way, Kirk's ship had been boarded, most likely by a shapechanger.

Which meant Worf was correct.

The *Belle Rêve* was now an enemy vessel.

Picard had no choice but to treat it as such.

"It's Spock, all right."

McCoy put his medical tricorder away, looked over at the Emergency Medical Hologram.

"I concur," the hologram said, and closed his own tricorder.

Kirk looked down at his old friend, still lying on the deck in engineering, where Norinda had somehow conjured him up even as she'd vanished. Spock was breathing, his eyes were open, but he was completely unresponsive. "What's wrong with him, Bones?"

"Well, from his brain-wave patterns," McCoy said, not sounding totally convinced, "he could be in a deep meditative state."

"Meditating?" Kirk said. He'd had occasion to disturb Spock's meditation in the past; on a starship, a crisis could erupt at any time. But always, Spock had been able to emerge from his state of intense concentration within a minute or so, and he'd usually been able to speak during the process. What was different this time?

"No sign of transporter trauma?" Kirk asked.

McCoy shook his head. "He wasn't beamed in."

"But he was . . . reconstructed here," Kirk said, trying to puzzle it out for himself. "I've read of cases of transporter comas . . . the brain's quantum state isn't quite reestablished perfectly, and—"

The hologram interrupted him. "Captain, it's been more than a century since a legitimate case of transporter catatonia has been reported in the literature." He looked down at Spock, pursed his lips. "I suggest smelling salts."

McCoy grinned at the hologram. "A man after my own heart. I have some in the infirmary."

And then Spock moved.

"Bones!" Kirk said.

Awkwardly, Spock got to his feet, eyes open and unblinking, staring straight ahead as if completely unaware of the two men and the hologram before him.

Kirk couldn't restrain himself. He grabbed Spock's arm. "Spock! You're back! You've been gone a year!"

But Spock's only reaction was to slowly turn his head until he looked directly at the main exit.

He pulled away from Kirk, walked toward the door.

McCoy and the hologram both had their tricorders out again, scanning Spock as the door slipped open and he stepped into the corridor.

"Now what's wrong with him?" Kirk demanded as he followed Spock toward the turbolift.

McCoy glanced up from his tricorder. "From these readings, it appears he's still meditating."

The hologram peered over McCoy's shoulder at the tricorder's display, deeply intrigued. "Remarkable. An almost complete suppression of all conscious thought."

Kirk suddenly felt certain he knew what Spock was doing.

McCoy caught the look of realization on his face. "What is it, Jim? What do you know that we don't?"

But Kirk had no time to share his discovery. Among her many other abilities, Norinda possessed a telepathic sense. If Spock knew something that he didn't want Norinda to know, he was quite capable of using his formidable mental discipline to keep that knowledge from his conscious mind and thus from her perception. And then Kirk realized that if Norinda *was* using her telepathic sense on him instead of Spock, she now knew what Spock was attempting, as well.

Spock stepped onto the turbolift with Kirk, McCoy, and the hologram crowding in with him.

Kirk touched his combadge. He had to keep Norinda off the ship, and from what he had just witnessed, he could make a good guess about what she was using as her access point. "Scotty—take the warp core completely offline."

"*Too late*," Scotty replied from the bridge. "*I just saw a surge in the standby relays. It's drawing power again, and I don't know what source it's using.*"

Over the thrum of the turbolift, Kirk felt the Cochrane generators beginning to pulse through the ship.

"Scotty, eject the core if you have to, but don't let it power up!"

Scott's next words were just what Kirk had hoped wouldn't happen.

"Captain—the tendrils are back! They're growing over the core!"

Norinda had looked into Kirk's mind and *had* learned what Spock was attempting to do. She was coming back to stop him.

"Now what?" Picard asked as he studied the sensor scans from the *Belle Rêve*.

"Their warp core appears to be coming online again," Worf said with suspicion.

"Get Geordi on those readings," Picard ordered. "Stand ready to drop shields and use our tractor beams to push the *Belle Rêve* free before her core explodes."

"This could be another trick, sir."

Picard shook his head. "It might've worked when we were the only ship within range. But the *Tucker* and the *Garneau* can lay down a crossfire to keep Kirk from going to warp."

Then La Forge reported from engineering. "*Captain, I'm watching the scans of the* Belle Rêve, *and they're in real trouble.*"

"Give me details," Picard said.

"*I'm seeing multiple attempts to eject the core . . . they've depressurized their engineering hold . . . but the breach is about to go critical.*"

233

"What is going on in that ship?" Picard asked. But his crew had no answer.

The turbolift doors slid open onto the bridge. Kirk sprinted out to join Scott, glanced back to see Spock heading slowly but deliberately for the life-support station.

"I've done all I can," Scott said. "But it's as if the core has a mind of its own."

Kirk followed Scott's gaze to the center viewscreen, still displaying a visual sensor image of engineering.

A tangled mass of tendrils fully encased the core. Flashes of blazing golden light shot through a few small gaps between the tendrils as the core pulsed in its run-up to full power.

And with each flash, a tendril peeled off from the main body, bent down to the deck, and rose up as a humanoid.

Among them, Kirk saw Norinda take shape, once again in admiral's uniform. Others joining her wore Starfleet uniforms from more than a decade earlier, specialist colors bright on their shoulders.

"Are *any* of those human?" Kirk asked.

"If they're movin' around in a vacuum, ye can be sure they're not," Scott said, stoutly unafraid. He checked his controls. "We're ten seconds from breach, sir. And there's nothin' can be done. . . ."

For just an instant, Kirk felt sorrow well up in him, not for himself but for all who had trusted him, whom he had now let down. Bones and Scotty, the holographic doctor, and most of all, his son.

But just as quickly as it arose, that sorrow vanished as Kirk remembered—

"Spock!"

He wheeled to see Spock at the life-support station, methodically making adjustments to one of the settings on the console.

Before Kirk could even think to wonder which settings Spock was changing, he knew the answer, even if he didn't understand it. He felt his own weight double, heard Scott's chair creak, McCoy's annoyed exclamation of protest.

Kirk chose an empty chair, dropped into it with a bone-jarring thud.

"Spock . . . ?" he gasped.

Kirk struggled to draw breath as his body grew even heavier, his shoulders slumped forward. All around him, he could hear console cabinets groan, some small popping sounds.

Spock had set the ship's artificial gravity to at least three times Earth normal and it was still increasing.

Kirk fought for breath in the unexpected onslaught.

McCoy was lying flat on the deck, apparently unconscious.

The hologram was unaffected by the change in gravity and stood over his fallen fellow physician, tricorder in hand.

"Captain!" Scott muttered. "Look!"

Kirk fought to turn his head toward Scott. The engineer's hand trembled on his console as he strained to point to the viewscreen.

Kirk blinked slowly, painfully. The shape of his eyes was being distorted by the increasing gravity, making his vision blur.

But with extreme effort he focused on the humanoid forms in engineering and saw them decomposing. In their place, twisting pillars of black sand devolved into smoke, fading from existence along with the tendrils that had swarmed the warp core.

Free of their influence, the ship's computer now accepted Scott's override commands.

The pulsing light in the core slowed and dimmed as once again it shut down.

The breach had been averted.

Kirk slumped in the chair, concentrating on each hard-won breath.

"Gravity, Spock?"

"As I calculated," Spock answered calmly, "four times Earth normal is sufficient to prevent the Totality from reaching us."

Kirk tried to nod in understanding and instantly regretted it. His chin remained on his chest, and the back of his neck paid the price.

"Reach us from where?" Kirk grunted, forcing his head up so he could see Spock again. The Totality was so unlike anything in this universe, he concluded that they could have only come from some other dimensional realm, some other reality.

But Kirk was not Spock.

"They are from here," Spock said. "The Totality arose in our universe."

Kirk blinked as dark stars flickered at the edge of his vision. "But they're so different. . . ."

"On the contrary," Spock said, betraying no sign that he also was being subjected to four times Earth gravity. "They are the life-force that inhabits ninety-six percent of the universe. It is we, chemical-based biological life, that occupy the remaining four percent.

"This is their universe, Jim. To them, we're the extremophiles, life as they do not know it, or understand it. In effect, we are little more than parasites that the Totality feels compelled to uplift or exterminate.

"They will allow us no other fate."

24

There were five ships now in that cold dark region. Earth's sun was just another point of light, too far and too dim to reveal the vessels as they held their positions at relative stop. They were perceptible only because they blocked the stars. Around their dim shapes slowly drifted ice clouds and the slow, tumbling rocks and debris from stars that had died billions of years ago, yet now provided the raw material of life for a new round of star-building that would lead to a new generation of life.

The *Belle Rêve* remained locked to the *Enterprise*. To Picard, the two ships joined brought to mind images of fossilized prehistoric beasts, each with a death grip on the other, trapped forever in their unyielding battle from which neither could emerge the victor.

The other three ships were spectators to that frozen

conflict. The *Tucker* and the *Garneau* had been joined by the *Titan*. The *Belle Rêve* would never withstand their combined assault, and yet, as long as it remained close to the *Enterprise*, it could not be attacked.

It was a true stalemate, an unexploded bomb, a tidal wave cresting slowly, almost ready to break.

It couldn't last.

Not if the galaxy was to survive.

"Dark matter?" Picard repeated.

On the viewscreen, Kirk confirmed what Spock had said, his words measured and slow. "Dark matter *and* dark energy." Both men on the *Belle Rêve* looked haggard, faces sagging in the high gravity they had chosen to endure. "It makes sense, Jean-Luc, and you know it."

Picard thought over the explanation Spock had presented and wasn't surprised that there *was* a logic to it.

Hundreds of years ago, in the troubled times leading up to the Third World War, humans had discovered that the majority of the universe was primarily composed of a mysterious unseen substance and almost imperceptible force that the physicists of the day had called dark matter and dark energy. Over the ensuing centuries, the concept fell in and out of favor as numerous theories of quantum cosmology were continually refined, one version leading to another as more and more discoveries were made. But always in the equations lurked two vast unknowns with changing names: shadow mass, quintessence, the Higgs sieve, dimensional braiding, deSitter particles, and etheric drag among others.

But today, Picard knew, in this modern era of technology unchained, multiphysicists had turned to the past. Once again researchers called forth those first, simplest, and self-explanatory terms—dark matter and dark energy—to identify that still unquantifiable but overwhelming portion of space that composed the sum total of the universe, except for stars and their galaxies.

Now, as when the concepts were first discovered, they remained a source of wonder. The approximately four percent of the universe that was composed of ordinary matter and energy had given rise to life while the rest of the void was barren.

But now Spock was saying that the Federation's finest minds were wrong. That life was not limited just to those few precarious environments on planets and moons, and a handful of comets and asteroids. A different form of it existed throughout *all* the unseen and unknowable regions of the universe. In fact, that life-force had spontaneously arisen from dark matter and dark energy as surely and as invariably as biological life arose from the chemistry of warm and wet physical environments.

The only place, Spock said, where dark-matter life could not emerge was in the minuscule parts of the universe where sporadic clouds of hydrogen gas coalesced into stars and galaxies. Those small regions of space-time apparently created such extreme conditions that even dark-matter life believed it was impossible for any other form of life to arise in them.

Spock had explained nothing less than the mystery of the Totality and its origin and motive. As the aeons had passed, dark-matter life spread through the universe, avoiding the pockets of normal matter and energy hostile to its existence, eventually becoming the linked sentience of the Totality. In time, projections of that combined life-force—the equivalent, in Spock's opinion, of biological individuals—developed techniques for penetrating and exploring the extreme environments where life as they knew it could not exist. But, as they were startled to discover, it did.

The Totality had found light-matter life: life as humans and other biology-based entities know it, formed from hydrogen clouds and the stars that arose from them. But the Totality also realized that this light-matter life, though capable of evolving a limited intelligence, seemed regrettably unable to perceive the true nature of the universe. So, driven by the desire to bring enlightenment to those poor beings confined to a mere sliver of the universe, the Totality took on the noble task of reengineering the harsh environments of coalesced hydrogen. They sought ways to eliminate the disruptive stars and galaxies that trapped and confined light-matter life. Their ultimate goal was positive and compassionate, Spock said: Absorb all stunted, extremophile life-forms into the vast, universe-wide shared sentience of the ultimate reality.

Spock repeated his conclusion for Picard's benefit. "The Totality believes it is bringing peace and joy to the universe, one galaxy at a time. The Kelvan Empire of Andromeda was the latest to be 'saved.' Now it is our galaxy's turn."

Picard glanced down at the small communications screen that had folded out of his command chair. Will

Riker appeared on it from the bridge of the *Titan*. He had heard everything, looked concerned. "I have a question for the ambassador," he said.

"Please," Spock answered.

"What's the connection between gravity fields and warp bubbles?"

Spock appeared to welcome the opportunity to explain in further detail. Picard followed most of his explanation, but trusted that his crew could enlighten him if he missed something significant.

"Dark-matter life," Spock said, "arises from the quantum foam of existence. It is a natural and inevitable result of the universe's underlying structure, no different from the sea of virtual particles and vacuum energy continually being produced out of what we erroneously call 'nothing.'

"But the conditions most conducive to this form of life require flat space-time. Strong gravitational sources create dimensional distortions."

Picard saw the connection. "Which is why the Totality avoided stars and galaxies for so long."

Spock confirmed Picard's conclusion. "However," he continued, "the *subspace* distortions created by our warp technology cancel out gravitational distortions. That makes almost any warp generator based on Cochrane's theories a portal for the Totality to reach within our gravitational wells."

Riker followed the logic and was able to answer the last part of Picard's question. "So by increasing our local artificial-gravity field, we basically pinch those dimensional openings closed."

"Simplistic, but correct," Spock said.

Picard looked at Troi and she nodded. "Everything Spock's told you, he believes."

"Ambassador," Picard asked, "you claim all this information was given to you by the Totality?"

"Not given," Spock said, "but it was . . . available during my experience in their realm."

Despite the burden of four gravities, Kirk managed to look impatient. "Jean-Luc, we can go into details later. Right now, I have to get to Earth."

"Fine," Picard said. He was as eager to end this stalemate as Kirk appeared to be. "Drop your shields, let us beam you aboard, and we'll continue this discussion in transit to Command."

Kirk's expression tightened. "You haven't been paying attention. Right now, my ship is the only one we can be sure has no projection of the Totality on board. If you want us on the *Enterprise*, you're going to have to increase your own gravity settings."

Before Picard could object, Worf did it for him.

"Sir, at four gravities we will not be able to effectively respond to any attempt by Kirk to escape or attack."

"I heard that," Kirk said, and there was little doubt his patience was at an end. "As far as I'm concerned, the only reason you could have for resisting an increase in gravity is because the *Enterprise* has already been infiltrated and compromised."

Picard sat back in his chair, secure in knowing that with three other ships in place to back up the *Enterprise*, Kirk had run out of options.

"Jim, it could also be inferred that the only reason you could have for refusing to allow us to confirm your identity is because *you* have been compromised."

Kirk's voice hardened. "Jean-Luc, Spock just told you how to fight back against the Totality. We drove Norinda from this ship. I'm trying to take critical information to Starfleet that could provide an even greater tactical advantage. I'm not the one who's been compromised."

Picard tugged at his jacket. "I understand your frustration, but the fact is, I have the advantage. The only way out is for you to trust me. The sooner you do that, the sooner we can get your information to Starfleet, and the sooner you can return to Vulcan to find your son."

Kirk bit his words off, one by one, for emphasis. "You don't have the advantage. As long as this ship remains at four gravities, I can go to warp without the Totality interfering. Even if I tear your ship apart. I'm giving you one minute."

Troi leaned closer to Picard. "No question. He's prepared to inflict casualties."

In response to Kirk's barely contained rage, Picard felt himself go cold. "And I'm prepared to accept them."

Kirk and Picard locked eyes, viewscreen to viewscreen.

"Fifty seconds," Kirk said.

"You won't escape the other ships," Picard warned.

"Then at least I'll die free."

The immovable object. The irresistible force.

Two beasts locked in eternal combat, each prepared to accept death before defeat.

"Forty seconds . . ."

Kirk could barely breathe. It took all his strength simply to sit upright. But he would not relax his posture. He would not let Picard see any sign of weakness.

At his engineering console, Scott had almost lost his voice. The holographic doctor had administered tri-ox and mitochondrial enhancers to everyone, but four gravities took a constant toll.

"Warp core comin' online, Captain," he croaked. "No sign of any interference. . . ."

Kirk was aware of Spock at his side, adjusting a communications control. "Jim, are you certain this is necessary?"

Kirk had to struggle to enunciate clearly enough to be understood. "You've been away, Spock. I believe the Vulcan authorities have been compromised by the Totality. And if it can happen there, it can happen on Earth, and on the *Enterprise*."

Spock didn't argue the point, though Kirk couldn't be certain if that was because he accepted the argument, or because exhaustion was also claiming him.

Then, without warning, the image of Picard on the center viewscreen dissolved into subspace static.

"Scotty . . . ?" Kirk began to ask. Had the Totality devised a new method of entering normal space-time?

But before his engineer could answer, the cause of the static was revealed as a new and unexpected image appeared.

*   *   *

"Captain, I have broken in on both transmissions," Tuvok said. "You are now on the viewscreens of the *Belle Rêve* and the *Enterprise*."

This time, Riker didn't even try to hide what he was feeling, and it left no room for any of the respect that he should be showing two more senior captains.

"You two will stand down right now or I swear I'll open fire on both of you!"

Kirk appeared on the left side of the main viewscreen. It was as if he had not even heard Riker's threat. "This isn't your fight, Captain," he rasped. "Thirty seconds, Jean-Luc."

"Why is this a fight at all?!" Riker demanded.

Picard was on the right side of the screen, jaw clenched, eyes piercing. "Will, I'm counting on you to stop Kirk as soon as he drops out of warp."

"No!" Riker shouted. "The universe does not revolve around you two alone! We're all of us on a Starfleet mission and there is another way to resolve this!"

Riker took some comfort in seeing Kirk and Picard finally react to what he said, both momentarily losing their stern demeanor.

"Twenty-five seconds," Kirk said. "Convince me."

"*I'll* increase gravity on the *Titan*! It'll be the neutral ground. And when you're both convinced that this ship hasn't been compromised, I'll beam everyone over for identity confirmation and a *sensible* discussion about how to proceed." Riker turned to Tuvok. "Mister Tuvok, is Kirk's warp core still online?"

"It is."

Riker glared at the two captains on the viewscreen as he gave his orders to Tuvok. "Very well. Target the *Belle Rêve* and the *Enterprise*. All banks, full barrage."

Then Riker made his ultimatum as clear as he could. "Captain Kirk, Captain Picard, you've heard my offer. But if you two are so determined to tear apart your ships, allow me to lend a hand."

"Phasers locked," Tuvok confirmed.

"Captain Kirk," Riker said, "it's your move."

25

Picard regarded Troi with concern. Even he could infer from her expression that the counselor was troubled.

"I've never sensed Will so angry," she said quietly.

Picard's guilt deepened. How many times had he told Riker to always look for another way out, a way to defuse a situation rather than stubbornly insisting on proving a point?

And here was the student instructing the teacher.

"All right," Kirk said from his side of the *Enterprise*'s viewscreen. "I'll agree to stay put. And you'll agree to let me run a complete sensor sweep of the *Titan* to monitor the gravity readings."

From his side of the viewscreen, Riker gave a tight smile. "Acceptable. Captain Picard?"

"I should have thought of that myself, Will."

"We both should have," Kirk said.

Picard nodded. He understood, as he was sure Kirk did, that that was as close to an apology as either of them would ever make, or need to make.

Riker quickly gave his orders. All crew on the *Titan* were to police loose objects and brace for increased gravity. The precautions were little different from the turbulence drills that were a regular part of starship life.

Within two minutes, all decks reported they were secure.

"Tuvok," Riker said, "increase gravity throughout the ship by four hundred percent." He looked at the viewscreen where Kirk and Picard waited. "Captain Kirk, start your sweep."

Already feeling the first tug of increased mass, Riker took his chair, bracing himself as artificial gravity plates below his bridge stepped up their cascade of Casimir particles to manipulate inertia.

"Two gravities," Tuvok announced calmly.

Riker heard faint creaking from the deck and a few of the bridge consoles as they responded to the building gravitational load. He felt the subtle change in the almost subliminal vibration of the ship's structural-integrity field as it sent bracing energy through the superstructure.

"Three gravities," Tuvok announced, and alone of all others on the bridge, he was the only one still on his feet, the only one who didn't sound affected by having his apparent mass triple. "Three point five . . ."

At the conn station, Ensign Lavena suddenly called for a replacement and slumped from her chair to the deck, lying awkwardly against her hydration suit's stiff dorsal spines where they protected her twin gill crests. "Apologies, Captain," she said haltingly. "Suit's pressure adjustment . . . not functioning . . ."

Commander Vale stomped heavily to the conn as if she bore two hundred kilos on her shoulders and slammed down into Lavena's empty chair. With a grunt of effort, she swung her hands to the controls, standing by.

Lavena lay on the deck to the side of her chair, the liquid gurgle of her gills audible, labored, even through her suit. From his vantage point, Riker could see that the water in the suit had pooled around her. The suit's distended shape gave the appearance that she was melting into the deck.

Riker concentrated on moving his head to the side, intent on locating any crew who might be near a critical equipment locker. Lavena needed extra water injected into her suit at once.

A blank-faced ensign sat on the deck staring at nothing, his legs straight out before him, his back to a wall of equipment lockers.

"Ensign!"

The young man did not respond.

Riker searched his memory. The young man was one of the few humans on board, fresh from the Academy. Riker had met him briefly, spoken to him at the orientation assembly . . . the name flashed before him.

"Ensign Doyle!"

Three things happened then, ensuring that Riker would never forget the young man's name again.

First, Doyle turned his head quickly and easily to look at him.

Second, like Tuvok, who'd been born and bred in the higher gravity of Vulcan, Doyle was not breathing with effort.

And third, just as Tuvok reported four gravities had been reached, Ensign Doyle came apart.

Riker stared as the ensign split into squared-off tendrils as if he were being pushed through a sieve, each cubelike segment losing color as it unwound to the deck, transforming in turn to grains of what looked like black sand that slowly lost definition and substance until there was nothing left, not even a stain.

The *Titan*'s bridge crew gaped in silent shock. The only word spoken was from Tuvok. "Fascinating," he said.

"Captain Kirk . . ." Riker finally managed to gasp in the crushing pressure of four gravities. "Did you see that?"

"More importantly," Kirk replied, also struggling to speak, "Jean-Luc, did *you* see that?"

"Indeed, I did," Picard said with difficulty. "I . . . I'll stand by to be beamed to the *Titan* at your convenience, Will."

Riker summoned the strength to poll the deck commanders throughout his ship. In addition to Doyle, seven members of his crew had dissolved: two humans, the others alien.

The conclusion was inescapable: Despite the medical monitors and constant surveillance, the Totality had infiltrated the *Titan* completely undetected.

To Riker, that meant one thing and one thing only.

Each Starfleet vessel, starbase, and installation must now be considered occupied territory.

* * *

Kirk, Picard, and Riker—three generations of Starfleet's finest—returned to Mercury at warp, on board Kirk's *Belle Rêve*.

When challenged, they refused to beam down to meet with the members of the Provisional Starfleet Command. Neither would they explain themselves over open communication channels.

The enemy was everywhere.

Instead, their messenger was the Emergency Medical Hologram. He had no physical body that could be duplicated by the Totality. The details of his one physical attribute—the advanced-technology holographic emitter—had been mapped and measured by Starfleet down to the molecular level. Though its sophisticated components could not be duplicated by twenty-fourth-century technology, the emitter itself was easily checked against existing records for alterations.

In less than an hour after the EMH beamed down to the Vostok Academy deep beneath the surface of Mercury, he returned with Admiral Janeway.

To avoid injury to the admiral, Kirk had his engineer set the *Belle Rêve*'s transporter room to one gravity for her arrival. Once Janeway had positioned herself on a chair from one of the staterooms, Scott, working from the bridge, slowly brought the gravity up to the safe setting—four times Earth normal.

To the relief of the three captains—and the EMH—the admiral, though distinctly bothered and uncomfortable, maintained her integrity. She did not disintegrate into black sand and disappear.

A few minutes later, their meeting took place on

the bridge, where the console chairs offered headrests and better support. Spock and Scott were present as well. McCoy had retired to the infirmary and a diagnostic bed, monitoring the bridge discussion over a communications channel.

Following captains' orders, the EMH was prepared to administer tri-ox and other pharmaceutical aids to the admiral upon her request. But since Janeway still hadn't determined if this was another ruse on the part of an enemy other than the Totality, she refused.

The holographic doctor remained by Janeway's side nonetheless, helpfully explaining that *he* was convinced by the captains' story and that he was certain she would be, too, soon enough.

Then the admiral, with a scientist's skepticism, listened as the three captains told her their tale.

Kirk assessed Janeway's reaction as the sensor log from the *Titan* played back on the central viewscreen.

When Ensign Doyle, by decomposing and vanishing, was revealed as a projection of the Totality that had presumably been somehow reabsorbed, the admiral's expression did change from neutral, to concern.

But she was not yet convinced.

Kirk caught Picard's eye, signaling his unspoken query. They still needed to make their case.

Janeway shook her head, carefully, in the punishing gravity. "Interesting, but it doesn't make sense."

"It *is* a completely unknown form of life," Riker argued. "It stands to reason that it might not behave according to logic."

Janeway turned her gaze to Spock. "No objection to that, Ambassador?"

"I am curious to know why you believe what you've seen doesn't make sense, Admiral."

Kirk's experienced eye and ear told him that Spock was impatient with Janeway's caution.

"Many reasons," Janeway said coolly, indicating that she would not be rushed into agreement. "The most important one is that given the power of this so-called Totality, why did they limit their attack to denying us warp travel? Why haven't we been completely overrun by them?"

Kirk had spoken with Norinda often enough to know the answer. "They don't want to force us to do anything."

Janeway frowned in disbelief. "You say they want to wage a war without using force, which they do by destroying hundreds of our ships, and inflicting thousands of casualties? Come on, Kirk."

Kirk tried to shrug, but under four gravities, his shoulders didn't budge. "The Totality is convinced that once we truly understand what it is they're offering us, we'll embrace it—without a fight."

"And," Janeway asked, "they're offering us what, exactly?"

"The chance to join them," Spock said.

Janeway's reply dripped with cynicism. "And become one with the universe."

Spock, impervious to such emotion, focused on the facts. "Admiral, they believe they *are* the universe, and in a way, they are correct."

To Kirk, it seemed as if Janeway momentarily lost

her struggle to ignore the extreme circumstances of their rendezvous. Even talking under four gravities was the equivalent of a heavy workout. She paused for a long moment, took a deep breath as the holographic doctor unobtrusively aimed a tricorder at her, just to be sure she was holding up. "Ambassador, where *exactly* were you this past year?"

Spock replied easily, maddeningly in control of his breathing and his speech. "I existed in a realm of shadow matter. My personality remained intact; I had an illusion of my body with which to interact with an illusory physical environment constructed to put me at my ease. But I was aware of other minds around me, as if I were in a constant state of residual mindmeld with uncountable individuals." He looked at Kirk. "And, when I was given the opportunity to meditate, I found myself able to sense the minds of others who remained in this dimensional reality."

"It worked, Spock. You got my attention."

Spock acknowledged Kirk's confirmation with an almost imperceptible nod. Then he looked back to Janeway. "And underlying the experience, at a distance yet always beckoning, I felt the mind-force of the Totality, urging me to take the next step to total absorption."

"Absorption into what?" Janeway asked after a long moment of silence.

"The Totality itself," Spock said.

"A group mind?" Janeway grimaced. Kirk felt sympathy for her. It had been hard for all of them to truly comprehend. "Like the Borg?"

"No, Admiral. I am familiar with the collective,

and this experience was unique. Where the Borg are driven by the need to assimilate individuals and have them work for the continued growth of the group, the Totality is not driven by anything except its own immediate existence. It has no goals, no purpose, only awareness."

Janeway struggled to raise a hand to rub at her temples. "I thought their goal was to bring us into the fold."

"That is correct," Spock agreed. "But not for the sake of conquering us, not for obtaining our resources, but merely because . . . they feel sorry for us."

Janeway stared at Spock, baffled.

"Admiral," Kirk said, taking pity on her, "what it all comes down to, what it's always been about since the first time I encountered Norinda, is that the Totality only wants to help us."

Janeway looked to Picard and to Riker. "You both go along with this?"

Kirk wasn't surprised to see that his fellow captains were uncomfortable accepting his summation.

"Whatever the Totality is," Picard said, clearly choosing his words carefully, "it's a life-form that we've never encountered. One that inhabits a realm our minds never evolved to comprehend. I don't think it's critical what their motives are, however accurately or imperfectly we understand them." He glanced at Kirk as if offering an apology. "What is critical is putting an end to what they've done to us.

"Spock has given us a way to drive them off our ships and enable us to travel at warp again. And Jim has a database of information collected by the first

Starfleet vessel to encounter the Totality as it traveled from Andromeda to our galaxy."

Janeway looked back at Kirk, now thoroughly confused. "Which vessel?"

"The *Monitor*." His hand and arm trembling from the effort, Kirk drew Marinta's copper-colored message player from his jacket. "This is their last transmission. I believe it contains information that'll enable us not only to resist the Totality, but to fight back."

Janeway pursed her lips in satisfaction. "So you do admit that we're in a war?"

"We are," Kirk said. "But they're not." He knew how Janeway would react to what he was going to say next, but that didn't stop him. "You see, the whole reason they're reaching out to us, attempting to communicate instead of just overwhelming us, is that the Totality loves us."

As Kirk expected, Janeway didn't appear to believe a word of what he had said. If she'd been capable of rising from her chair to mock him, he suspected she'd have done so.

"How do you propose we fight 'love,' Captain?"

Kirk said nothing, but tightened his hold on the message player, hoping the answer was somewhere in its contents.

Because right now, he had no answer for the admiral.

And he knew that, until he did have that answer, he would never see his son again.

26

When it had to, Starfleet moved quickly.

The provisional Starfleet Command agreed with Kirk's reasoning and did not transmit any information concerning the Totality's newly discovered weakness. The presumption was that every Starfleet vessel had at least one agent of the Totality on board as a spy, so Command would do nothing to warn them of what was to come.

Instead, just as in the days of Cochrane and the first great wave of human exploration, decades before the discovery of subspace radio, word went out by messenger.

One by one, starship commanders stationed in Earth's home system were visited by three representatives from Command and given verbal orders. One by one, the commanders issued orders for their crews to brace for increased gravity. By the dozens, crew on each vessel broke into black cubes and sand as the gravity load reached four hundred percent Earth normal.

On the ships that had been cleared of Totality projections, warp cores were brought back online, and once again starships set off at factors far beyond the speed of light.

Their first objectives were those vessels stranded between the stars. Ships that had managed to shut down and retain their warp cores were told to increase their gravity, then resume their warp travel for Earth.

Those that had ejected their cores were also instructed to increase their gravity settings, then wait for a refit team from the Starfleet Corps of Engineers. In the meantime, any urgent supply needs were noted, and any passengers with critical skills required for the fight against the Totality were allowed to transfer to warp vessels—Janeway's holographic doctor among them, checking that key personnel were able to function adequately under the gravitational strain.

The Spock Defense, as it came to be called, spread out from Sector 001 at warp nine. Special diplomatic envoys carried the information to the Klingon and Romulan Empires.

But even as the Federation's competitors were given help, one world of the Federation remained out-of-bounds.

Just as the Totality had first focused on the twin worlds of Romulus and Remus to establish a beachhead in this galaxy, another world appeared to have been chosen for their second attempt.

So it was decided to give the Totality one safe harbor to which they might withdraw. One planet on which they might feel protected. One planet that Starfleet could attack in force when the time came.

Thus, no Starfleet vessels traveled to Vulcan.

The strategy was cold, calculating, and endorsed by those senior Vulcan diplomats in Earth's home system.

Spock had given Starfleet a strategy for exposing Totality spies and keeping Starfleet facilities free of infiltration.

Kirk had given Starfleet the *Monitor* transmission, and in its secrets Starfleet scientists and engineers were convinced they had found the secret to creating weapons to drive the Totality from Federation space, and then the galaxy.

Vulcan would be the first battleground and, if all worked as planned, the last.

All it would take was time.

And that was the one thing Kirk didn't have.

Alone in his cabin, Kirk believed the only thing keeping him sane was the continual exposure to four gravities. Every movement required thought and planning. Exhaustion was a constant. The mere struggle to breathe and eat and make his plans with Spock, McCoy, and Scott left him little time for worry. Even less time for despair.

He was certain Norinda didn't want to harm his son.

But her means and motives, her actions and goals,

all seemed to shift over time, as if the Totality wasn't constant.

That meant Joseph might be safe for now.

But he wouldn't be safe forever.

Which was why, in less than twenty hours, the *Belle Rêve* would set off for Vulcan with the newest weapon in Starfleet's arsenal—a localized gravity projector.

A team of Starfleet engineers had created the device in less than a day, with Scott telling Kirk they'd done so simply by modifying two portable antigrav carriers to operate out of phase—the same technique Kirk had had Scott use to generate an artificial-gravity field outside the hull of the *Belle Rêve* during its battle with the *Enterprise*. The significance of mismatching the phase of the antigravs was that doing so caused their gravitational distortions to manifest at a distance, instead of on the surface of their contact plates.

The science of the device had been known since Kirk first joined Starfleet. He still had fond memories of the late-night gravity races he had excelled in at the Academy, when teams of midshipmen would compete to see who could toss a classmate strapped to antigravs the farthest and fastest around the main grounds late at night—without being caught.

But antigravs had given way to tractor beams. Because tractor beams were able to move objects by means of directed gravitons more efficiently than gravity-field generators, the technology had never been pursued.

Now, however, it was possible to use the jury-rigged device, just slightly larger than a standard phaser rifle, to create a meter-wide region of four gravities at a range of between three to twenty meters.

Kirk looked forward to using it on Norinda the next time their paths crossed. It wouldn't kill her. It wouldn't even harm her, Spock had confirmed. It would simply drive her away.

Away from him, and away from his child.

And when he had accomplished that, Kirk told himself, maybe then he could concern himself about the fate of the Federation.

All that mattered to him now was Joseph.

Joseph was what kept him from sleeping this night.

Kirk lay stretched out on his bunk in his cabin. He wore a small medical oxygen mask at McCoy's insistence to ease the effort of breathing during the night. But eyes open or closed, he saw only nightmarish images of Joseph decaying into black sand, slipping away from him and into Norinda's false embrace.

He knew he'd do anything to prevent that from happening.

His door chime sounded, startling him from his dark thoughts. He and Spock were to meet at 0600, still hours away.

"Lights," Kirk said to the computer, and his cabin brightened. "Identify."

A familiar voice came over the hidden cabin speakers.

"Jean-Luc. I trust I'm not disturbing you."

Kirk felt laughter bubble up in him that never reached the surface. The effort was too great. When *hadn't* Jean-Luc disturbed him in one way or another?

It wasn't that they didn't get along, he'd realized long ago. It was because they were so much alike.

"Give me a minute," Kirk said. Then he wrenched himself onto his side, placing his arm for a shove into a sitting position. He inhaled deeply three times, tugged off his oxygen mask, and with a grunt of exertion swung his legs off the bunk, pushed forward, and sat up.

He instantly slumped, catching his breath, supporting himself with both arms on the bunk's edge. His feet ached where they'd slammed into the deck.

"I'm disturbed now," Kirk said. He straightened his shirt; in four gravities, undressing for bed was a waste of effort. "Come in."

The door to the corridor slid open and Kirk was surprised to see Picard standing there as if four gravities was completely normal.

"Are you wearing an exoskeleton?" Kirk asked, annoyed that somehow Picard wasn't suffering as much as he was.

Picard waved Kirk over. "Step into the corridor."

Kirk gritted his teeth, but stood up and moved as smoothly as he could to the open door, willing his legs not to buckle under him.

Then he stepped through the doorway and experienced a sudden, intense wave of vertigo, as if the deck had given way beneath him.

And then he was light. His arms, lifted, buoyant. His knees no longer grinding and complaining. The sensation was almost as if he were floating.

"What's wrong with the gravity?" Kirk asked,

though he felt like rejoicing at the release of tension in his body.

"Starfleet's been experimenting," Picard answered with a grin, which disappeared almost as quickly as it had appeared. "We've been spreading word to the ships in the system about Spock's discovery. There've been cases of duplicated crew disappearing on every vessel whenever gravity's been increased. With the surveillance recordings the ships have been making, we've been able to go back and see where some of the substitutions have taken place."

"Engineering," Kirk said as he realized why gravity in the corridor was back to normal.

"Exactly," Picard confirmed. "Warp cores, powered up, are the Totality's pathway into our ships and facilities. As long as we keep four gravities set in every engineering department, we're safe from infiltration."

For a moment, Kirk was impressed. Then he remembered the effort he'd expended just to walk out to the corridor. "Then why was my cabin still set for four g's?"

"Starfleet orders—all command staff have to be placed in a four-gravity environment four times each day and before each strategic meeting. Just to be sure."

Now Kirk grinned, gestured to his cabin.

Picard clearly realized what Kirk wanted, frowned, but didn't argue. He braced himself in the doorframe, carefully stepped into the cabin. His shoulders sagged, the color draining from his face.

Kirk stayed in the corridor. Misery did love company.

"How long does Starfleet recommend command

staff remain in a four-gravity environment?" he asked innocently, adding, "I could go get some coffee, be back in an hour."

"The effect is apparently instantaneous," Picard said tightly. "So a minute is considered adequate."

Kirk decided he had had enough fun. "I'm convinced," he said, relenting. "Come out."

Picard stepped out of Kirk's cabin and rocked for a moment in the corridor, regaining his balance.

Kirk refrained from smiling. It was time to get down to business. "Since it's two hundred hours, I'll take a wild guess and say that Starfleet's come up with something critical that you've been asked to tell me."

Picard nodded. "Let's get that coffee."

27

"Earl Grey, hot," Picard said to the replicator in the *Belle Rêve*'s small galley.

"Actually," Kirk said behind him, "you don't want to do that."

"Yes, I do."

A steaming cup of tea appeared in the dispenser slot.

Kirk gave Picard a look of commiseration as if daring him to give it a try.

Picard sipped the tea. Cringed.

Kirk pointed to a wall locker. "I have real teabags in stasis pouches."

With relief, Picard put his teacup into the recycler and ordered boiling water. A few minutes later, he tried the fresh-brewed tea and smiled. "Much better."

Kirk sipped his own Vulcan espresso. "So?" It was all

the shorthand the two captains needed to start their conversation.

Picard began. "Starfleet Intelligence put their best analysts on the *Monitor* transmission. They've extracted a wealth of data already, and believe there's a great deal more."

"What kind of data?"

"The *Monitor* recorded the energy signature of a major projection of the Totality. Larger than a starship. A phenomenon they called 'the Distortion.' At the time, the *Monitor* was in intergalactic space, hundreds of thousands of light-years from the nearest star."

Kirk saw why those sensor readings might be valuable. "A perfect environment for the Totality. Local gravitational effects in that region would be insubstantial at best."

Picard nodded. "The projection is so large, we can actually see the dimensional interface between the Totality's realm of dark matter and our own normal space-time."

Kirk could see that Picard was building to a moment of truth. "And that's valuable because . . . ?"

"The dimensional energy signature is unique, and . . . it's been seen before."

Kirk waited.

"The *Monitor*'s deflector systems automatically went to full power as the Distortion closed in," Picard said.

"Which means the Distortion registered as having a physical presence."

Picard agreed, then added, "But the *main* sensors made no sense of what was before them. In fact, the bulk of the data we've recovered comes from analysis of the Distortion's optical properties only—how it appeared to ripple the light of galaxies behind it, how it appeared visually on the viewscreen. . . . At first, the crew thought they were seeing a cloaking device in action."

Kirk looked down at his espresso, trying to understand why what Picard was saying sounded familiar.

Picard continued as if prompting Kirk. "Other than the deflectors being triggered and recordings of the Distortion's visual appearance, every sensor scan reported density negative, radiation negative, and energy negative."

Kirk looked up with those words playing back in his mind, so tantalizingly familiar. "It's been a long time . . . but I'm sure I've heard those readings before." But he couldn't place the memory.

"I actually looked them up," Picard said, "almost three years ago."

Now Kirk was truly confused. "That's before any of this happened."

"But after you told me about your first run-in with Norinda."

Kirk nodded. "I remember. When we were in the desert on Bajor."

Picard nodded. "On vacation."

"What's the connection?"

"You told me how Starfleet had ordered you to locate Norinda's ship after they'd tracked it traveling at an impossible velocity."

"That's right. It was off the warp scale we used back then. Factor fifteen, I think."

"At that factor, where did they think it had come from?"

Kirk shrugged. This was all so long ago. "They were afraid to say it at the time, but it seems they were right. It was extragalactic. From—" And then as if he had been hit by a phaser beam, Kirk remembered where he had heard those readings for the first time.

"The galactic barrier."

In the early days of faster-than-light exploration, a handful of ships had tried to penetrate the mysterious energy barrier that surrounded the galaxy, and they had failed.

But after Starfleet had confirmed that Norinda's ship had indeed arrived on a trajectory from outside the galaxy, Kirk had been ordered to retrace her route. So it was that in the first year of his original five-year mission on the *Enterprise*, Kirk had reached the barrier and attempted to pass through it.

The effort had cost him the lives of three crew, including his best friend, Gary Mitchell.

And yet, in subsequent years and subsequent attempts, the *Enterprise* had managed to penetrate the barrier and survive without ill effects.

In debriefings, one theory raised by Starfleet Command suggested that the barrier had somehow "recognized" the *Enterprise* from its first attempt, and so had allowed it to pass.

Another theory held that the galactic barrier was weakening. Though at the time, since no mechanism had ever been found to explain its existence, whatever might be causing it to fade away also defied analysis.

Kirk saw the puzzle pieces fall into place, even

though the picture they formed wasn't yet complete. "Starfleet thinks there's a connection between the Totality and the galactic barrier?"

Again Picard nodded. "From the ongoing research into the phenomenon, there've been several compelling theories advanced that suggest the barrier is an artificial construct, perhaps put in place as much as four billion years ago."

Four billion, Kirk thought. That span of time was also something he had heard before.

Picard continued. "About six years ago, my crew took part in an experiment to penetrate the barrier by means of an artificial wormhole."

Kirk wasn't aware of that attempt. "Did you succeed?"

Picard's reply was enigmatic. "It's a long story, and by order of Command, off the record."

Kirk knew better than to try to get Picard to defy orders. "Where does that leave us?"

Picard took a sip of his tea, as if trying to put off what he had to say next as long as possible.

But time was up.

"Jim, this is extremely difficult for me."

Kirk went on alert. Nothing good ever came from a conversation that began with those words.

"Go on," he said.

"Starfleet Intelligence has identified a pattern which concerns them."

Kirk pushed ahead. "I take it I'm part of the pattern."

Picard nodded. "You were the first to make contact

with Norinda. A few months later, you passed through the galactic barrier, something that had been impossible up to that time. Then you made contact with Norinda on Remus."

"I stopped a civil war between Romulus and Remus that could've spread to two quadrants. And it wasn't all my doing, Jean-Luc. You were part of it, too."

Picard didn't respond to Kirk's interruption. He continued as if what he was saying had been rehearsed.

"And now, you've had contact with Norinda again, this time on Vulcan—a planet which Command believes is as you described it: under Totality control."

Kirk didn't like where this was going, and he could see Picard didn't either. "What's the final conclusion, Jean-Luc?"

"The Totality has demonstrated the ability to kidnap and absorb whoever they want, whenever they want. What seems to connect their victims is a victim's perceived ability to counteract the Totality's actions—as if they set out to eliminate potential enemies before launching their main attack.

"They've also demonstrated their ability to replace virtually anyone with a precise duplicate, again to undercut our ability to fight back."

Kirk didn't understand what Picard was trying to say. "What's your point?"

"Jim," Picard said bluntly, "this is what concerns Command: Why haven't they taken you?"

Kirk sat back on the galley bench, almost knocking

over his small cup of espresso. "They've tried. Norinda's tried. On Remus. At the Gateway. On the Vulcan space station."

Picard studied Kirk with a skeptical expression. "And yet you, of all the hundreds, perhaps thousands, of individuals whom the Totality's gone after, are the only one who's managed to evade them."

Kirk shook his head, couldn't believe what Picard was implying. "Jean-Luc, I escaped on the space station because Vulcan security guards rushed in and used their phasers against Norinda."

"Vulcan authorities," Picard said somberly, "whom you've already suggested are Totality projections."

"A setup?" Kirk asked. "Is that what Command thinks?"

"Truthfully," Picard answered, "Command doesn't know what to think. But they are concerned that you've had extensive interactions with the Totality, yet have been left in peace. They need an answer, Jim."

Kirk stared at his friend in open disbelief. "I've fought Norinda and the Totality each time our paths have crossed. I risked my life, and the lives of my friends, to bring Starfleet the information they need to fight the Totality. I am not a collaborator."

Picard wasn't swayed, repeated the question. "Then why do they leave you alone?"

Kirk had had enough. He jumped to his feet, using action to burn off his sudden frustrated anger. "I don't know and I don't care. I've done my duty. I've got the information and the equipment I came for. And now all I want to do is go back to Vulcan and get my son."

Picard rose calmly.

"I'm sorry. I can't let you do that."

Kirk was incredulous. "You have to."

"Jim, you'd do anything to save your son, wouldn't you?"

"Of course."

"That's why we can't risk letting you contact the Totality again."

Kirk made fists at his sides. "You think I'll reveal Starfleet's strategy to the Totality in exchange for my son."

"That's one possibility."

"The other one being that I've been feeding information to the Totality all along."

Picard didn't answer and Kirk knew his conclusion was correct.

"Do you honestly think that little of me? That I could be a traitor?"

"Honestly? You're not known for playing by the rules."

"The only rules I've broken are the ones that deserve to be."

"Who makes those decisions?"

Kirk threw out his hands in exasperation. "*We* do. The people on the edge of the frontier. The people who do things that no one's ever done before. Explorers, starship captains, you and me, Jean-Luc."

Picard's expression became almost wistful. "Once, perhaps, but . . . We're from two different ages, my friend. It's not the rules that've changed. It's the playing field."

"Give me a chance and I'll change your mind," Kirk said.

But Picard shook his head sadly. "Starfleet's preparing a task force to retake Vulcan. We'll find your son and get him back to you."

Kirk knew then that if Starfleet attacked the Totality and succeeded in making it withdraw, Joseph would be taken from him. Norinda would see to it personally.

Not for spite or revenge, but because Starfleet was right.

There *was* some special connection between Kirk and Norinda.

Kirk didn't know what it was, but he was certain Norinda did.

And to ensure that Kirk would seek her out and find her again, she had equipped herself with the perfect bait.

Joseph.

"I'm sorry, Jim."

"So am I," Kirk said.

"Will you come with me now? They'd like you on Mercury till this is over."

Kirk shook his head. "I don't think so."

Picard sighed, not looking for a confrontation. He tapped his combadge. "Picard to *Enterprise*."

The two captains held each other's gaze.

After a few seconds, Picard tapped his combadge again. "Picard to *Enterprise*."

"I'm surprised you haven't read the specifications for this ship," Kirk said. "Specifically, the equipment it has for blocking unauthorized communications."

Picard frowned, tapped his combadge. "Picard to

Starfleet Command." No response. "Picard to any station."

Nothing.

"Sorry, Jean-Luc," Kirk said, and meant it. "But I like to be prepared. Now, are you going to come with *me*?"

Picard's eyes widened. "Where?"

"You already know that answer," Kirk said. "If I can't change the rules anymore, then it's time to change the game."

28

Riker stared at Janeway in disbelief. "Are you certain Picard wasn't taken by the Totality?" he asked.

Janeway sat on the edge of her desk, gingerly. It was old, battered, something from a miner's office. Despite the fact that warp travel was possible again, Command had no plans to move off Mercury until the threat of the Totality had been eliminated. For the duration of that campaign, the abandoned mining complex attached to the oldest section of the Vostok Academy would continue to be Starfleet's provisional headquarters.

"With the gravity safeguards we have in place at every point of entry and exit, it's not possible," Janeway said. "I sent Jean-Luc to the *Belle Rêve* to return with Kirk—"

"Arrest him?" Riker interrupted.

276

Janeway's eyes narrowed at his choice of words. "Technically, no. We're concerned about Kirk, not convinced. We just wanted to keep him out of harm's way."

"And out of contact with the Totality."

"A precaution," Janeway confirmed. She looked at Riker more closely. "You seem troubled, Captain."

"James T. Kirk, a traitor? The idea that someone in Command could think that's possible . . . I do find it troubling."

"Not a traitor," Janeway said. "A loose cannon."

"As far as I know, that's exactly why you signed him on to command a Q-ship. You didn't have any trouble trusting him enough to be a covert agent for Starfleet Intelligence."

Janeway's voice did not lose its conversational tone, but her next words were cutting. "I imagine you had a special command relationship with Jean-Luc. As his first officer, it would be your duty to question his orders and discuss alternatives. But right now, you're a captain addressing an admiral. You and I do *not* have a special command relationship."

Riker clenched his jaw. "Yes, Admiral."

"To get back on topic. Two hours ago, the *Belle Rêve* broke orbit. Jean-Luc is not here. Neither is Jim Kirk."

Riker kept all inflection from his voice. "Maybe Kirk convinced Picard to join him."

"To do what?" Janeway said sharply. As uneasy as Riker was with the current situation, the admiral was clearly even more provoked. Riker was well aware that Kirk had that effect on some people. He revised that thought: most people.

"I don't know Kirk as well as Jean-Luc does," Riker

said. "Or as well as you probably do after this past year. But it seems obvious that the only reason Kirk returned to this system and tried to run the embargo was to get help for rescuing his son. I *do* know Jean-Luc, and that would be a compelling mission."

Janeway shook her head and spoke firmly. "Captain Picard's a Starfleet officer and this is a time of crisis—billions of lives are threatened. It's inconceivable that he'd abandon his ship and his duty to save one child."

Not for the first time, Riker felt a huge divide between Janeway and himself. Perhaps it was because she had risen through the science ranks, while he had come up on the command track. Perhaps she still carried scars from her perilous voyage through the Delta Quadrant and the losses she'd endured. But whatever had forged such an unyielding attitude in her, she definitely saw the universe in terms more extreme, more black and white, than he did.

He wondered how many crew a captain had to lose to gain those scars, to embrace that all-or-nothing approach to command.

Riker hoped he was fortunate enough never to find out.

"Since you ask, Admiral," he said, "I have no difficulty accepting that Captain Picard would attach great importance to the life of a single child, no matter whose child he was. And since it appears that Kirk's son is being held by the Totality, I'm not sure that I see how a decision by Jean-Luc to face the Totality can be considered abandoning his duty."

Janeway's eyes flashed, as if he had overstepped

himself again, but this time she stayed silent, listening. So Riker seized the opportunity, kept talking.

"As for abandoning his ship, if Jean-Luc considers Kirk's mission to be dangerous, it wouldn't be the first time he's shouldered extra risk to protect his crew. I frankly don't see the need for concern. At least, not with what we know at present." Riker forced himself to smile at the stern admiral, so she wouldn't overreact to his next suggestion. "Have you attempted to establish contact with Kirk's ship?"

Janeway's retort was swift. "All warp vessels are under subspace radio blackout and you know it."

"With apologies, Admiral, a simple inquiry to determine if Jean-Luc's aboard Kirk's ship would reveal nothing of our plans to take on the Totality."

"No subspace," Janeway snapped. Then she shook her head, moved off the desk, and stood for a moment as if collecting her thoughts. Riker watched, waiting, as she directed her gaze upward to the low, sagging, stained ceiling. Dark wires trailed down from a broken tile in the far corner, tangling and twisting until they disappeared into a chipped-open hole in the floor. It was all too easy for Riker to believe he was back in the primitive, imperfect days of the twenty-second century when this facility had been constructed. It might have been an exciting era for exploration, but living conditions on worlds that weren't M-Class left much to be desired. Mercury was no exception.

"You know, Captain," Janeway said, her eyes meeting his directly, "I'm not so sure you're right for this assignment."

Riker started, confused. He thought he'd been

summoned to discuss overall strategy and fleet disposition prior to the main advance on Vulcan. "I beg your pardon, Admiral. What assignment?"

"Recovering Jean-Luc and stopping Kirk."

Riker tried to keep the indignation from his response. "I'm perfectly suited to that task."

Janeway showed no sign of agreeing with him. "Because . . . ?"

"I agree that Kirk's no friend of Starfleet Command these days, but . . . he trusts me."

The admiral appeared to consider that as she began to pace. "The impasse between Kirk and Jean-Luc . . . you broke that."

"I offered them a way out of a no-win situation," Riker said, encouraged.

Janeway halted, turned. "What if Jean-Luc isn't Kirk's prisoner as I believe? If Kirk's managed to convince Jean-Luc to help him storm Vulcan to try to rescue his son—"

"Which I believe is more likely," Riker interjected.

"—how can I be sure Kirk won't convince you to switch sides, too?"

"We're all on the same side, Admiral. Kirk just has a different approach. More direct."

"It sounds as if you approve of what he's doing."

"I understand what he's doing. There's a difference."

"You think you can talk Kirk out of moving on Vulcan on his own?"

"Is it really important that he doesn't do that?"

Janeway seemed taken aback by his question. "Yes, Captain, it is. Kirk knows how we've managed to drive the Totality off our ships. He knows about the gravity-projector weapons. That information could be plucked from his mind by telepathy, *or* he might freely exchange it for his son."

Riker wanted to object, but truthfully, when it came to the safety of Joseph, Riker couldn't be certain how far Kirk might go. It *was* within the realm of reason that he might reveal Starfleet secrets, especially if he could convince himself that the revelation would cause no real harm.

Janeway studied him, seeming to intuit his thoughts. "So you *do* understand the importance of the mission."

Riker nodded, gave his reluctant confirmation. "Stop Kirk from making contact with the Totality and recover Jean-Luc."

"Then you have your orders." Janeway walked around the old desk, and took her seat. She activated a padd, then paused, without looking up at him, her fingers still on the padd controls.

"And you'll take the *Enterprise*."

Riker didn't conceal his surprise. "What about the *Titan*?"

"It's not ready for warp, the *Enterprise* is. And I presume you know that ship as well as, if not better than, your own." Janeway's tone was brisk, impersonal.

It was clear to Riker that he was being dismissed.

"Aye, Admiral."

"Good hunting, Captain."

"What are you really planning to do?" Picard asked.

Kirk ignored the question, put Picard's dinner tray on the small silver desk beside the bunk.

"I know how much your son means to you," Picard tried again, "but I still can't believe you'd jeopardize the existence of . . . well, of all life in this galaxy for his sake—not when there're other options."

Kirk sat down on the edge of the bunk, facing Picard across the small guest cabin. "Starfleet options?" Kirk asked.

"Jim, you have to know you'd have a better chance of saving Joseph if it was part of a concerted attack on the Totality."

"I don't know that at all, Jean-Luc. Neither do you."

Picard weighed his next words carefully. He estimated they were still twelve hours out from Vulcan. If the *Belle Rêve* arrived at that world and it did turn out to be under Totality control, then Starfleet's plan of attack would be in danger of being exposed. Somehow, he had to convince Kirk to change his mind and stay out of the Totality's reach.

"Jim, honestly, what can one man do against them?"

Kirk shrugged. "One man? I'm not sure. But you said it yourself: For some reason, the Totality leaves me alone."

Picard felt an icy chill move through him. "Jim, *are* you working with them?"

Kirk looked at him, eyes intent. "You know me better than that."

Picard shook off his misgivings. "You're right. I do. But then . . . have you any theories to explain why they treat you differently from anyone else?"

Kirk nodded.

"Well?" Picard asked.

"They're telepathic. Better you don't know. Just in case."

"In case they capture us?"

"In case they capture you."

"You truly don't think you're in danger from them?"

Kirk shook his head. "A year ago, I would have said yes. I was no different from anyone else. On Remus, Norinda tried to . . . to absorb me into the Totality, the same way she did Spock. But . . . she wasn't able to."

Picard tried to remember back to what he had heard then, on the communicator channel while in orbit of Remus. He thought back over the reports he had read after his debriefing at Starfleet Command. He didn't recall any mention of an attack on Kirk.

"You didn't include that in any of your after-action reports."

"It wasn't important."

"Jim, how could it *not* be important? If Norinda attacked you and that attack failed, then clearly you came up with some defense against her—a defense that could help us defeat the Totality."

"I know."

"So what was it? What did you do?"

"Me? Nothing."

Picard didn't understand. "But, you were alone with her. I mean, Spock was there . . . that's when we lost him and—"

Picard stopped in a moment of shocked realization.

Kirk hadn't beamed down to face Norinda alone. Norinda had demanded that someone else accompany him.

"Jim . . . was it *Joseph?*"

The words came from Kirk as if being torn from his heart. "Joseph stopped her. When I couldn't and Spock couldn't, he could."

Picard was astonished. He knew that Norinda had wanted Joseph under her control, but he'd assumed that was because she and her followers were trying to foment unrest between Romulus and Remus, and Joseph, hailed by some as the new Shinzon, fit into their plans. When Norinda had vanished and her divisive *Jolan* Movement had collapsed, Picard had expected that everything would return to normal.

"I think it's time you tell me what's so special about your son," Picard said.

Kirk's slight hesitation told Picard that if he didn't have an answer, at least he had suspicions.

"Jim," he urged, "Joseph could be of the utmost importance to the future of the Federation."

"He's a child."

"We're at war."

Picard's challenge went unanswered. He tried again, still urgent, but reassuring. "If you tell me what you know, all of Starfleet will work to keep your son safe."

Kirk's face was like stone.

"You're asking me to send my only child to war."

Picard couldn't speak as a father, only as a starship captain, and in that role it sometimes seemed he had been a soldier as often as an explorer. So as a soldier, he said simply, "If that's what it takes to win, yes, I am."

Kirk turned, went to the door, and it slipped open before him.

He paused there, looked back at Picard, face drawn by some terrible inner conflict that Picard would not dare presume to understand.

"He's my child, Jean-Luc. How can I place him in danger? How can I risk losing him?" Picard could see there was something more Kirk wanted to say, but this wasn't the time. "I love him," he said quietly. "I'll find another way to fight."

Kirk stepped into the corridor. The door slid shut and locked behind him.

Picard wondered if Kirk, in his parental anguish, had found the answer to Janeway's question: *"How do you propose we fight love?"*

Faced with the extinction of all life in the galaxy . . . perhaps all life in the universe . . . Kirk could not, would not, risk the one chance life might have to survive.

Was that the secret of the Totality's power? The secret that revealed why it couldn't be defeated?

Perhaps there *was* no way to fight love.

If so, the poets had known it all along.

Love did conquer all.

29

S.S. BELLE RÊVE
STARDATE 58571.1

When Kirk had had the *Belle Rêve* refit at Admiral Janeway's expense, he had equipped four small cabins with workbenches, computer consoles, and universal equipment racks, turning them into labs. They had become a favorite of the researchers he invited aboard, not the least reason being that the cabins he had chosen all had forward-facing viewports.

Eight hours out from Vulcan, Kirk found Spock in the largest of the four. He wasn't surprised. It was the best lab, with the best view, and even after a lifetime of serving in Starfleet, Spock was looking out the viewport at the stars.

"Will we ever get tired of them?" Kirk asked as he entered.

Spock stood with his hands behind his back, kept staring ahead as the stars streamed by above and below and to each side. "In the past, I found them peaceful."

Kirk stood beside Spock, puzzled by what his friend had left unsaid. "But not anymore?"

Spock angled his head, pursed his lips in consideration. "I spent a year within the Totality. They see stars differently—the equivalent of death. I still have echoes of that perception. It is an intriguing dichotomy, to be drawn to something, yet fear it."

Kirk smiled. "I can think of a great many things that fit that description." He looked away from the stars for a moment. "What does the Totality know of death?"

Spock didn't answer at once, and Kirk didn't hurry him. Spock had explained that he found it difficult to put into words what he had experienced during his time in that other realm.

"They do know of nonexistence," Spock finally said. "Not as a life-force overall, but as projections."

"Projections? That's their equivalent of individuals?" Kirk asked. "So they do know personal death?"

Spock nodded, eyes still fixed on the stars. "The projections do take on individual attributes, especially the more time they spend apart from their realm. Some become bolder than others. Some more thoughtful."

"Did you interact with any?"

"A few," Spock said, "though it was difficult. We had no real points of reference in common. Most times, I felt them around me, observing me as I interacted with other personalities that had been drawn into their realm."

"The people they had captured?" Kirk asked.

"Abductees, yes. As well as those they had replaced." Spock turned to Kirk, and as he spoke Kirk felt it was almost as if Spock was still trying to make sense of what he had experienced. "I found the range of their reactions to be . . . surprising."

"How so?"

"For some, there was a great deal of fear. The Totality took images from our memories, to create illusory environments that they hoped would put us at our ease. But the settings that resulted were far too confusing. A disturbing blend of places the abductees had been in the past, mixed with places they had only dreamed of, or imagined."

"Did you experience anything like that?"

Spock nodded. "My first experience of the Totality took place in a reconstruction of the mountains overlooking my family's estate. I was a teenager, and Norinda appeared to me as . . . someone I knew."

Kirk heard the hesitation in Spock's voice, and as a friend, he understood it was a memory Spock didn't want to discuss.

"Of the people you encountered," Kirk asked instead, "were there any who weren't afraid?"

"Some felt they were in an afterlife that corresponded to their religious beliefs. Most of those were surprised, but content. But others . . . as I said, there was always that presence, unseen, unfelt, but trying to pull us further into the experience. Out of our reconstructed environments and deeper into the Totality."

Kirk knew Spock well enough to understand what he wasn't saying.

"You were tempted," Kirk said.

Slowly, almost reluctantly, Spock gestured to the viewport. "It was much like these stars, Jim. Peace. Understanding. Belonging."

Kirk found that unexpectedly amusing. He turned away from the viewport, found a place to sit on one of the consoles. "How many worlds have you and I visited where the leaders told us they had the secret of a perfect society?" He laughed. "And all we had to do to achieve perfection is not ask any questions."

Spock kept his attention on the stars. "This wasn't the same."

Kirk didn't like the sound of that.

"You . . . believed it?"

Spock looked at Kirk with an almost apologetic expression. "I felt it. I felt . . . there was something more to understand, if only I would let down my guard and accept what they offered."

"Why didn't you?" Kirk asked.

Spock didn't answer.

"Spock?"

Spock bowed his head. "I don't know."

Kirk got up, moved closer to his friend. "Were you afraid?"

But Spock shook his head. "Not in the way you might think." He turned away from the stars then, as if he had seen enough. "Others went."

"Went?" Kirk asked. He didn't understand.

"Deeper into the Totality," Spock answered. "Some

of the crew of the *Monitor*. Some of the scientists who had been kidnapped, the Starfleet personnel who had been replaced. They felt the pull of the Totality and . . . they embraced it."

"What happened to them?" Kirk asked.

"That is the question," Spock said. "There is no way to know. Their minds . . . vanished from my awareness."

"You think they were killed?"

"No," Spock said with certainty. "I think they simply moved on to a realm of existence that we can know nothing about."

Kirk found that idea disturbing. "The ultimate reality of existence."

Spock nodded sagely.

Kirk was loath to ask his next question, but he knew he must.

"Do you think it's true?"

Spock shook his head. "You said it yourself. How many worlds have we visited where someone claimed to have that ultimate truth?"

Kirk sensed the hesitation in his friend, as if Spock didn't want to say anything to upset him.

"The Totality's not a world," Kirk said. "From everything you've told us, the nature of the universe makes the Totality inevitable."

Spock nodded. "But the nature of the universe also makes biological life inevitable, wherever conditions are suitable."

"A handful of planets," Kirk said. "A few moons. Places where the temperature is warm enough and wet enough long enough for chemistry to become biology. But for the Totality . . . it's the very structure of space and time that creates it. Everywhere."

Spock nodded slowly, as if Kirk were saying everything he dared not say himself.

Kirk looked at the stars through the viewport, anxiety growing. "What is life but the search for answers?"

Spock's words were quiet, measured, shocking. "In the Totality, we may have found them."

Long moments passed.

And then Kirk said, "I can't accept that."

Spock gave no indication that he was ready to argue the point. "You weren't there."

"That's what I mean," Kirk said. "According to what you've told me, you weren't there, either. Not where the 'truth' was being revealed. You said you felt the invitation. You saw or experienced people who accepted it. But they disappeared. If there is an ultimate truth, don't you think it'd be something that could be shared? Don't you think someone should be able to come back and explain it to us?

"But if it's like passing through the subspace event horizon in a black hole . . . a boundary from which no information can ever return . . . it might as well be death."

"Still," Spock said softly, "I wonder."

"That's the difference between the life we are and the life the Totality represents. We don't know the answers, so we go looking for them. The Totality claims to have the answers, but the only way *we* can hear them is by stepping into a black hole and *hoping* the Totality was telling the truth."

Spock looked at Kirk, and Kirk could see the wry humor in his friend, invisible to anyone else. "Ah, but why would Norinda start telling the truth now?"

But Kirk didn't laugh, didn't even smile.

"Was it hard to resist?" he asked.

"Yes," Spock said.

Kirk looked at the stars, wanted them to move faster.

If Spock found the Totality hard to resist, then what chance did a child have?

30

The Vulcan home system has no cloud of cometary debris. Over aeons, the gravitational dance of the Eridani stars has scattered all orbiting masses, except for the innermost planets that circled the largest of the three—Vulcan's sun.

But like every other member of the Federation, in response to the threat of the Totality, the Vulcans had established their own system-wide embargo. Thus, twelve light-hours out from its destination, the *Belle Rêve* was challenged by Vulcan Space Central.

Kirk sat ready in his command chair as all eyes on the bridge turned to him, waiting for his reply, and his orders. Scott was at navigation, McCoy at tactical, Spock at Kirk's side.

"What should I tell them?" Scott asked.

Kirk knew it didn't matter what he said. The result would be the same no matter what reply he gave. "It's been what, two hundred years or so since a Vulcan ship fired on an Earth vessel?"

Scott and McCoy looked alarmed, as if they expected Kirk to call for general quarters.

Spock replied with apparent disinterest. "Two hundred and twenty-seven point five seven years. It was at the time of the Vulcan Reformation."

As always, even if he should be used to it by now, Kirk was in awe of Spock's command of history.

"Let's not have history repeat itself," Kirk said. "Scotty, open a channel to Vulcan Space Central. Put it on the viewscreen."

With relief, Scott acknowledged the order.

A reserved-looking Vulcan female with short white hair appeared on the screen. A moment later, she raised an eyebrow, high, which told Kirk he had shocked her.

"James T. Kirk?" the Vulcan inquired.

"Correct," Kirk said. "I request passage for my ship and my crew."

The Vulcan's gaze shifted as she saw who else was on her screen. "Spock," she said with a knowing edge.

Spock politely inclined his head to her, said nothing. Kirk had already let him know what he thought they'd be facing. Conversation was not required.

"Ultimate destination?" the Vulcan asked.

"What does logic tell you?" Kirk replied.

The Vulcan smiled then, confirming Kirk's suspicions—she was no more a Vulcan than the security guards he had faced with Marinta.

"Drop out of warp at one million kilometers and continue at impulse," she said. "You'll be met by escort craft and directed to the proper coordinates."

Kirk returned the woman's smile. "Tell Norinda I'll see her soon."

The woman's un-Vulcan smile faded. "She'll be waiting, James. Vulcan Space Central, out."

The viewscreen snapped back to a view of the stars at warp, one orange star at the center of the screen brighter than the others.

"Mister Scott," Kirk said, "how long till we arrive?"

"Twenty-two minutes, sir."

Kirk stood up from his chair, gave it a last look. "It's fitting."

Spock gave Kirk a curious look.

Kirk explained. "Passing command to Jean-Luc. From one captain of the *Enterprise* to another."

"What're you mumbling about this time?" McCoy asked. He pushed himself up from his duty station and joined Spock at Kirk's side. He still hadn't completely recovered from the strain of two days spent under four gravities.

"You're just dropping me off, Bones. Then you'll be letting Jean-Luc out of his cabin and giving him command of the ship."

McCoy reacted with as much surprise as the duplicated Vulcan had shown—though in his case, he didn't hide it. "Who came up with that harebrained scheme?" He stared fixedly at Spock as if he already knew the answer.

Kirk looked past Spock and McCoy. "Scotty, are we still being pursued?"

"Aye, that we are. Th' *Enterprise* is three hours behind and closing fast."

"My fight's with Norinda," Kirk said to McCoy. "Jean-Luc's fight . . . your fight . . . the whole Federation—"

"The Totality," McCoy said in resignation.

"All I want is my son back." Kirk put a hand on the arm of his chair. "The person who sits here, he needs to want more."

McCoy snorted in disdain. "You think this tub and one starship can defeat the Totality?"

"It's not one starship, Bones, it's the *Enterprise*. Spock knows what to do. Jean-Luc will coordinate the ships. And in a little less than a day, the Totality will be an unpleasant memory and you're going to be looking after Joseph again."

McCoy furrowed his brow. "I don't like the way you said that. Why aren't *you* going to be looking after Joseph?"

Kirk had made his decision and his peace. He didn't need to or want to talk about either. "There's only one way Norinda's going to release Joseph." He knew how difficult this would be for his friends. "So his future is going to be up to you and Spock and Scotty because—"

"Don't say it," McCoy warned.

Kirk heard the anger in McCoy's voice, the frustration, knew the love that both emotions sprang from.

But he had to tell his friends the truth.

"This time, I won't be coming back."

*　　*　　*

It was night in Shi'Kahr, and the boulevards were quiet.

Kirk had anticipated as much.

Tall buildings surrounded the plaza where Scott had beamed him, directly to the coordinates he'd been given. The buildings' windows blazed with lights. The cityscape before him glowed with russet, red, and amber—the rich colors of the smooth-skinned towers that rose all around him. Their flowing corners and smooth contours harkened back through the centuries to the birth of Vulcan architecture, when primitive structures had been formed from simple clays and baked in the sun.

Vulcan would always be a world of tradition, ensured by the fact that mind-melds kept ancient memories alive for generations.

Kirk wondered if mind-melds were the reason this ancient city, Vulcan's capital, was so quiet tonight.

Had the word gone out, flashing from mind to mind, that the governing authority no longer existed, its politicians and civil servants replaced by duplicates? Did Vulcans huddle in their homes, meditating, seeking the solace of logic in the face of the Totality? Or had the Totality's own telepathic energies found Vulcans to be open receptors, their minds defenseless before an enemy that turned their own strengths, their own intellects, against them?

It was not a question he could answer. It was not a question he wanted to answer. There were others better equipped than he to undertake that struggle.

Tonight, in the vast and dark and silent city, he had only one goal, one purpose.

He walked across the empty plaza toward the glaring beacon of light that stood out so prominently from the subdued tones of Shi'Kahr.

Ahead of him, constructed with the bold angles and sharp corners of presumptuous human architecture, bathed by banks of light that matched the blue-white spectrum of Earth's sun, was the great hall of Starfleet Command's Joint Operations Center.

Vulcan Space Central was headquartered there.

And it was there, he'd been told as the *Belle Rêve* had been escorted into orbit, that he was expected.

The warm dry wind of the Vulcan night made his dark jacket flutter. He heard the fabric snap against the inductance barrel of the gravity-projector weapon he carried strapped to his back.

Kirk's boots made staccato echoes as he drew near the wide, brilliantly lit walkway that ran from the plaza to the building's entrance.

No one barred his way.

Even the guard kiosks, usually staffed at all times, if only for ceremonial reasons, were empty.

Kirk glanced down at the combat tricorder strapped to his wrist.

He wasn't even being scanned.

Either the Totality already knew everything there was to know about him and what he carried with him this night, or Norinda had decided that in no way could he ever represent a threat.

Kirk looked forward to changing her mind.

He entered the blinding white building, walking

beneath the gleaming silver emblem of Starfleet Command.

One last time, he thought.

The entry hall was empty, and it shouldn't have been.

On an ordinary day, or night, hundreds of beings would be in motion across the polished white marble floor, some hurrying, some walking slowly in hushed conversation, many in Starfleet uniforms, others in alien garb.

But it was as if Starfleet had already been defeated.

The only sound in the cavernous space was the white-noise rush of the fountain, where a cascade of clear water shimmered down a carved stone replica of the great seal of the Federation.

Kirk had been given no exact instructions, other than to arrive at this building. Another person might have waited in the desolate hall with its towering glass walls and arching, light-studded ceiling.

Not Kirk.

Since there was no one here to greet him, he walked directly to the moving stairways leading to the upper level. Banks of bronze-doored turbolifts were there. They would take him to the command level.

The moving stairways were motionless.

He took that to be a good sign because he knew they operated by gravity control. The Totality obviously had reason not to have operational gravity generators nearby.

Kirk climbed the sleek, static stairs.

As he reached the upper level, a single turbolift chimed.

Its open door was an invitation.

Kirk accepted, entered. The lift dropped.

The swift ride lasted thirty seconds, long enough to take him five hundred meters underground. Time enough for Kirk to recall that the Vulcans had been insulted when humans had insisted on burying Starfleet's regional command center beneath half a kilometer of dispersal shielding. Where was the logic, Vulcans had protested, in thinking that an enemy could penetrate far enough into the Federation, and then far enough into the Vulcan home system, to be a threat to this center?

But after V'Ger had come within seconds of obliterating Earth, and the Vulcans had done a quick check of how many space probes *they* had lost mysteriously over the centuries, their objections quickly faded.

There was logic in being prudent, after all, they decided.

The turbolift door opened.

Kirk stepped into a small entrance foyer, saw a series of three varicolored emblems worked into the polished white floor.

One was a stylized IDIC showing Mount Selaya, marked with Vulcan script. Another was the Starfleet emblem. The last was a variation of the Federation seal, ringed in English and Vulcan script.

Kirk walked across them, heading for the sliding translucent partitions that shielded the command center beyond.

He had been here before, several times, and even

as an active Starfleet captain, then admiral, he had been challenged by armed guards on this level.

Tonight, it was as deserted as the city above.

For a moment as he paused before the partitions, Kirk wondered if there were any Vulcans left at all on this world. Could it be possible that they had *all* been absorbed into the Totality?

The silhouette of a hand appeared on the partition directly in front of him, glowing green—the color of Vulcan blood and thus a sign of warning.

He placed his hand against the silhouette.

The partition slid open.

He stepped into the command center for Vulcan Space Central—a dark, domed room constructed like a stadium-size version of a starship's bridge.

Kirk scanned the multiple display screens on the far side of the curved wall. Each screen—ten meters tall, fifteen wide—showed complex moving graphs and charts related to orbital space around Vulcan and her planetary system. Banks of silver-gray workstations rose in graduated tiers, ringing the outer wall, looking in to the center and to the main screens. And there, in the center, he counted nine chairs on a raised dais. Each of the chairs was balanced on a single pointed stalk instead of multiple legs—a rare case of Vulcan technology employed strictly for aesthetic effect. Each also had small display screens and input padds angled out from its arms.

Kirk knew that more than a hundred technicians, and Starfleet and Vulcan Planetary Defense personnel, should be working here at any given time.

But even this facility was deserted.

He stepped up on the dais.

On each of the nine chairs, the small display screens rolled with static, as if they had all been taken offline.

As if this center no longer served a purpose.

It took Kirk only a moment to decide that that was the message Norinda wanted to send him: According to the Totality, *nothing* here was necessary anymore.

That last thought had just settled in his mind when Norinda spoke quietly behind him.

"You're right, James."

Kirk jumped forward, spun around, swinging his gravity weapon from his back to aim it at—

Norinda wasn't there.

He slowly turned on the dais. No sign of anyone.

Her voice fluttered in his ear again. "Why do you resist?"

Kirk snapped around.

No one. Nothing.

He was being toyed with. Taught a lesson.

"I'm not resisting," he called out, and his words echoed in the empty room. "I'm here."

"With a weapon?" He couldn't tell where Norinda's voice came from. It was as if she were invisible.

"We need to talk," Kirk said. He pointed the weapon to the ceiling, keeping it ready, but not threatening.

"That's all I've ever wanted," Norinda said.

"Show yourself," Kirk demanded.

Norinda's light laughter echoed through the empty center. "Say what you truly mean, James."

"Show me my son."

"I'll show you Joseph," Norinda's voice whispered. "But he's not your son anymore. . . ."

Those words constricted Kirk's heart, even as the hiss of a sliding door spurred him to instant action.

He turned again, weapon held ready, to see light from a corridor flood into the room, capturing someone in silhouette and shadow before it.

The figure walked forward, familiar, but different.

The door slid shut, the glare of the outside light was ended.

"Joseph . . . ?" Kirk said, in recognition, in doubt.

The dark skin was right, the dappling, the ridges . . . his mother's gently upswept pointed ears.

But his son was taller, broader in the shoulders, no longer a child of twelve . . . older, a teenager, almost a man.

"Joseph," Kirk said again as his son stepped up on the dais. "What's happened to you?"

The boy—the youth—looked down at his hands as if seeing them for the first time and noticing that he had changed. "Nothing that isn't supposed to," he said.

His voice was deeper. His eyes dark, so like his mother's.

"Father," he said.

Somewhere in his being, Kirk registered the word as a form of address, not a term of endearment. Not the breathless shout of "Dad!" or the happy, childish cry of "Daddy!"

He had been apart from his son for less than a week, but it might as well have been five years.

Kirk quickly glanced around the command center

303

again, saw no sign of Norinda. "It's time to go," he said.

But Teilani's child, Kirk's son, the sum total of their life and love and legacy, was no longer theirs. No longer Kirk's.

"No," Joseph said. "My place is here . . ."

Kirk could not drive the next words from existence.

". . . with Norinda."

And like a shadow becoming real, a shifting patch of darkness rose up from the dais and floated into a column that became the creature Kirk had met so long ago, in the Mandylion Rift.

Absolutely beguiling, enchanting, desirable, and deadly.

She laughed as she embraced Kirk's son, and claimed him.

Kirk knew it was the sound of victory.

31

Having is not so pleasing a thing as wanting.

It was an old Vulcan saying, and it was foremost in Riker's thoughts as he sat in the captain's chair on the bridge of the *Enterprise*. It was the command Riker had always wanted, but now that it was his, he felt he was an interloper.

Because the *Enterprise* was more than a ship. Indeed, he had served on two vessels to bear the name. But the crew had remained the same, as had the captain.

The first time Riker had declined a command of his own, he had done so for no other reason than to advance his career. Far better to be the executive officer on any of the *Galaxy*-class starships than commander of a smaller ship that would never be given a mission to push out beyond the edges of the Federation's frontier.

But twice more during his posting on the *Enterprise*, command had been offered and Riker had declined. Both times, he knew, it was because his career path had been redefined. He didn't want to be commander of just any starship—he wanted to live up to the ideals and the tradition of the *U.S.S. Enterprise*.

Then came the day when he finally realized that Picard and his *Enterprise* should never be separated.

When Jonathan Archer had retired from Starfleet, his *Enterprise* had been given a place of honor in orbit of Pluto, and millions had walked its corridors since, awed by the history that ship had seen and made. Kirk's last *Enterprise* had likewise been retired with no thought of giving it to another commander.

With that realization, Riker had sought and been given command of the *Titan*.

Yet scarcely a year later, Picard's *Enterprise* was his.

Sitting in Picard's command chair, reflecting on the ironies of his own desire, watching the bridge staff work efficiently, he became aware of Troi watching him.

She smiled, and he knew she understood exactly what he was feeling. "You're only borrowing the ship, Will. You did it before. And you gave her back."

Riker accepted her encouragement. When Picard had been assimilated by the Borg, Riker had been temporarily promoted to captain of the *Enterprise*. At the time, no one had thought it would be possible to reclaim a drone from the collective, but Picard had returned to them. Riker hoped the same miracle might be accomplished when it came to recovering someone from the Totality. Certainly, the return of Spock suggested it was possible.

But everything would depend on what it was the Totality truly wanted. And for now, Riker couldn't be sure.

Long-range sensors had revealed that the *Belle Rêve* had passed through the Vulcan embargo without slowing, and even now was in orbit of that world.

Riker had no doubt that Kirk was intent on confronting the Totality, and he feared that in some way the Totality was intent on confronting Kirk. Riker had no way of knowing what drove the Totality, though he could understand why a father would be driven to the act of desperation Kirk had embarked upon. But what was inexcusable was that Kirk had either kidnapped Picard, or convinced him to assist in the foolish, hopeless endeavor.

Riker looked around the dark bridge of the *Enterprise,* already feeling the grief of loss.

Who would command her now?

"Captain," Worf growled from the tactical station. "We are receiving an emergency subspace transmission."

Riker sat forward in his chair. All Starfleet vessels and allied ships were operating under subspace-radio blackout in order to keep the secret of gravity adjustment away from the Totality as long as possible. But an emergency subspace message from Command could

mean that something new had been discovered—
a tactic, perhaps, that couldn't wait.

"From Admiral Janeway?" Riker asked.

Worf, as always, was gruff and to the point. "No. It
is from Captain Picard. He is under attack."

Twenty seconds after Kirk had beamed down, the
Belle Rêve had gone to warp directly from orbit of
Vulcan.

It was a maneuver forbidden because of the havoc
it played on the planet's sensor and communications
networks. The two vessels that had escorted the ship
to a geosynchronous orbit within range of Shi'Kahr
were taken by surprise.

Spock had no wish to warn them of his plans, so,
unlike Kirk in his confrontation with Picard, he had
ordered the *Belle Rêve* to warp without any de-
tectable initialization period.

But in less than a minute, the escorts had apparently received their orders and gave chase.

In the command chair on the *Belle Rêve*'s bridge,
Spock watched the two Vulcan vessels closing relentlessly on the center viewscreen. He knew his ship
could outrun them, given time.

But for what Kirk had asked him to do next, time
was not a variable.

In his locked cabin, Picard was a caged animal.

He had felt the *Belle Rêve* drop into normal space
and seen Vulcan through his viewport. Then, only a
minute after settling into orbit, the ship had slammed
back into warp.

Now he heard phaser volleys impinging on the shields.

Kirk, he decided, either had gone crazy or was dead.

His door chime sounded.

Picard turned from the viewport and the streaking stars, folded his arms in disdain and defiance. "What is it?"

The door slid open to reveal Doctor McCoy, the frail physician with an attitude at least as tough as the *Belle Rêve*.

"Time to abandon ship?" Picard asked.

"I already asked that question," McCoy said with the barest flicker of a smile. "But Spock says that wouldn't be logical."

"Spock?"

"He's keeping your seat warm, Captain." McCoy nodded to the open door. "You're wanted on the bridge."

Chief Engineer Scott lacked the piloting expertise of Captain Sulu, but finesse and precise maneuvers weren't needed to break through the Vulcan embargo the second time around.

Between the *Belle Rêve*'s original design specifications and Scott's year's worth of tinkering and improvement, the ship had no need to evade Vulcan fire; it had only to keep flying, shields shedding phaser energy and quantum-torpedo disruptions like sea spray from the back of a breaching whale.

"Well done, Mister Scott," Spock said.

"I wish I could take all the credit for it," the engineer replied, not looking up from the flight controls.

"But that's the sorriest attempt at an embargo I've ever seen."

Spock understood. According to the sensor readings displayed on the right-hand screen, only the original two escort ships remained in pursuit of the *Belle Rêve*. None of the picket ships on embargo duty appeared to have warp capability. From their delayed responses, none appeared to have realized that the *Belle Rêve* was attempting to leave the system.

To Spock, the logic of the situation was clear. "I believe that means not every ship in the system is under Totality control. The vessels ordered to enforce the embargo evidently were not warned of our approach, and I suspect one reason for their lackluster attempt to stop us is that their commanders are questioning their orders."

Scott glanced back at Spock. "I'm still takin' some credit for gettin' us through that mess."

"As well you should, Mister Scott."

The turbolift opened and Picard stormed onto the bridge. He quickly took in the images on the three viewscreens. "What's our status?"

"Shields at ninety-five percent," Scott answered crisply. "Holding at warp-eight-point-five. Our two Vulcan friends in pursuit are closing at eight-point-six."

Picard turned to Spock. "Why aren't we outrunning them?"

"They're to be the subject of an experiment," Spock said, "for which we will need the assistance of the *Enterprise*."

Spock could see Picard working to control his frustration. "And the *Enterprise* is where?"

"Rendezvous in thirty-eight minutes at our present heading," Scott said. "Provided we can break subspace radio silence t' let them know that's what we're planning."

Spock got up from the command chair, gestured to it.

Now Picard seemed more confused than angry. "Why do you need me for any of this?"

"Captain Kirk described his last encounter with you on his approach to Earth. We have no time for the same distrust to impede what we must do now."

"Which is?" Picard asked.

"Destroy the Totality. Preferably in time to save Captain Kirk."

Picard's confusion escalated. "Doctor McCoy said Jim's on Vulcan."

"And Vulcan, for now, is the maw of the beast. Please, Captain, contact the *Enterprise*. There is a way to fight the Totality, but we must act quickly and definitively, before they have time to develop a countermeasure."

Picard took the center chair, though Spock could see he was still skeptical of what he'd been told.

"Mister Scott," Picard said, "open a channel to the *Enterprise*."

McCoy coughed from his console. "On this ship, that's my job."

Picard waved his hands in dismissal. "Then . . .

carry on, please." He stared pointedly at Spock. "And I want to know *everything* that Jim has planned."

Spock gave a small Vulcan shrug. "I am prepared to tell you. But Jim has warned me, you're not going to like it."

Picard sighed. "Of that I have no doubt."

Spock began his briefing.

32

All things ended, Kirk knew.

Nothing made that more clear than holding a newborn baby. The promise of a new life by definition meant the end of the old.

With love, James T. Kirk and Teilani of Chal had joined their lives to create Joseph, their vanguard to the future, their declaration of faith that there would be a future and that those would be the days worth living for, better even than the present.

So Kirk had known there would come a day when Joseph would stand apart from him, a child no longer, but a participant in the great chain of humanity that stretched from the chaos of the unknowable past to the wonder of an inconceivable future.

But he had never imagined the day would come like this, with his child *taken* from him.

A thousand pleas and warnings raced through Kirk's mind as he saw his son embraced by a monster so beguiling, no child could be expected to see through her disguise.

But all Kirk could say in the emptiness of the command center was "Joseph, no . . . not like this."

Joseph smiled at Kirk as if in pity, the future looking down at the past. "You know I don't belong with you," he said.

"That's not true."

Joseph traced the ridges of his forehead, his finger trailing to a pointed ear. "Look at me. I'm not like you. I'm not like Mother."

"No child is," Kirk pleaded.

Joseph's smile vanished, his face became hard. "I'm not a child."

Kirk closed his eyes as he struggled to think of a response. And when he opened them again, he knew there was nothing more he could say.

Norinda had changed.

In the past, she had taken on the form of the female most attractive to the male she communicated with. Kirk now realized the reason for the tactic: sex was a driving force of biological life, and so that was the one overpowering attribute the Totality had sought to command.

In the past, when Norinda had appeared before Joseph on the *Belle Rêve* and on Remus, she had appeared as Teilani, breaking Kirk's heart, but calling up lost memories of comfort and maternal love no child could resist.

But Joseph had said he was no longer a child, and

Kirk saw that was true because Norinda now appeared as she had in the surveillance images captured at the Gateway.

Her skin was dark like Joseph's, her forehead ridged, her temples dappled, her ears pointed, all like Joseph's. She had willed herself into a female version of whatever species Joseph was, and Kirk instinctively knew that was the reason his child, for whom not even McCoy could predict a gender, had become, at last, a male.

"Can't you see what she's doing?" Kirk asked.

Norinda leaned her head against Joseph's shoulder. "He knows exactly what I'm doing," she said. "Love, James. It's all that the Totality offers, all that the Totality is." She looked at Joseph with admiration and wonder. "I love him."

Kirk could see Joseph swept up in the emotional power and appeal of Norinda's devotion.

"I belong," Joseph said, his voice husky with desire.

"Not with that thing," Kirk said.

Norinda glared at him, eyes narrowed. "Don't interfere."

Kirk studied her, and his next question was obvious.

"Then why don't you stop me?"

Norinda didn't answer, glanced at Joseph, stared again at Kirk as if in indecision.

Kirk pressed his advantage though he still didn't understand why he had one.

He held out his hand, taunting his son's captor.

"You've been trying to take me into your realm,

315

like you did to Spock. So go ahead. Here I am. No resistance!"

There was enough about Norinda that was human that Kirk could see in her eyes that there was nothing more she wanted to do than to claim him.

But she didn't reach out to him.

Kirk seized the moment, just as he had when he had rushed the Vulcan officer in the marketplace, counting on even one second's delay to give him the advantage.

He swung up his gravity weapon and fired it point-blank at Norinda.

But Joseph was Kirk's son and instinctively jumped between the weapon's barrel and Norinda.

If he had expected to take a phaser blast or projectile impact, he was mistaken.

There was no energy beam, no distortion of the air, but Joseph suddenly cried out in pain as he doubled over, his legs collapsing as he was subjected to a gravity load almost four times stronger than Vulcan normal.

Kirk felt sick at having hurt his son, clicked off the weapon at once, but then charged between the improbably balanced chairs to fire at Norinda from the side.

He caught her as she leapt off the platform, trying to escape.

She slammed into the dark acoustic floor tiles as if she had fallen eight meters, not one.

Kirk stepped slowly to the side of the dais, keeping the humming weapon trained on Norinda's body.

He saw the edges of her begin to darken, begin to

crumble into black sand, as if she were being charred by volcanic flames.

She pushed herself up, tried to crawl out of range.

She left a trail of darkness, reverting to her shadow form.

Kirk allowed himself a moment of triumph.

He had been ready to sacrifice himself for his son. But now he would have another chance. There was still time.

And then Joseph hurled himself at Kirk and drove him off the platform to the floor.

Kirk gasped as he hit and rolled, his son's mass crushing him as he landed on top.

A sharp pain in his lower chest told Kirk he'd snapped a rib.

Stars of pain exploded in his vision as he attempted to draw a breath. Then the pain of his ribs was eclipsed by the pain in his hand as Joseph, instantly back on his feet, kicked the gravity weapon out of Kirk's grip.

Kirk hugged his hand to his chest, wincing as he realized his index finger was broken.

Then, as if Kirk were no more than a child himself, Joseph grabbed his jacket and hauled him to his feet.

Kirk wavered. The control room spun around him. His hand throbbed and each breath set fire to his chest.

"You can't control me anymore," Joseph said. His face had darkened with rage and exertion. His other hand was clenched into a fist.

Kirk refused to accept the evidence of his eyes.

"I didn't give you this anger," he told his son.

"Think back . . . think back and remember . . . all I offered you was love and acceptance. You *always* belonged."

Joseph hesitated.

"Think for yourself. She's been manipulating you," Kirk said. "Controlling you. . . ."

Norinda, restored, stepped up behind Joseph, ran her hands over his shoulders and onto his chest, pressed against him as if for protection. "He's lying again," she whispered. "Everything he says about me is a lie because he's jealous."

"I want to live my own life," Joseph said.

"You can't with her," Kirk warned. He shot a quick glance to the floor to locate the gravity weapon. It was three meters away, and its operating lights still glowed. "She'll absorb you into the Totality."

"Liar," Norinda said, as if Kirk's claim was of no importance. Then, so quickly that the movement was a blur, her arm shot out, stretched into a black ribbon, and *shattered* the gravity weapon, sending its components tumbling and sparking across the dark floor, leaving Kirk defenseless.

Joseph didn't seem to notice. He kept his attention on his father, eyes burning with the indignation of youth. "Then why hasn't she done it?"

For a moment, pain and desperation fell from Kirk. Joseph was right. *Why* hadn't Norinda acted against Joseph?

Kirk had assumed that she had taken Joseph to use as bait to capture him. But now that Kirk was here, she had taken no action against either of them.

The answer came to Kirk like a lightning bolt.

Norinda couldn't claim either one of them.

Kirk knew she had tried to take him into her realm of dark matter on Remus, but other than his arm momentarily appearing to corrode into darkness, nothing had happened.

Kirk stood straighter, filled with the power of knowledge. He ignored the pain in his ribs, in his hand.

"Because she *can't* harm us," Kirk told his son. "There's something about us, you and me. Maybe our genes. Maybe something alien I was exposed to in Starfleet." A smile played over Kirk. Wasn't that what Starfleet Medical had said about McCoy's astounding longevity? That he had been exposed to something in his career?

It had to be the same explanation for Kirk. There *was* something special about him. Something *he'd* passed on to his child.

"You're finished," Kirk said as he began to advance on Norinda. "*I'm* the weapon that will keep the Totality away."

Joseph stepped forward in confrontation. "Stay away from her."

"I know what she's like, Joseph. I know how she can distract and confuse—"

Kirk suddenly gasped as Joseph struck him in the face.

"You don't know a thing about her," he said.

Kirk put his hand to his face, the shock of actually being struck by his child more painful than the physical blow.

"Joseph, no. . . ."

The youth stepped closer, punched Kirk again in the chest, turning his broken rib into a white-hot steel lance.

Kirk choked with the pain, stepped back in agony. "You don't understand . . ." he said, his voice faltering.

He had never felt so old, never felt such a failure.

"If you want to go after her," Joseph said, still advancing, powerful, unbowed, with all the force and assurance of youth, "you have to take me out first."

He stood there then, hands at his sides, making no attempt to protect himself.

Kirk was within arm's reach of Joseph.

He could never defeat his son's strength, evade his speed, or match his endurance.

But Kirk had years of Starfleet combat training. He had learned the Eighteen Strikes of Vengeance from a Klingon Master. Spock had taught him how a sudden, sharp blow to any one of six nerve clusters could bring down any human.

Kirk could not defeat Joseph in any kind of fight. But with his experience, all he had to do was raise his hand against his son once, and Joseph would be unconscious before he hit the floor.

One strike. One hit.

Against his own child.

To do so would be inconceivable.

There were no rules to change, no new game to play.

Kirk had finally met the one opponent he couldn't defeat, because it was the one opponent he would never harm.

Joseph appeared to sense his father's acceptance of defeat.

"In time, you'll understand," Joseph said.

"I already do," Kirk said with sorrow.

Norinda slipped up against Joseph, turned his head to hers, kissed him deeply.

Kirk looked away.

Norinda laughed.

"Don't worry, James," she said kindly, "you'll feel better soon."

Kirk looked back at Norinda, wondering what she meant.

"It's time for you to receive your gift."

Kirk was confused. That's what the Totality called it when they captured humans and brought them into their realm.

"Accept," Norinda said as she walked toward Kirk, arms outstretched. "Embrace," she said, and her arms dissolved into black tendrils that flowed through the air like smoke to wrap gently around Kirk.

"Be loved," she said.

Pain danced like electricity across Kirk's skin as he felt himself dissolving in Norinda's grasp.

Her face was so close to his, changing back to the human form it had when he had first met her.

"That's right," she said in a childish, teasing voice, "you were wrong. There's nothing special about *you* at all."

Overcome by defeat, Kirk felt his body decay into nothingness as he was absorbed at last into the Peace of the Totality.

33

"Surrender?" Riker said.

On the viewscreen of the *Enterprise*'s bridge, Picard appeared to be as pleased with the strategy as his former first officer.

"For this to work," Picard explained, "we have to get close enough to the Vulcan ships to take them off-guard." His voice and image sparkled with interference, and there was a definite time lag between exchanges. Instead of using subspace, the *Enterprise* and the *Belle Rêve* were communicating by laser transmissions—an old but effective method of evading eavesdroppers. In this case, the eavesdroppers were the two Vulcan cruisers chasing Picard's vessel, within minutes of arriving, weapons armed.

"It isn't quite what I had in mind for my first command action on this ship," Riker said.

Picard smiled ruefully. "Just don't get too used to that chair."

Riker returned the smile. "Is there anything else Geordi needs to know?"

"Just follow Mister Scott's lead and . . . hope for the best. *Belle Rêve* out."

Riker tapped his combadge. "Geordi, did you get all that?"

La Forge answered from engineering. *"Sure did, Captain."*

"Think it'll work?"

"Could get tricky if they try to board us while we're attacking. But if Starfleet's tested it, I'm ready to give it a shot."

Riker was tempted to remind La Forge that Picard had said the artificial-gravity distortion techniques had been tested "in simulation," but he decided not to add any additional distractions to what was already a complex situation.

When Spock had returned from the realm of dark matter with the knowledge that gravity was what kept the Totality away from the stars and galaxies, he had provided the key to the new strategy. Then Starfleet's Department of Advanced Research had demonstrated proof of concept at Mercury, for using projected gravity fields as a weapon. Now Admiral Janeway was spearheading the crash program to use the new technology to engage the Totality at Vulcan, and, if need be, drive them from the Federation one world at a time.

Somehow, Riker wasn't surprised that in the midst of such an enormous undertaking, James Kirk had found a way to apply it to a personal mission. He had also been heartened to learn that Picard really had been kidnapped by Kirk. But he was even more pleased that Picard had since made up his mind to do anything he could to help his fellow captain recover his son. And if Kirk's personal quest offered the chance that the Totality could be defeated at the same time, so much the better.

"We are being hailed by the Vulcan cruisers," Worf announced.

Riker exchanged a look with Troi, gratified to have her at his side again. He saw that she was ready, straightened his jacket, and told Worf to put the signal onscreen.

A sallow young Vulcan in a combat helmet appeared.

"*U.S.S. Enterprise,*" the Vulcan said coolly, "you are infringing on Vulcan territory. Drop from warp and prepare to be taken in tow."

Riker knew he had to appear to surrender for Picard's plan to work, but he had to make it look good. So with practiced offense, he refused the demand. "We're well outside your system's territorial boundaries."

"In the current situation, new rules apply. All ships traveling at warp are presumed to be enemy vessels. Drop to impulse or be fired upon." Despite the deadly threat he made, the Vulcan's tone remained crisp and uninvolved.

Riker feigned annoyance. "We're on a rescue mission."

"Provide details."

"We've been asked to rendezvous with a private vessel, the *S.S. Belle Rêve*."

Riker was certain he saw the Vulcan's face tighten. He caught Troi's eye. The nod she gave was imperceptible to anyone but him.

"The *Belle Rêve* and her crew are guilty of criminal actions within the Vulcan system. If you persist in aiding them, you will be considered accomplices."

Riker gave an impression of shifting uncomfortably in his chair. Adopting an air of extreme reluctance, he addressed his conn officer.

"Ensign Choyce, take us to impulse."

Riker returned his attention to the viewscreen and the Vulcan. "I take it you want to scan us."

"You will be boarded and searched," the Vulcan said.

"I will file a complaint with Starfleet Command," Riker threatened.

"That entity no longer exists."

"Captain," Worf interrupted, following his script. "The *Belle Rêve* has been hit."

"Damage?" Riker asked, as if it were of utmost concern and not part of Picard's plan.

"They have lost warp engines," Worf replied. "Shields are fluctuating."

"There're Starfleet personnel on board that ship," Riker said with a hint of anger, knowing how that typically human emotional display would annoy a real Vulcan.

"They are reporting injuries," Worf said loudly. "Severe burns. They are requesting emergency medical aid."

Riker stood to face the nameless Vulcan on the viewscreen. "I'm responding to that request. If you want to board and search this ship, you're going to have to do it when we reach the *Belle Rêve. Enterprise* out."

Riker gave a quick cutting gesture and the viewscreen returned to showing the stars at warp. He looked over at Troi and she applauded lightly. "Bravo. He believed every word."

Another time, Riker might have taken a bow. But he was about to take the *Enterprise* into battle.

"Ensign Choyce, set a course to the *Belle Rêve*. Maximum warp. Hold station at five kilometers when we arrive, and so the Vulcans don't get suspicious if they scan us, alert transporter control to operate as if they're preparing for medical evacuation."

"Aye, aye, sir."

Riker turned to Worf. "What are the Vulcans doing?"

"Following. Weapons are armed, torpedoes are loaded."

Riker waited a few moments, then, "If they haven't shot at us by now, they're going to wait to see if we follow through on what we said."

Worf bared his teeth in an unsettlingly predatory smile. "Then we have them."

Riker wasn't as convinced as Worf, but he had long ago learned the folly of arguing with a Klingon.

"Th' *Enterprise* is droppin' from warp," Scott said.

Picard watched the viewscreens carefully. A moment after the *Enterprise* streaked to relative stop, the two Vulcan cruisers completed the same maneuver.

"Distance to targets?" Picard asked.

"Five kilometers port and starboard," McCoy answered. "They've sandwiched us."

Picard tapped his finger on the arm of his chair. "We have to turn that around."

"We're being hailed," McCoy announced. "It's the Vulcans."

Picard looked at Spock, standing at his side. "Any suggestions?"

"Resume laser communications with the *Enterprise*," Spock said.

"This close," Picard cautioned, "the Vulcans will detect the transmission."

"Correct," Spock agreed. "But they will not be able to decipher its content unless they intercept it."

Picard grinned as he saw the end result. Lasers were a line-of-sight communications method. "One of those two ships will have to position itself between us and the *Enterprise*."

"Captain," Scott said, "the Vulcans are gettin' a wee bit peeved. They want us t' open a channel or they'll fire."

Picard stood to be better prepared to play his part for the Vulcans. "Doctor McCoy, establish a laser com link with the *Enterprise*. Transmit sensor data, anything in the library . . . just be sure to encrypt it to make certain the Vulcans will be curious."

"Vulcans do not need to be 'made' curious," Spock observed.

"If those *are* Vulcans," Picard said. "Onscreen, Doctor."

A stern Vulcan appeared on the center screen. Picard was surprised to see that he wore a battle helmet, as if he expected to take part in personal combat at any moment.

"I demand to know why you fired on me," Picard said angrily.

"Demand?" the Vulcan replied. He almost smiled. "Drop your shields and prepare to be boarded."

Picard continued playing his role, wondering how long it would be before the Vulcans noted the laser link.

"I will do no such thing. You have no authority in open space."

The Vulcan was about to respond to Picard's challenge when he abruptly looked offscreen as if someone had just arrived with an important message.

It was the right message.

"*Belle Rêve*, you will cease all laser communications with the *Enterprise* at once."

Picard hoped Spock's logic was sound as he forced an escalation. "We don't have any laser-communications capability."

The Vulcan glared at him from the screen. Then McCoy announced that the Vulcan ship to starboard was moving in at high speed, and just as quickly as that had positioned itself directly at the midpoint between the *Belle Rêve* and the *Enterprise*, blocking the laser link between the two craft.

Picard tapped the control that cut viewscreen communications. "Is he where we need him to be?"

"Precisely," Spock said.

"Fire," Picard ordered.

For the first time since the war with the Totality had begun, light-matter life fought back.

* * *

The attack was crude, the weapon of choice imprecise.

Had the *Enterprise* and the *Belle Rêve* attempted such a tactic on a Romulan warbird, after a few seconds of confusion the Romulans would have laughed and adjusted their shields to make themselves impervious to further annoyances.

But a few seconds was all that Picard and Riker needed.

So far from the Vulcan sun, there was little to see in the darkness of interstellar space.

The *Belle Rêve* and the *Enterprise* could be noticed only by their running lights, effectively invisible against the vista of stars.

The Vulcan cruiser might have been glimpsed, traced by the glow of its impulse engines as it dropped into position between the two Starfleet vessels. But once it was in place, its running lights and the soft illumination from its viewports were lost against the tens of thousands of other points of light that made up the galactic band of stars.

The energy that the *Enterprise* and the *Belle Rêve* directed against the Vulcan ship was equally invisible.

Each ship altered its artificial-gravity generators to project toward the other, out of phase. The phase shift was precisely tuned so that the peaks of the Casimir wavelengths met at the coordinates of the Vulcan ship, where they amplified each other, creating a dramatic increase in local gravity.

At this point in the attack, an observer might have

seen flashes of light as interior conduits collapsed within the Vulcan ship and multiple explosions strobed behind its viewports. A few more seconds, and the ship was easily discernible because of the detonation of its port nacelle.

Then the heavens were ignited by multiple quantum-torpedo bursts and phaser fire from the second Vulcan cruiser.

But the light show didn't last long.

The second cruiser made the mistake of coming to the assistance of the first. When it was between the two Starfleet vessels, it was also caught in the gravity waves.

More explosions followed.

The cruisers were crushed.

And when they were scanned, no evidence of any physical bodies was found, because there had been no real Vulcans on board either ship. Only projections of the Totality.

The Federation strategy was a success.

As soon as Leybenzon confirmed that there had been no casualties, cheers erupted on the bridge of the *Enterprise*.

"Break radio silence," Riker told Worf. "Send a message to Admiral Janeway: It worked."

Picard appeared on the viewscreen, definitely pleased. "Well done, Will."

"To us both."

"Ready for round two?"

"I'm ready for as many rounds as it takes."

Picard grinned. "See you at Vulcan," he said.

* * *

Explosions still erupted from the tumbling ruins of the Vulcan cruisers as their fuel and energy systems broke down and consumed themselves.

But even those small, sporadic flashes were eclipsed by the sudden glowing starbows of two ships jumping to warp.

The first skirmish in the battle of Vulcan had been fought.

It was not the last.

34

THE TOTALITY
STARDATE UNKNOWN

There was something Kirk knew he was forgetting.

He heard water rushing, and at least that sounded familiar.

He turned to see a stream curving gracefully through a grove of shade trees. He looked up to see the sun, saw a domed roof instead, hundreds of meters high, studded with lights.

I've been here before, he thought.

There was so much that was green and growing. The scent of life was strong, comforting.

He took a deep breath, reveling in the sensation.

And then he remembered.

His rib had been broken.

His finger had been snapped.

But he felt no pain.

"It's nice, isn't it?" Norinda asked.

Kirk wheeled to face her and saw instead a Reman, towering, gray and cadaverous, with fangs and bat-like ears.

"I'm on Remus," Kirk said. He remembered now. It was just last year. The Federation thought Spock had died in an assassination attempt. Kirk had come to find the truth.

But he couldn't remember if he had found it or not.

The Reman who was Norinda stared down at him with curiosity. "What is truth, James?"

"Not this," Kirk said, and he rejected the illusion.

The Reman exploded into black sand.

Kirk covered his eyes with his arm, and when he looked out from cover again—

—it was dawn, bloodred, long black shadows like clawed wounds carved through the mound of scattered debris and small fires.

I've been here, too, Kirk thought. And though his body still felt no pain from his injuries, his heart ached as he stared at the destruction around him. He tried to remember why that should be so, why this landscape should cause him such anguish.

Two figures approached, shadows against the rising sun.

He thought of Bajor then. Of how, two years ago, he and Picard had marched across the desert by the Valor Ocean. But this wasn't Bajor, and this moment was earlier.

He wondered how he knew that.

The figures came closer: a young Vulcan woman, an old Ferengi male.

But he wasn't a Ferengi, Kirk remembered.

He was . . . he was . . .

The old Ferengi coughed and pointed a black-nailed finger at Kirk. "If I *were* a Preserver," he laughed, "given the task of educating an entire galactic Federation to prepare for its future among a universe of other federations . . ."

Kirk didn't hear the rest of the familiar, haunting words, because he suddenly, painfully, understood where he was.

Halkan.

All around him were the ruins of the starship that had claimed his Teilani's life.

He sank to his knees in the red soil and wept as the full memory of this place and this time returned.

Standing over him, the old Ferengi who wasn't a Ferengi, yet was older than any human mind could comprehend, cackled on. "To have the power to preserve life and improve the conditions in which it can flourish, and yet *deliberately* choose not to accept your responsibility to *exercise* that power . . . Captain Kirk, I submit that despite what you see around you, there is no greater tragedy than *that*."

Kirk looked up through his tears to see the Ferengi's dark and ageless eyes gazing down at him, looking through him.

What else had he said on the plain of death?

Something about Kirk having been chosen?

About Teilani having been chosen?

"Joseph . . ." Kirk gasped as a pattern formed just out of reach.

Then the Ferengi was gone, though no transporter had claimed him, just as had happened so many years ago, leaving Kirk alone with his grief, and with the young Vulcan.

She looked at him in bewilderment. "You can have anything, James. Be anywhere. Feel anything. And yet you choose this?"

Kirk blinked against the bright morning sun of this world, and in that moment the young Vulcan became Norinda.

Kirk stood, drawing strength from the loss he had experienced here, because in *this* illusion, Norinda had not become Teilani.

In the same moment that realization had formed within his mind, Norinda shattered into black and shadows streamed past Kirk until—

—he squinted in the bright lights of the museum, no longer startled by the abrupt change of scene.

He looked around to get his bearings, stopped in horror as he saw the small, stuffed, mummified body of Balok. The diminutive alien's mouth was molded into a permanently twisted smile as he perpetually contemplated the glass of *tranya* that had been wired to his hand.

Kirk was in a chamber of horrors.

And he knew who had created it.

He had.

His other side.

The Emperor Tiberius who had brought Earth and Vulcan to abject ruin in the parallel universe that was a dark reflection of Kirk's own.

And yet, Kirk knew, it was to this chamber, the lair

of Tiberius, that he had come willingly to barter for Teilani's life only six years ago.

Heavy footsteps sounded behind him. Metal upon stone, the sound of jackboots in any age.

Kirk knew he was in a dimension other than ordinary existence. He knew Norinda was searching through his memories, trying to find a time and a place he'd accept as his new home in her realm.

That knowledge strengthened him.

He turned to face Tiberius again, to stand up to that other side of himself and once again make peace with him, as he had in the past.

But there was no mirror for him to look into.

The person who approached was Norinda.

"This is wrong, James. I give you love and you surround yourself with . . ." She looked around the museum cases filled with atrocities. ". . . with such ugliness."

Kirk felt even stronger. How had he ever found Norinda desirable?

"I know exactly why I'm here," Kirk said. "And I know why you never will."

Norinda's face tightened in pain and confusion and flew apart as—

—the holographic sign floating overhead flashed BIENVENU VOYAGEURS A TRAVERS LE TEMPS / WELCOME TIME TRAVELERS.

Kirk laughed in the shock of recognition. He saw the crowd surrounding him dressed in formalwear, heard the excited conversation, the music, the clinking of crystal, and knew exactly where he was: Île Ste-Hélène, Montréal.

It was almost seven years ago and he was on his first trip back to Earth since the ill-fated launch of the *Enterprise*-B. Meeting old friends. Even confronting Janeway's duplicate from the parallel universe.

He knew that in this here-and-now Teilani waited for him in their home on Chal. She had urged him to take this journey and return to Earth, never dreaming of the consequences: Joseph's conception; their wedding; her death.

But here he was again, near the beginning of his unexpected second chance, feeling the promise of life still to come. He realized he wouldn't change these moments even if he could. With great sorrow had come great joy, and perhaps that was the way of things.

Janeway of the other universe approached him then, dressed as a server, carrying a tray of drinks through the crowd.

Kirk wasn't fooled for an instant.

"It's because you're not in control," he said, continuing their conversation.

The Janeway duplicate became Norinda.

"I'm trying to give you love!" she pleaded in frustration.

Kirk marveled at her ignorance.

"But I already have it," he told her.

Norinda gave up the debate then. She fought his resistance in the only way she could, the only way left to her after so many years as a projection into Kirk's realm, out of touch with her own.

* * *

Kirk's life sped before him in ever faster strobes of re-created experience, as if flashing in time to the beating of enormous wings.

He was a child again, running in fear through the snow on Tarsus IV, chased by Kodos.

His mount thundered across the beach of Chal, and he exulted in the scent of the sea, the heat of the sun, the purity of the blue sky, white sand, and the love of Teilani riding at his side, long hair alive in the wind.

He was in his parents' farmhouse. The Romulan assassins hunting him. Seeing Teilani for the first time in the kitchen, tasting their first kiss.

Telling Spock and McCoy he was retiring, going to Chal to find Teilani, to uncover the mystery of that world and its people, to find love.

On the rocks at Veridian with Picard, that first time they had met face-to-face, the long fall, the shadow of death approaching, but seeing at last it was Sarek.

The Borg. Destroying the machine world to save Picard. Losing himself in an energy beam that brought him—

—to Chal again, to Teilani, to battle the virogen plague that had scarred her beauty.

* * *

In the flashing of light and darkness, in the stream of all the experiences he had ever had, new knowledge was born: Kirk realized the secret that was being revealed, part of it, at least.

Teilani . . . All things led to Teilani.

Just as Teilani led to Joseph.

And Joseph led to—

Norinda cried out in heartrending anguish and the whole of the Totality's realm joined in her denial.

Another flash and Kirk was on the bridge of his own *Enterprise*, Gary Mitchell at the helm as the ship approached the galactic barrier.

For a moment, Kirk was puzzled that Norinda had found this event, a memory that had no connection to Teilani or to Joseph.

Why is this here? Kirk thought.

He glanced around the bridge as it had been at the beginning of his first five-year mission. It was so new, the crew so young.

Then he saw the anomaly.

Doctor Elizabeth Dehner, the psychologist who'd been lost on this mission with Gary. She was present, but as Norinda.

"No," Norinda said. She stood transfixed by the seething purple energy of the galactic barrier on the viewscreen.

"Not again!" she cried with the full force of the Totality and—

* * *

—when the explosion of darkness ended, Kirk was back where it had all begun.

Norinda's ship, at a time when he had just been given command of the *Enterprise.*

Kirk realized now how much of her ship Norinda had reproduced on Remus—the domed environment filled with a hundred shades of green; each breath bringing with it the rich perfume of a jungle in flower, lush plants, sparkling rivers; a wall of luminescent blooms, interwoven clusters of scarlet and saffron.

He understood that connection now, between what he had seen in his first months on the *Enterprise* and what he had seen just last year.

Norinda didn't know it, but the appeal and power and mystery of life in Kirk's realm had already conquered *her* before the Totality could conquer the rest of the universe.

"I don't understand," Norinda said.

She appeared before him as she had that first time. Swathed in a diaphanous wrap that glowed with the colors of the jungle-flower wall, her dark hair lustrous, flowing, like a windswept shadow.

"You never will," Kirk said.

"But I have so much to offer you."

"What you offer is deadly to us."

She looked at him in silence, then repeated, "What you offer is deadly to us." A single tear left a glistening track down her flawless cheek.

Kirk had no way of knowing whether Norinda was parroting his words or truly understood that each of their realms was fatal to the other.

Kirk almost felt sorrow for her.

He had come to Vulcan, walked knowingly into her trap, fully prepared to give his life to save his son.

Then, when she had absorbed him into the Totality, letting him know he was wrong in his conclusion and that there was nothing special about him at all, he had accepted death. He was prepared to let go as long as he knew Joseph would be free.

But in trying to entrap, beguile, confuse, and possess him, she'd accomplished the opposite of what she had hoped to gain.

"No . . ." Norinda wept as Kirk's thoughts became clear to her.

"Even here, there's nothing you can do to control me," Kirk said quietly. "I have Teilani in my heart, I have my son, and I always will."

This time, the explosion was like a supernova.

It was dark and cold when Kirk could see again.

He scented fertilizer, the old-fashioned kind, and it made him think of his family's farm and of—

He looked around in shock at the so-familiar old buildings.

He heard the hiss of sprinklers watering the immaculate lawns.

He saw the statue of Zefram Cochrane reaching to the low-hanging clouds of San Francisco and the hidden stars beyond.

He was on the grounds of Starfleet Academy as it had been ages ago, when he had been a teenager, as Joseph was today.

"Are *all* your memories the same?!" she demanded.

Kirk knew then that he had her.

There *was* a way to fight love: with more love. Real love. Family, friends, and lovers.

Kirk had those—all of those—waiting for him in his realm, in his life, and in his memories.

The lesson had been taught. To him, if not to Norinda. He would not accept death. He was ready to fight.

This time, Norinda was not the only thing that exploded.

Everything did, and—

Kirk was in nothingness, with no frame of reference, no illusory environment. All he was aware of was that he was aware, and that he could still hear Norinda.

I tried to bring you here by choice, James. It's easier that way.

Kirk knew what she meant. Spock had described it.

Norinda was taking him deeper into the Totality, past the point of no return, to show him the ultimate secret.

Or to show him death.

35

With Captain Picard and the *Belle Rêve* leading the way, the *Enterprise* blazed through the Vulcan embargo and not one ship fired on them. Whatever technique the Totality used to communicate in normal space, their system was in disarray.

And if, as Picard suspected, only the command levels of the Vulcan defense forces had been infiltrated and replaced by projections of the Totality, then he was certain that mutinies would already be under way among the Vulcan crews.

But fighting individual projections was something to be undertaken another day.

For now, Picard's goal was to take out the Totality's leader in this realm. And all evidence pointed to that leader being Norinda.

Picard set course for Vulcan and the city of Shi'Kahr,

343

where, according to plan, Kirk would already have engaged the enemy—*if* he had survived.

Kirk was aware of nothing but himself.

He didn't feel weightless; neither did he feel the pull of gravity of any kind.

He felt no sensation of air on his skin. He didn't breathe. He couldn't hear his own heartbeat.

For a numbing, endless moment, he feared he was dead, the horror of his situation amplified by the thought that he might be conscious of his nonbeing forever.

How long would he—could he—last in this situation and retain his sanity?

He wondered if this was the ultimate truth of reality promised by Norinda: the gift of madness.

Then, vaguely, as if he was looking in the wrong direction, he became aware of a light just out of view.

It sparkled at first, then flared, its aura brightening.

He heard the growing buzz of equipment. The light shimmered like a viewscreen out of focus.

He sensed his body again, a familiar sensation of sharp sparks of electricity playing over his flesh, the constriction of clothes as if they had suddenly appeared out of nothing.

Kirk gasped and felt air explode from his mouth as the pain of his fractured rib returned, followed by the ache of his broken finger.

Gravity pulled at him. He felt himself falling.

He swung out his arms, preparing to brace for impact, and only then did he realize that someone—something—was grasping his legs, trying to hold him back.

At the same time, something else pulled on his forearms.

He thumped against a hard surface. He used the resistance of it to bend forward, wrenching one arm free of the thing that gripped him, then his leg.

Kirk's vision blurred as smeared and out-of-focus images began to whirl around him, faster, faster—

A masculine voice rang out.

"Leave my father alone!"

A swirling, disorienting vortex of black particles spun itself out of existence—leaving Kirk behind, saved by the one he'd come to rescue.

Joseph.

Picard was at the *Belle Rêve*'s navigation console, piloting Kirk's ship. For the gravity weapon to work, each move the *Belle Rêve* made had to be coordinated with the *Enterprise*. As much as Picard respected Mister Scott's engineering expertise, this was war.

The two starships closed on Vulcan, and this close to the Totality's base, they took fire.

Picard was getting used to the smaller ship's capabilities, though, and he guided it through twisting dives and maneuvers to draw the worst of the phaser blasts coming from the Vulcan ships, flipping back or spinning into hundred-and-eighty-degree turns to catch an attacking ship as it passed between his craft and the *Enterprise*.

In each encounter, success took only seconds. Together, the two ships created a focused field of increased gravity that instantly drove the Totality projections back to their dark-matter realm.

Ship after ship fell before them, some emptied entirely of their crews, others staffed only by puzzled Vulcans who had seen their commanders dissolve into black and vanish.

As the *Belle Rêve* and the *Enterprise* flew on, closing relentlessly on their target, McCoy and Scott relayed critical information to the Vulcan vessels now free of Totality control: Increase the local gravity around their warp cores to the equivalent of four times Earth normal, and the dark-matter projections would be locked out forever.

The nightside disk of Vulcan filled the center viewscreen.

Picard picked out the glittering web of lights that identified Shi'Kahr.

Entering orbit was not an option.

He transmitted to Riker to brace the *Enterprise* for atmospheric entry.

They were going in.

Kirk grimaced as he pushed himself up to sit on the hard floor of the command center. He was cold, shaking. Grimly, he diagnosed himself: His symptoms were those of internal bleeding. It would be only a matter of minutes before he succumbed to shock.

But even in that precarious condition he felt safe, because his son stood beside him, facing down their common enemy.

Norinda.

She stood five meters away, naked, as if trying one last time to reach deep within the most primitive parts of her adversaries' brains to enthrall them.

Her features shifted like a living sculpture, from the young humanoid woman Kirk had first met, to the female version of Joseph's own appearance. But the perfection of both guises was marred by troubled frowns of nervous indecision.

"You promised me you wouldn't hurt him," Joseph said. Kirk was pleased to hear something new in his son's voice; this form of Norinda's appearance, so close to his own, had lost its power over him.

"I wasn't hurting him," Norinda said plaintively. "I was giving him the ultimate gift."

"He doesn't want it," Joseph insisted. "You said you'd leave him alone—like me."

Norinda took a step forward, arms outspread, offering herself as if she couldn't comprehend how Joseph—how *anyone*—could refuse her.

"I *have* to leave *you* alone. But no one else. Not even James."

At that, as if suddenly sensing danger, Joseph moved to shield Kirk.

"Then you lied to me," Joseph said.

"Only because I love you most," Norinda confessed. She extended a hand to Joseph, as if wanting to draw him closer. "Let me show you how much."

"Dad . . ." Joseph said, and that tentative appeal from his child broke through Kirk's exhaustion and injuries. He lurched to his feet as a narrow tendril of black writhed from Norinda's outstretched hand and within seconds took on a separate form.

Teilani, young, vibrant, unscarred, as she'd been when Kirk had followed her to Chal.

Now Teilani faced Kirk as Norinda faced Joseph,

both apparitions reflecting the pain of rejection, both reaching out in supplication and hope.

Their voices blended in an eerie harmonic.

"I bring you love," they promised.

Then their arms uncoiled like pillars of smoke, and without thought Kirk pushed Joseph to one side and threw himself to the other as the tendrils swirled into the empty space where father and son had been.

Breathing hard, dizzy to the point of nausea, Kirk knew he couldn't evade another attack. He was certain that Norinda knew the same.

But still he watched in apprehension as each of the projections produced a slender tendril that uncoiled from their hands. The tendrils met and merged to grow again, and *another* Teilani took shape, her face fuller, stomach swollen, just as she had appeared when she had been pregnant with Joseph.

The younger Teilani, the older, and Norinda, they advanced on Kirk in precise and unnatural lockstep.

"Embrace. . . ." they said together.

Before entering the Vulcan atmosphere, the *Enterprise* and the *Belle Rêve* neutralized eight additional sentinel ships. But past that point, no other vessel challenged them.

Picard smiled in grim triumph as he pictured hundreds of Vulcan vessels suddenly and inexplicably having their gravity jump to four g's, no doubt startling even the Vulcan crews as they watched the duplicates among them dissolve away. Scott and McCoy had been successful in relaying their critical information to the Vulcan fleet.

Ionized trails of superheated plasma marked the trajectories of the *Belle Rêve* and the *Enterprise* as they continued unimpeded.

Shi'Kahr grew on the horizon.

Kirk moved back as the thing that was young Teilani extended her formless arms to wrap around him. The instant one of them solidified against his back and began to urge him forward, he shifted and twisted, and threw his attacker against the other two.

Seizing his moment of freedom, Kirk scrambled back and rolled behind a bank of workstations on the first tier, shouting for his son to run.

The moment he reached cover, Kirk stole a glimpse across the open floor, checking the disposition of his enemy, searching for Joseph . . .

. . . and where there'd been three versions of humanoid females, Kirk now saw *six*.

Teilani, young and beautiful. Teilani, pregnant, older, scarred, but full of beauty within. Norinda as he had first encountered her. Norinda as a Reman. Teilani in the clinging black flightsuit she had worn the day they had first met. And most cruelly, Teilani in her wedding gown.

"*Be loved. . . .*" the shadows of lost loves pleaded. "*Be loved,*" they entreated, one voice in many bodies, no longer an invitation but a near-deafening command.

The air in the command center changed as the rustle of tendrils and the shifting of bodies grew louder. Kirk stayed hidden, unwilling to risk betraying his position to see how many more beings Norinda would become in her relentless quest to have him accept her.

But the sound of footsteps approaching told Kirk he hadn't managed to hide at all.

Shadows fell upon him. Dozens of them now.

Kirk used the last of his strength to stand, to face them.

But then the creatures cried out as one in anguish, turned away from him, back toward the platform at the center of the chamber.

Kirk stared after them in wonder.

Joseph had waded into the mass of projections, all different forms and guises of Teilani and Norinda, some even an intermingling of the two.

Instantly, the supplicants converged on his son, and as if a ripple of heat or an atmospheric distortion had roiled through the command center, one after another they shifted and changed into reflections of the female of Joseph's species.

"Be loved!" they begged, demanded.

At the same time, more and more of them arose, as in the ancient tales of dragon's teeth spawning invincible armies, compelled by the primal emotion that drove the life-force of their reality.

Kirk knew he was witness to the smothering power of love frustrated, passion denied, and that logic and force of arms could hold no sway over either.

But somehow, his son could.

Kirk edged out from cover, preparing to go to Joseph's side. Despite his son's apparent resistance to the Totality, Kirk didn't know how either he or Joseph would or could escape this confrontation and if they would survive, together.

Then a familiar golden light played over another curved bank of workstations. A familiar musical note chimed.

As quickly as that, the game changed once again.

Jean-Luc Picard had beamed in.

36

Picard took only seconds to assess the situation, and he was appalled.

He was also startled to hear Kirk call for him.

Picard ran for the workstations where Kirk crouched. He glanced over his shoulder to see scores of creatures resembling Norinda tear apart other workstation tiers with the terrible focus of the Borg. They were clearly searching for something, or someone.

Picard ducked down beside Kirk, took in his condition, knew it was bad. "You look awful."

Kirk smiled as if nothing were out of the ordinary. "Good to see you, too."

Picard had no time for pleasantries or sparring. He estimated that the mass of beings disassembling on the far side of the command center would reach their position in only minutes. "What are those creatures?"

"Norinda," Kirk said. He coughed suddenly, winced, and pressed a hand to his side.

"All of them?"

"She's desperate," Kirk said. "She's so convinced that we have to love her, that she's trying to become a version of herself that we can't resist." Kirk gave Picard a wry smile. "But that's not how it works, is it?"

"This is hardly the time for a philosophical discussion of love."

"Then what *are* you doing down here?"

Picard shook his head. Trust Kirk to try to find humor in the most dire of situations. "The gravity projectors are working, but the dispersal shielding protecting this place . . ." Picard shrugged.

"I'm surprised you could even beam in," Kirk said. Picard could see he was becoming paler, struggling to keep his eyes open.

"Beaming in we can do—the *Enterprise* is hovering two hundred meters over the operations center."

"The *Belle Rêve* . . . ?" Kirk asked with effort.

"Standing by." Picard and Kirk both started as a horrendous crash of metal echoed in the center. "What're they doing?"

"Looking for Joseph," Kirk said, coughed again. "But he'll be safe . . . I know he will be. . . ."

Picard didn't understand where Kirk's assurance came from, didn't want to argue with him. He pulled a tricorder from his belt, spoke urgently. "Look, Jim, we can't beam anyone out past the shielding." He held up the tricorder. "So I need to set this on a target, to be a beacon for the *Enterprise* and the *Belle Rêve* to use to focus their gravity weapons."

"Then you're going to have to get it as close as you can to the original Norinda."

Picard frowned. "How can I tell which one's the original?"

"All the others have grown from her," Kirk said. "She'll be somewhere in the center." He tugged at the combat tricorder strapped to his own wrist. "Use this one—it has a strap."

Picard took it. "I'll be right back."

Kirk forced a grin. "I'll be here."

Picard peered over the edge of the workstation, saw more than a hundred Norindas, all resembling Joseph to varying degrees, half of them ripping apart the center in their search for the youth, half wandering without purpose, as though they'd been abandoned.

But there, in the center of the room, looking back and forth frantically as if lost, Picard saw one Norinda who *was* more familiar, more human than the others.

He had his target.

Dozens of Norindas turned to meet his charge.

"*Yes!*" they called out to him with chilling conviction. "*Be loved!*"

Even as Picard sprinted toward them he could see the danger he faced—a living barrier of hands raised to grasp, to tear . . . some of them already beginning to lose definition, dissolving into the black formless substance that could somehow extract people from this reality and absorb them into the Totality's realm.

But Picard didn't falter.

The brave crews of two ships waited above for his signal.

A galaxy waited to know if it would live or die.

He kept running.

The hungry, driven throng engulfed him.

"Accept! Be loved! Embrace!"

Picard dove forward, over one, past another, slid across the hard floor, then fought his way to the center of the maelstrom and leapt to his feet in front of the Norinda he recognized.

For a moment, the encircling, swaying vortex of creatures kept their distance while the first Norinda reached out to Picard as if to caress him with relief and adoration.

"Yes, Jean-Luc! You understand! You'll tell James and Joseph and all of them!"

She touched his face and Picard shrank back as Norinda slowly and subtly began to shift her appearance to resemble Beverly Crusher.

"I love you so much," Norinda crooned as her fingertips made electric contact with his skin. "I want to give you so much."

The shock of gazing into familiar eyes that could not be Beverly's was enough to catapult Picard into action, and at once he slapped the combat tricorder to the creature's slender wrist.

An instant later, the creature's touch burned against his face as Norinda's arm rippled into a column of swirling dust and the tricorder, with nothing physical to support it, dropped to the floor, lost in the shadows.

"Why?!" she cried, inconsolable. "Why do you beings deny all that you love?"

Picard began to move back as Norinda sobbed before him, wrapping her arms around herself, racked by grief.

For a moment, as he saw her pain, understood her anguish, his heart went out to her, and then—

—more hands than he could count took hold of him, forcing him to the floor, holding his legs and arms immobile.

Picard cried out in surprise more than pain. He tried to tear himself away but there were too many of them.

He could only look up to see the original Norinda, no longer Beverly, moving toward him, eyes soft with tears.

"*Embrace. . . .*" all the Norindas murmured at once, their voices resonating like prayers in a temple. "*Be loved. . . .*"

The hands that gripped Picard tightened, riveting him in place.

Norinda loomed over him.

"Why don't you understand?" she asked, full of sorrow and incomprehension.

Picard prepared himself for what would come next—dissolution into her realm, into nothing.

His last thought was of Beverly.

Until a familiar voice broke through the moment of defeat.

"Norinda!"

Kirk's voice echoed above the others.

Picard peered past the forest of Norindas to see Kirk staggering closer, each step a struggle.

"Let him go!" Kirk shouted. "You only want me! You've always wanted me!"

Picard struggled uselessly, helpless to aid his friend as black tendrils snapped from the multitude to snare Kirk and drag him forward.

The Norindas deposited Kirk on the floor beside Picard. There was no need to hold the new captive down. Kirk's strength was exhausted. Where he sprawled now was where he would die.

"Brave attempt. . . ." Picard said through clenched teeth, fighting the pain of the hands that imprisoned him. "Incredibly stupid . . . but brave nonetheless."

"You would've done the same for me," Kirk said hoarsely.

"Oh, probably not," Picard said.

The two captains looked at each other, began to laugh through their pain.

"I do want you, James . . ." all the Norindas said.

"Then take me," Kirk said. "I give myself to you."

Picard watched in amazement as Norinda's desolate expression changed to one of transcendent joy, and she became the only Norinda to speak.

"James . . . do you love me?"

"I understand you," Kirk said. "I understand what's driving you. I can't hate that. I can't hate you."

Norinda held out her arms to him. "Will you be embraced in love?"

"I have loved and been loved. And that's why I'm

357

giving myself to you, so you'll leave all the others I love unharmed."

Norinda hesitated, uncertain. "But I want them, too."

"Love carries a price," Kirk said. "If you truly want to make all the others happy—"

"Yes! I do!" Norinda interrupted.

"—then take me," Kirk continued, "and give the others their freedom."

"*No,*" the Norindas sighed in unison. "*They will be alone. . . .*"

The one Norinda stepped closer to Kirk and Picard. "*I* will be alone."

"You'll have me," Kirk said, roughly, urgently. Picard knew his friend was fading.

"Not enough," Norinda said. Picard heard Kirk sigh as the one Norinda began to lose form. "*Never enough,*" the Norindas sadly chanted.

A slow cloud of darkness moved toward Picard and Kirk. The negotiation was over. Norinda's reversion was complete and they were in the presence of the basic, primal, all-encompassing Totality, all-encompassing desire.

Picard glanced at Kirk. "Well, I never wanted to die in bed. . . ."

Kirk grinned weakly. "I never wanted to die. . . ."

STOP.

Picard didn't understand where that command had come from. It wasn't spoken, but somehow he had sensed it.

LET THEM GO.

The one Norinda coalesced into her humanoid form, stepped back.

FACE ME.

All the Norindas turned from their captives as one.

Picard raised his head as he was released.

There was someone else in the command center now.

It was Joseph.

And once more he had *changed*.

37

Kirk heard the voice that was not a voice, and he recognized it.

It brought him from the darkness that was poised to claim him. He had to know, he had to see his son one last time.

"Jim, look . . ." Picard said in awe.

He helped Kirk sit up. He helped Kirk see what was before them.

Joseph and the one Norinda.

Surrounded by her duplicates, she was a transformed creature, solid once again, human once again, collapsed on her knees before Kirk's son, consumed and defeated by the unyielding need she had tried to force on all life.

Joseph had also been transformed, and Kirk blinked back weary tears.

The harsh masculinity Norinda had brought forth in his child had softened. Joseph was himself again, neither one gender nor the other. His ridges, his ears, all the marks of distinction that had echoed the myriad species of his genetic makeup, had also blurred, until there was nothing more to point to, to call out a difference.

The thought came to Kirk unbidden—an ancient wisdom revealed: *Infinite diversity in infinite combinations.*

Never had he understood that more than at this moment.

A perfect being . . . he thought in wonder.

NO, the voice answered him. JUST A BEING.

Norinda's voice was petulant, defensive. "You can't win this time!"

Her body began to change again, taking on its formless bulk of black cubes, black sand, primordial matter in constant motion.

This time . . . ? Kirk thought. How long had this battle been raging? How many times had these foes met?

Norinda had become a waving mass of writhing tendrils snaking through the air, darting at Joseph, seeking to draw him into her embrace.

But Joseph stood unflinching, spread his arms to her as if to offer no resistance.

As if in the face of her love, he offered love in return.

Kirk saw the combat tricorder on Joseph's wrist—he had made himself the target for Starfleet's new weapon, though Kirk didn't understand how his son could have known of that plan.

Then Joseph began to *glow*.

For a moment, just a moment, Kirk felt unreasoning fear.

Then he recognized the spectrum of that energy his son produced, that his son was part of.

Picard fumbled for his own tricorder, took readings as the purple light from Joseph filled the huge room.

"Density . . . negative," Picard read from the tricorder's small display. He changed a setting. "Radiation negative . . ."

Kirk didn't need a tricorder to know what the last reading would reveal. Neither did Picard.

"Energy negative," they said together.

Joseph was light.

Norinda was darkness.

Kirk knew he witnessed a battle that was older by far than his first encounter with the Totality, older by far than Earth itself.

"The galactic barrier . . ." Picard said.

Kirk understood. "Built as a defense . . . four billion years ago, when only one species lived in this galaxy."

BEGONE FROM HERE, the voice said.

"Never!" Norinda cried in defiance.

Her tendrils flickered hungrily toward Joseph, but exploded into inky mist at each contact with the energy that surrounded him.

Joseph's form could be seen no longer. He blazed with the same energy that fueled the galactic barrier—the same energy Kirk had seen on the first mission to take him past the boundaries of Earth's frontiers and for the first time to truly go where no one had gone before.

Kirk held up his hand to cover his eyes, but that light could still be seen.

Then Kirk realized that even as his child achieved victory, he himself had lost.

Even the simple act of holding up his hand was impossible.

Strength melted from him. His arm fell to his side. He could no longer sit up. He stretched out on the dark floor, each breath more difficult than the one before, knowing that soon he'd draw his last.

It was time for him to die.

And then . . . he saw Jean-Luc on the floor beside him, also gasping for air.

"Jean-Luc," Kirk said, "you've got to hold on."

"I will," Picard replied as if puzzled by Kirk's concern. "The gravity increase will only last a few seconds."

"Gravity increase?"

"The *Enterprise* and the *Belle Rêve* must've finally locked on to the combat tricorder. We're in a projected gravity field."

If Kirk had had the strength, he would have laughed.

Picard gave his friend a questioning look. "What . . . did you think you were dying?"

Kirk gazed up at the rich purple light that filled the command center, a glorious light, he realized, that had followed him all through his career.

"Not today," he said. "Never today."

And then the light intensified beyond anything Kirk had experienced before, erasing all the Norindas, filling him, his vision and his heart, becoming a radiance so bright and pure he knew that even Teilani might see it, and know that their love still survived.

"Teilani," Kirk whispered as the light took him, "we won. . . ."

38

AFTERMATH

Most of the abductees returned from Norinda's dark realm. Exactly how, no one could say. But the colonists of Delta Vega, once an old mining station, awoke the morning after the events on Vulcan to find almost a thousand newcomers standing in confusion in the fields and forests surrounding their colony's Central City.

Starfleet Command came to the conclusion that Delta Vega had been chosen to receive the abductees because, in the Alpha Quadrant at least, it was the closest Class-M planet to the galaxy's edge and thus to the galactic barrier. Though this assumption implied that some intelligence had done the choosing, Starfleet did not address the issue. At least, not in their public analysis.

With reports of other abductees being returned to the Klingons and the Romulans, researchers were now expecting, over the decades and centuries ahead, to hear similar stories from cultures with whom the Federation had yet to make first contact.

Some abductees were still unaccounted for. As Spock had said, some of the personalities he encountered in the realm of dark matter apparently accepted the invitation to go deeper within the Totality. None of those people had yet returned, the captain and crew of the *U.S.S. Monitor* among them. They were explorers, so perhaps their decision was understandable.

Initial follow-up reports suggested that perhaps as many as four hundred Starfleet personnel had been replaced by projections. But more than five thousand replacements occurred on Vulcan. Strategists were arguing vehemently over why Vulcan had been singled out by the Totality for such extensive infiltration. The majority view was that the Totality, in its blind faith in its mission, had decided that logic alone would encourage Vulcans to accept their invitation.

Not one Vulcan did. Each of that world's abductees returned.

There was interest also in what happened when the *Enterprise* and the *Belle Rêve* succeeded in their gravity attack on Shi'Kahr: When Norinda was reabsorbed and vanished, every other projection, whether in Starfleet or other agencies, dissolved. For a few months, at least, Starfleet intended to continue random gravity increases on starships and starbases, just to be sure no new projections attempted to infiltrate. However, there was reason to believe the Totality could never again attack: Readings from hundreds of subspace observatories confirmed that the galactic barrier had undergone a dramatic change in just a matter of days, becoming stronger than ever before, as if it had somehow been recharged. Quick calculations indicated that the increased negative-energy range of the barrier was enough to prevent the opening of any new portals to the dark-matter realm.

Privately, Starfleet Command was beginning to consider the barrier in a new light. Rather than a navigational nuisance that kept Starfleet vessels *in*, it was seen as a welcome phenomenon that kept something *out*.

While Starfleet's public report did not address the issue of how the recharging of the barrier might have occurred, a small handful of Starfleet personnel, active and retired, felt they knew the answer.

A month after the events on Vulcan, the group gathered in a small clearing on an ocean world named Chal. In the clearing was a half-built cabin, an old tree stump still buried in the ground, and a simple grave marked with a polished stone and the dedication plaque from a starship called *Enterprise*.

A new marker had been added near the grave. It was inscribed in four languages: Standard, Vulcan, Klingon, and Romulan. There was no body beneath it because no body had been found, and neither did anyone expect to find one.

In one of those languages, the marker read simply:

JOSEPH SAMUEL T'KOL T'LAN KIRK OF CHAL
WITH LOVE

For those who knew, it was memorial enough.

Epilogue
Palimpsest

U.S.S. ENTERPRISE NCC-1701-E
STARDATE 58582.5

The yellow lines of the graviton grid grew faintly luminescent as the light dimmed in the holodeck. Usually, Kirk was impatient with holographic reconstructions; why relive something of the past when there was so much of the present and the future still to experience?

But McCoy had convinced him that this reconstruction was worth his time. As had Jean-Luc.

The doctor and the captain both stood with Kirk now, as did Doctor Crusher, Spock and Scott, Admiral Janeway, and the holographic doctor.

The black walls and floor and ceiling of the holodeck remained unchanged, marked only by the glowing grid, no artificial backdrop required for what it was to display.

And then the reconstruction took shape. A humanoid

figure. Female. Clothed in a simple white robe. Her scalp hairless, her features vaguely unformed, yet somehow complete.

Kirk glanced at Jean-Luc, saw his friend smile in recognition. This was a reconstruction he knew well.

"You are wondering who we are," the humanoid began. The voice was artificial, Kirk knew. In its original form, it spoke in the language of whatever computer system it found itself in, so it could be understood by any suitably advanced species. *"Why we have done this; how it has come that I stand before you, the image of a being from so long ago."*

For all that he had heard about this message, Kirk was still surprised by the clarity of it, and by the understatement: "so long ago."

The humanoid continued. *"Life evolved on my planet before all others in this part of the galaxy. We left our world, explored the stars, and found none like ourselves.*

"We were alone.

"Our civilization thrived for ages. But what is the life of one race, compared to the vast stretches of cosmic time? We knew that someday we would be gone, and that nothing of us would survive. So we left you."

Picard had told Kirk the story, how twelve years ago a human archaeologist had put enough of the puzzle pieces together that Picard had been unable to resist completing it.

The end result had been a momentous chase across the quadrant, vying with Cardassians, Romulans, and Klingons to be the first to uncover this message from what was now called, by some, the Progenitor race.

"Our scientists seeded the primordial oceans of many

worlds," the humanoid said, *"where life was in its infancy. These seed codes directed your evolution toward a physical form resembling ours—this body you see before you. Which is, of course, shaped as yours is shaped. For you are the end result. The seed codes also contained this message, which we scattered in fragments on many different worlds."*

Kirk knew that just this part of the message had offered a solution to one of the great mysteries of extraterrestrial life that had arisen from Zefram Cochrane's first voyages of exploration—why nature seemed to favor the humanoid form. In a galaxy where Tholians and Medusans and Horta had all evolved and succeeded as intelligent yet wildly divergent species, why were their forms not echoed on other worlds, while humanoids seemed to have evolved independently on hundreds?

The answer, this message had revealed, was that most if not all humanoid species shared a common origin.

The humanoid was nearing the end of her message. *"It was our hope that you would have to come together in cooperation and fellowship in order to activate this message. And if you can see and hear me, our hope has been fulfilled.*

"You are a monument. Not to our greatness, but to our existence. That was our wish. That you, too, would know life, and would keep alive our memory. There is something of us in each of you, and so, something of you in each other."

The humanoid paused, and Kirk saw in her face an expression of joy and of sadness.

Joseph's face.

The weight of his loss struck him anew. But seeing this memory, thinking that this might hold a clue to the mystery and the wonder of Joseph's existence, he also felt a thrill of happiness.

Joy and sadness both together. Was there anything more human?

Then the humanoid said her final words.

"*Remember us. . . .*"

She faded then. As if in respect, the lighting in the holodeck remained subdued.

"A message from four billion years ago," Picard said.

"Just about the time life was showing up on Earth," McCoy added.

"And the approximate time frame in which the galactic barrier was established," Spock said.

"Do you really think it's possible?" Scott asked. "That such a thing could actually be *built*?"

Janeway kept her gaze on the empty space where the humanoid had been. "What's always troubled me about this is that they were so incredibly advanced, yet they knew they were dying." She looked at the others. "How do you know that you're dying as a *species,* and yet be unable to take any action to prevent extinction?"

"Unless," Kirk said, "they knew why they were dying, and that the only defense would take too long to complete."

The holographic doctor made a show of stroking his chin. "You're suggesting that the Progenitor race we've seen here was attacked by the Totality, and built the galactic barrier to save not themselves, but . . . their children."

"That's what parents do," Kirk said.

"Unfortunately," Janeway countered, "there's not enough evidence to support that theory."

"I suppose not," Kirk said. It wasn't a point to argue.

Janeway started toward the holodeck's arch. "As fascinating as all this is, I have to get back to Command. Doctor."

The holographic doctor said his good-byes.

Janeway turned before she passed through the arch. "And Captain Kirk, the new modifications you wanted on the *Belle Rêve*—they'll be finished tomorrow. We've got something we need you to do on Andor. They've found something interesting buried in the ice."

Kirk smiled in acknowledgment, but said nothing.

In time, they had all gone on to their other duties and other lives, until only three remained. Kirk, Spock, and McCoy.

"So what do you say, gentlemen," Kirk began. "In the absence of evidence, was everything that happened destiny?"

Spock was unconvinced. "Destiny would imply an intelligence capable of interpreting an almost infinite number of facts in order to predict the likely outcome of events."

McCoy scowled. "Or just a damn good guesser, Spock. Don't make it harder than it has to be."

"Or was it just chance?" Kirk asked. "Joseph, Teilani, that Ferengi on Halkan . . . for that matter, my whole career in Starfleet?"

"You've got to admit all those things worked out pretty well," McCoy said.

"If they hadn't, Doctor," Spock added gravely, "then I doubt we'd be gathered here to discuss their advantageous results."

Kirk thought that over. "So you're saying things only make sense in hindsight?"

Spock tilted his head in thought. "I'm suggesting you've asked a question that cannot be answered."

"That's a depressing thought for the day," McCoy complained.

Kirk smiled, glad of the company of his friends. "Look at it this way, Bones: As long as there're unanswered questions, there'll always be something new to find out. Can you think of a better reason to get out of bed in the morning?"

Neither Spock nor McCoy could argue with that.

"So are you going to find out what the admiral has in mind for us next?" McCoy asked.

Kirk grinned, threw his arms around his friends, started walking with them to the arch and all the adventures that still lay ahead.

"Actually," he said, "I've been working on this new idea. . . ."

He told them all about it on the way back to the *Belle Rêve*.

It was a good one.

And within the hour they were back with Montgomery Scott, where they all belonged.

At warp among the stars. Their mission continuing.

As it always would.

STAR TREK®
ACADEMY
COLLISION COURSE

WILLIAM
SHATNER

WITH JUDITH & GARFIELD REEVES-STEVENS

Available now

1

That first night in San Francisco when it all began was cool and gray and thick with fog. Soft billows of it drifted over the Academy, causing its tall locked gates to phase in and out of visibility for the teenager dressed in black, lost in the shadows across Pacific Street.

His name was Jim Kirk, and he was seventeen years old, plus five months. There was no fear in him, and there hadn't been for three years.

From the safety of a dense bank of juniper, Kirk studied the Academy's Presidio Gate with disdain for what it represented, and with growing confidence for what was to come, based on what he *didn't* see. Blue-white floodlights played over the old stonework, revealing the slow tumble of the evening fog as it flowed unobstructed through ironwork. Beyond, low streetlamps picked out the curving path of Presidio Boulevard, their halos fading with distance into the night and the glowing mist that enshrouded the Academy's vast campus.

Just as he'd expected, there were no signs of guards or other watchers. After all, this was a perfect world. How could Starfleet even conceive of someone like Kirk doing what he planned to do this night?

"This is such a bad idea," Elissa Corso whispered.

Kirk turned to his girlfriend and grinned to reassure her. As far as he was concerned, this was the best idea he had had in weeks. But there was just enough fog-filtered light falling through the branches to reveal the worry in her eyes.

"Elissa, there's no one there."

"Not at the gate."

"So we'll be fine."

Elissa frowned, not convinced. Kirk took her hand. "Look, they've got no right to go after you, and you know it. Their system's at fault." He held up his homemade override, a jury-rigged homebrew concoction of transtator filaments mounted inside an old tourist translation device. To the untrained eye, it was little more than a dented metal tube, not much larger than a finger. But Kirk had been bashing transtator kits since he was four. The old dented tube had a few surprises inside.

Elissa reached out for the override. "No—you'll set off an alarm or something."

Kirk teasingly held the device behind his back, hoping to bring her just close enough for him to steal a kiss.

Elissa refused to play, but Kirk knew he'd won. She

couldn't resist his smile. Never had been able to. Her eyes were bright now, forgiving.

She slapped a hand against his chest. "What am I going to do about you?"

"Love me. What else?"

Elissa rolled her eyes, and laughed because he was right.

He kissed her and she didn't pull back.

"Hsst! Jimmy!" It was Sam; his timing, as always, awful.

Kirk waved one hand dismissively, used the other to sweep Elissa closer, not releasing her. Until a hand clamped on his shoulder.

"Give it a rest," Kirk's brother said. "I found one."

George Samuel Kirk was four years older, his sandy hair was longer, and he was thicker in the middle, running to fat. But tonight, clad in the same type of dark jacket, jeans, and boots that Kirk wore, most people would have a hard time telling the brothers apart, their resemblance was that strong, each his father's son.

Kirk reluctantly freed Elissa, who was by this time satisfactorily breathless, dizzy. "Okay . . . show me."

Sam held up a palm-size bicorder, the kind of commercial sensor anyone could purchase in a corner shop—and the kind Kirk excelled at modifying. The device's small screen displayed a quantum interference grid that looked like a random scattering of lurid purple sand. But Kirk saw in it what he needed to see—a repeating pattern.

"Good one, Sam." Kirk turned to Elissa. "What did

I tell you? When you think you live in a perfect world, you get sloppy."

Elissa only sighed, mercifully forgoing her usual protest to Sam. For some reason she'd been unable to explain to Kirk, his older brother made her nervous. Though Kirk always stood by Sam in public, privately he thought he understood what bothered Elissa. But tonight, if she'd decided to be cooperative, despite her misgivings and Sam's involvement, then Kirk certainly wasn't going to disagree. After all, everything he was about to do was for her.

At Kirk's signal, the three of them turned away from Pacific Street and the Presidio Gate to the Academy and moved quietly back through the juniper bushes to the overflow visitor's lot. This early in August, with regular classes still three weeks away and only plebes going through indoctrination at the Academy, almost all the vehicle slots were empty. Almost.

In a lot capable of holding two hundred vehicles, there were fifteen parked overnight. Three were rental groundcars anyone could access with a currency card; four were robotic transports likely waiting until normal business hours to make their automated deliveries. The eight other vehicles were the reason Kirk was here.

They were Starfleet staff cars—compact, aerodynamically sleek vehicles designed to carry four to six personnel on official business. A few had Academy markings, the rest had fleet designations. All of them—white, of course—gleamed in the lot floodlights. White was the color of truth and purity and all the other self-righteous qualities Starfleet claimed to stand for. But Kirk wasn't fooled. "Which one?" he asked.

Sam led the way. "Fifth one. It's got a K-series navigation interface."

Kirk walked past the other vehicles with the bicorder, feeling no concern about being detected in this lot. The surrounding foliage blocked any view from the streets, and the simple sensor repeater he'd set up on their arrival continued to send out an unchanging signal to the lot's surrounding security sensors, reassuring the monitoring computers that nothing was on the move here.

Kirk focused the bicorder on the K-series vehicle. It was a heavy-duty version of a civilian Sky Rover with four ground wheels instead of landing skids. He couldn't tell how many antigrav plates it had—they were out of sight on the vehicle's underside. But all he would need for his demonstration was one.

He waved Elissa over, showed her the quantum interference grid again. "Here's the problem," he told her. "The car's controller is protected by a Starfleet encryption key. Quantum entanglement algorithms. More possible code combinations than there're elementary particles in the universe. Unbreakable, right?"

"So I've been told." Elissa kept looking around as if she didn't trust his assurances about the sensor repeater. In contrast, Sam stood ready, waiting, his silence and stance conveying complete faith in his younger brother's technical prowess.

"Smoke and mirrors," Kirk said. "Maybe that's what they use on starships—those things are untouchable.

But on the small stuff like these cars—*and* the security lockouts at the Academy—look how the complexity of the key has been scaled down. There's a repeating pattern in there. See it?"

Elissa nodded.

"Ten million possible combinations, tops," Kirk said. He held up his override. "This'll sort through all of them in under five seconds."

Elissa looked at him askance. "If you figured it out, don't you think someone at Starfleet might have, too? Built in some safeguards?"

"You spent a year at the Academy and you still don't understand these people."

Elissa began to object, but Kirk acted quickly to cut off the argument he was sure she was about to make. "What it comes down to is this: If Starfleet is so damned perfect, then why are they accusing an innocent person of breaking into the lab?"

His girlfriend's eyes flashed with indignation.

"Did you steal the dilithium?" Kirk pressed on.

He could see her control herself with difficulty. "You know I didn't."

"Okay. So all I'm saying is, their system screwed up and this is why." With dramatic flair, he pointed his override at the staff car, pressed a single blue switch. "Watch."

Two small control lights flickered on the side of the override, changing from amber to red in a blur. A few moments later, less than the five seconds Kirk had predicted, the staff car's interior lights switched on and the door locks clicked.

Kirk gave Elissa a quick "I told you so" smile and she grudgingly nodded.

Sam was more enthusiastic, gave his little brother a punch on the shoulder. "Jim-*mee!*"

"Thank you, thank you," Kirk said to an imaginary cheering crowd. "And for my encore . . ." He pressed the blue switch twice and instantly the staff car's power cells activated and its suspension rose a few centimeters, ready to be driven.

"So much for Starfleet security measures," Kirk said.

He enjoyed Elissa's change of expression as she finally realized that everything he had been telling her the past two weeks was right.

She looked from the waiting staff car to the override. "It's really that easy?"

"It helps if you're a genius," Kirk said.

"And modest," Sam added with a laugh.

"Can I show the override to my conduct adviser?"

"That's the whole idea. You're innocent and this is the proof."

Elissa launched herself at Kirk and wrapped both arms around him in gratitude. "Thank you!"

Kirk winked at Sam, but Sam wasn't paying attention to his brother's sweet moment of victory. Instead, he was looking across the almost empty lot.

"Sam . . . ?" Kirk began.

That was when the floodlights brightened and an amplified voice blared, *"You! Stay where you are!"*

Elissa jerked away from Kirk. "You said we'd be safe! I believed you!"

Kirk saw three dark figures running across the lot toward them, palmlights slashing through the fog. It didn't matter, though. He'd already done what he'd set out to do. "We're still okay. They can't catch us." He turned in the opposite direction. "Let's go!"

But from the opposite direction, two more figures ran at them, rapid footfalls like an approaching avalanche.

"Oh, crap," Sam said.

Elissa was furious. "That's it. I'm expelled."

But Kirk refused to admit defeat. He never would. He grabbed Elissa by the shoulder. "I said I'd help you and I will!"

"How, genius?"

Kirk aimed the override at the activated staff car, jammed his thumb on the blue switch. The doors slid open. "Get in!" He pushed Elissa into the back seat of the car. His brother stopped him before he could jump into the driver's seat. "I'll drive!"

Kirk quickly moved Sam aside. "You get picked up again, they'll cancel probation, remember?"

Kirk slipped into the driver's seat, Sam beside him. Behind them, Elissa stared out through the rear windshield, pulsing halos in her hair where the flashing palmlights played over her.

"*Get outta the car!*" the amplified voice boomed.

"Seat belts," Kirk commanded, then punched the control to close the doors as the car lurched forward, tires squealing.

Now shafts of light flashed through the staff car's front windshield as Kirk swerved around the first three figures who'd charged them.

Sam turned in his seat as they sped past. "One of them's on a communicator!"

Kirk swiftly checked the console navigation screen. "Ten blocks . . . see that overpass . . . we can dump the car there, grab a magtrain." He glanced back at Elissa. "Then hit Chinatown for some pizza. Is that a plan or what?"

An even more powerful light blazed through the back window. "Apparently not," Elissa said.

The staff car's emergency-alert speakers blared to life. *"Unauthorized vehicle, this is San Francisco Protective Services. Pull over at once!"*

Elissa slapped the back of Kirk's seat for emphasis. "Do what they say. Now. Don't make this any worse for me."

"I made a promise," Kirk insisted. His hand moved to flip three red switches on the console.

Elissa leaned forward, panicked, knowing what the switches were for. "No!"

"Oh, yessss," Kirk said. Then he pulled back on the steering yoke and the staff car soared into the air, leaving the SFPS patrol car on the road.

Sam whistled. "You have any idea what you're doing, Jimmy boy?"

Kirk savored the thrum of the car's Casimir emitters as it climbed over the fog-smeared lights of San Francisco. "Always," he answered.

He banked into the night, punching through the fog layer until the stars suddenly filled the night sky above him. And for all the adrenaline and excitement of the moment, for all the thrill of flying, the glimpse of stars inexplicably swept him with regret.

"Always," he said again, shaking off the odd feeling, then whooped with the sheer joy of free flight as he barrel-rolled the car and dove back into the sheltering fog, turning his back on the stars once more.

Just as he had three years ago.

If you loved reading
William Shatner's
CAPTAIN'S GLORY,
try listening to it
on **audio**!

CAPTAIN'S GLORY
is available now on CD and
for download!

Praise for William Shatner's *Captain's Glory* audiobook:

"The indefatigable William Shatner reads his
ninth *Star Trek* novel, written with the help of
the Reeves-Stevenses. Few on planet Earth have
an equivalent grasp of the *Star Trek* universe.
Shatner not only knows the story lines intimately,
he puts all the passion of his Kirk character into
his reading....No one can be more counted on to
save the Federation than Captain James T. Kirk."
— *AudioFile*

Listen to free excerpts from *Captain's Glory* and other
audiobooks at www.SimonSaysAudio.com

SIMON & SCHUSTER
AUDIO